THE

BLIGHTED

SON

PETER HARRIS

CRANTHORPE
—MILLNER—
PUBLISHERS

First published by Cranthorpe Millner Publishers (2024)

ISBN 978-1-80378-225-6 (Paperback)

www.cranthorpemillner.com

Cranthorpe Millner Publishers

Printed and bound by CPI Group (UK) Ltd
Croydon, CR0 4YY

MIX
Paper | Supporting
responsible forestry
FSC
www.fsc.org   FSC® C013604

To my wife, Wendy

CHAPTER 1

Just before midnight on a bitter January night, two men and a woman appeared at the end of a long hospital corridor heading purposefully to the cardio-thoracic operating theatre.

One of the two men, heart surgeon James McCloud, a youthful-looking Scot in his late forties, was carrying a white box marked with a large red cross and the words "Human Organ". Inside, wrapped in plastic and packed in ice, was a donor heart he had recovered only an hour or so earlier from a brain-stem dead road accident victim.

Walking briskly alongside him down the corridor at Roundthorn Hospital in Manchester, was a specialist transplant nurse who had been with him during the organ recovery, and a uniformed hospital security officer.

Two other men, both dressed in hospital scrubs, who had been awaiting their arrival, stood at the other end of the corridor. One recorded their time of arrival in a spiral-bound notebook. The other took a series of quick-fire photographs.

Noting the time was journalist Edwin Benn, the medical correspondent of the national daily *The Informer*, who had been invited to witness the operation by the lead surgeon.

With him was his newspaper colleague, photographer Mike Wolff, who had worked with Edwin on several other medical assignments and was one of the few staff "snappers" not likely to faint at the sight of blood under the heat and glare of the operating theatre lights.

'Is everything on schedule?' Edwin asked the surgeon as they all walked into the operating theatre, aware that he looked anxious, even unusually stressed.

'Yes, except for the big delay on the motorway due to an accident. We had to call the police and arrange an escort,' he replied bluntly without stopping.

'Were you delayed long?' Edwin asked.

'Perhaps half an hour but luckily we made it in time. Will talk to you later. We need to get started.'

Edwin and Mike realised that it was not the right time to ask any further questions and withdrew to the back of the operating theatre, as the transplant team, led by heart surgeon Mr Jonathan Barr-White, moved into position around their anaesthetised patient. The patient's own unhealthy heart had already been removed, and he was being kept alive mechanically by a heart-lung monitor that pumped the blood around his body and breathed air into his lungs.

The gaping cavity in his chest was waiting for the new healthy donor heart to be plumbed in, in the hope that it would shortly begin to beat naturally, giving the patient the chance to lead a new and normal life.

All that Edwin and Mike knew was that the patient was James Karl Fisher; that he was fifty-two years old; lived alone following a divorce and, ironically, ran a health and fitness club called Big Jim's Gym. Some five months earlier, he had been diagnosed with dilated cardiomyopathy – severe cardio-arterial disease following a massive heart attack that had left his heart tissue irreparably scarred.

During a brief interview conducted before the transplant, the cardiologist had told Edwin that the patient likely had a genetic heart condition, which had manifested itself when he was pumping iron in his gym, attempting to lift heavier and heavier weights. Eventually, his heart could no longer take the strain.

Judging by the brief glimpses they had of the patient before all but the site of the operation was covered with sheeting, they concluded that he had the physique of a stocky, clean-shaven wrestler. As he moved carefully around the operating table taking impromptu images, Mike noticed what he thought was a dagger tattoo on his right bicep and another smaller tattoo that looked like a skull on the side of his neck.

'Looks like he could be an ex-soldier, a military guy of some sort,' said Mike.

'Very likely. We'll find out soon, no doubt,' Edwin replied.

As they spoke, the donor's heart was lifted reverently from its box and placed in position in the recipient's chest cavity. Edwin made another note of the precise time, knowing it would add contemporaneous reportage and drama to the article he would be writing for his newspaper. Photographer Mike, who had the advantage of being over six feet tall, held his

Nikon camera above his head and took more pictures over the heads of the team encircling the operating table.

Almost immediately, the lead surgeon confidently but painstakingly began attaching the donor heart to the open-ended matrix of blood vessels in the hope it would begin naturally to pump the patient's blood around his body, signalling that the initial surgical phase had been a success.

Under the heat of the theatre lights, beads of perspiration began to appear on the surgeon's brow and, every now and again, a nurse wiped them away and threw the tissues into a bin. Everyone worked methodically, knowing precisely what was required of them at any one time. Very little was said.

Some three hours after the donor's heart arrived, lead surgeon Mr Barr-White moved away from the operating table and walked over to Edwin and Mike who had remained at the back of the operating theatre at a discrete distance from the patient and the surgical team.

'I think it's high time for a coffee, gentlemen. If you'd like to follow me, we can go through to the surgeons' restroom.'

'I take it that all is going well, Jonathan,' said Edwin, who, as the newspaper's medical correspondent, had established a first-name relationship with Barr-White and his senior surgical colleagues.

'So far, no major hitches, I'm pleased to say. The donor heart, we know, was a good match and it is now beating on its own which is always a great relief. Sometimes we have to stimulate the donor heart into action electrically but there was no need for that on this occasion.'

'That's just wonderful. Is there much left to do now?' Edwin asked.

'Just close up the chest cavity and tidy up, as it were. I can leave that to the team. That's what they will be doing now.'

Inside the small restroom, the surgeon removed his face mask and poured himself a coffee from a flask.

'Relax, gentlemen... you don't need to wear your masks in here. Sit down and we can have a chat before I have to go back into theatre to ensure that all is well.'

Edwin and Mike followed his example and, after removing their masks, they each poured themselves a coffee and sat down in two easy chairs.

'There's some biscuits in the tin if you'd like something with your coffee,' said the surgeon, pointing to a biscuit barrel alongside the flask.

His casual, easy-going demeanour belied the fact that he had just stitched the heart of one man into the chest cavity of another, giving the patient, in all probability, his only chance of ever again leading a normal, active life.

'If you gentlemen don't mind, I'm going to have a pipe of tobacco,' the surgeon continued, reaching into the top pocket of his jacket hanging on the back of the door and removing a chunky well-used briar with a curly stem.

'Not at all. I used to smoke a pipe myself until a couple of years ago,' said Edwin.

'Some of my colleagues take a pretty dim view of it and as a medical man I know that I cannot justify it. I'm not setting a very good example, but there are times when there's no substitute for a pipe of tobacco.'

'I know just what you mean. I always used to tell people that I wasn't hooked on tobacco, just addicted to pipes. There's something very tactile about them: knocking out the ash, priming the bowl, filling it, patting down the tobacco – all that sort of thing. It's something of a ritual.'

As Edwin spoke, the surgeon filled the bowl of his briar with an aromatic Dutch tobacco and lit up, blowing out a cloud of smoke.

'I once read something about a famous author – can't remember his name – who said that for the pipe smoker, the world need never come any nearer than the end of the bowl. I could always relate to that when I smoked,' Edwin continued.

'I'll remember that,' said the surgeon. 'Now, what can I tell you about this transplant?'

Edwin switched into journalist mode. 'What happens next when he comes out of theatre?'

'Everything has gone pretty smoothly so far, so I would expect that he would be moved onto the ICU – the intensive care unit – where he will be put on a ventilator to help with his breathing, with tubes inserted into his chest to drain away any build-up of fluid from around his lungs and heart. He will also receive fluids and pain control medication intravenously.'

Edwin continued his questioning. 'How long would you expect him to be in the ICU?'

'Not for much longer than a few days, after which we will move him to a hospital room, where he is likely to remain for a week or possibly two and be carefully monitored for any signs of rejection. This, as you know, is the most serious cause of failure with transplant patients and it is vital that they are put on immunosuppressants to decrease the risk of the body attacking the donor heart,' the surgeon explained.

'For how long will he have to take immunosuppressants?'

'All transplant patients have to take them for the rest of their lives.'

'How long is it likely to be before he can receive visitors in hospital?' asked Edwin.

'As soon as we think he's well enough, we will allow him to have a limited number of visitors. In fact, there's every possibility that we can arrange – if he is willing – for you to come along and interview him on the ward in a couple of weeks, maybe even sooner.'

'I was going to ask you about that. We would most certainly like to have a chat with him when he is well enough. Presumably, we could also take photographs?'

'If he's agreeable, it would be fine by me and the hospital, I'm sure.'

'We'll be carrying the story of the transplant in tomorrow morning's paper, but it will be just the basic facts including some comments from yourself. It would be nice to know him as a person – his interests, his family, his background, likes and dislikes – that sort of thing. A human-interest story, I suppose, in a nutshell.'

Mike, who had not contributed to the conversation this far, interposed. 'We noticed he seemed to have a tattoo of a dagger on his arm and possibly another one, perhaps a skull, on the side of his neck. We were wondering if he was a military man?'

The surgeon drew on his pipe and blew a cloud of tobacco smoke into the air, giving himself time to contemplate his response.

'Now this is off the record; most definitely not for publication, gentlemen... He has several distinctly bizarre tattoos on various parts of his body and there are some that are rather unsavoury and provocative, to say the least. But we are not here to judge people's political or religious views, but simply to try and save their lives whether we approve of their morals or not.'

Edwin pressed him further. 'Jonathan, when you say provocative, in what way, may I ask?'

'This is not to go in the paper, I stress, but my colleagues and I, including the nurses, took the view that some of the tattoos were blatantly racist, even white supremacist. I don't feel I should say any more than that.'

'Understood. Let me assure you that nothing of that nature will appear in the article. In fact, we couldn't publish that sort of thing without giving him the opportunity to explain and, obviously, that's not something that would be possible just now,' Edwin reassured him.

'I can see that it's intriguing – we were all shocked to see his tattoos as well – but we are not here to judge him. He is simply a patient who required a new heart. When he is eventually back at home and has made a full recovery, I accept that there are circumstances in which it could become newsworthy. But not now,' the surgeon reiterated.

'Absolutely not now, I can assure you. But just out of interest, have you noticed anything, any little incident, that would seem to confirm your suspicions about his extremist views?' asked Edwin.

'There were the odd little things that were noticed, yes.'

'What sort of things, may I ask?'

'Well, when he was told he was being listed for a transplant, he seemed very keen that I would be doing it and not my colleague, Mr Jelani. And when he was on the ward, the nurses noticed that he only ever spoke directly to the White nurses. If he wanted something, he always asked them.'

'That's awful – hard to believe anybody could be like that...' Edwin paused. 'I know I really shouldn't say this but he really does not sound like the nicest person in the world, to put it mildly.'

The surgeon took another long drag on his pipe and patted down the tobacco with his index finger. 'I'm sure you are right but let's just leave it at that. Right now, he is nothing more than our patient and it's our job to try and give him a new lease of life. The type of life he leads is no business of ours.'

'Jonathan, let me just say that I am just planning on writing a straight news report about the transplant – nothing remotely controversial – and that would also be the case if and when we manage to fix an interview with him when he is well enough and back on the ward.'

As Edwin finished speaking, one of the transplant nurses tapped on the door and opened it simultaneously.

'Mr B, I think we are ready to move him out of theatre. Would you like to come back and check all is well before we move him through to ICU?'

Mr Barr-White stood up instantly, knocked the ash from his pipe into a metal waste bin and prepared to scrub up again before going back into the operating theatre.

'OK, gentlemen, I take it you have got all you need for the time being. I look forward to reading your article and seeing the photographs.'

*

After barely four hours sleep, Edwin drove to the office to compose his article for the following day's newspaper. But as arranged, before switching on his PC, he called the hospital to check that all was well with the patient. There were happily no problems.

'Let it run, Edwin,' said the news editor, Ross Hetherington, a moustachioed, heavy-smoking Scot in his late fifties. 'We're planning on using a few paras as a taster on page one and a double page spread inside with pics.'

'OK, Ross,' Edwin replied, contemplating a punchy intro.

The real life-and-death drama of the transplant was still very fresh in his mind, and once he was satisfied with his opening sentences, the article developed its own natural momentum, with chronological references to all the key stages, from the arrival of the donor heart to the patient's transfer to ICU.

It appeared the following morning under the banner headline: *Fitness Fanatic Big Jim Has Lifesaving Heart Transplant* and was accompanied by four of Mike's photographs, including one showing the tense moments when the heart arrived and another when the patient was returned to the ICU, on which it was possible to glimpse his face behind the matrix of tubes and face mask.

'Nice piece, Edwin,' said Ross, who, as usual, had an Embassy tipped cigarette drooping from the side of his mouth. 'When d'you think we'll be able to do a bedside interview with him for a feature follow-up? I'm interested in finding out more about this guy.'

'Could be in a week if all goes well, Ross. I reckon that we're going to get some interesting letters and calls from people who know him before then. I'll certainly be surprised if we don't.'

'You're probably right,' said the news editor, as the ash from the cigarette cascaded down his beige waistcoat.

*

Edwin's prediction proved to be right. Four days later, a steady stream of letters started to pour into the newsroom from readers. Most of the letters were sent anonymously from people who had either been victims of a catalogue of racist attacks in which he had seemingly been involved over several years or who knew of his criminal record.

One, in particular, stood out from all the others. It came from a native Barbadian man who said he had served a prison sentence in Liverpool at the same time as Fisher. He stated that, with the help of other racist accomplices, Fisher had subjected him to months of violence and abuse that had been largely ignored by the prison staff.

In a handwritten scrawl on school exercise-book paper, it read:

Just seen your article about James Fisher. All I can say is it was a waste of a good heart saving the life of that evil, Nazi bastard. Would have done the world a favour if they had let him die and rot in Hell. You should check out what he got up to when he was in Liverpool, all the time he did in jail, all the people he hurt. You should put that in your paper.

It was just signed "Joshua, Liverpool (originally from Barbados)".

There were other letters, all of them anonymous, that collectively added up to a conclusive indictment of Fisher's entrenched hatred of Jews and Blacks. One alluded to the fact that "he only ever allowed Whites to join his gym". Another referred to him "daubing swastikas on synagogues" and a third included a photocopy of a newspaper article which reported that he and others had been found guilty of throwing a pig's head into a Jewish delicatessen.

Edwin also took several phone calls, many of them from Black men and women living near Fisher's gym who reported how he operated a colour bar, restricting membership to White people only and how many of those were racist skinheads. Edwin was also told how, during his days on Merseyside, Fisher led and spoke at far-right rallies and had been photographed giving the Nazi salute.

It was indisputably damning evidence.

But, except for the sundry newspaper cuttings of court hearings and photographs of Fisher taken at rallies sent in by readers, the outpourings of vitriol that landed on Edwin's desk were unsubstantiated allegations that would need to be carefully checked.

Instinctively, Edwin's highly-tuned news sense told him that he was amassing a file of information that would eventually culminate in a big news story but, for the time being, would have to remain on hold. He had promised the surgeon and the hospital that as long as Fisher remained in hospital as a patient, his coverage would concentrate solely on the lifesaving transplant – and it was a promise that he had no intention of breaking.

Edwin also knew that any story that he may write would be incomplete without knowing the identity of the donor and, ideally, the donor family's reaction to knowing that their loved one's heart was beating inside the tattooed body of a man who championed the vile philosophy of Aryan supremacy.

There was always the risk that other national news outlets would also be tipped off about the unsavoury exploits of James Karl Fisher and run their own stories, but Edwin felt that the risk was minimal. He had been offered exclusivity to witness the transplant first-hand to help promote the pioneering work of the centre and its attendant fundraising appeal – and it was unlikely, he thought, that news desks elsewhere would make the link to the racist who lived on Merseyside many years earlier.

Nonetheless, slim though the risk was, Edwin felt that he needed to discuss his strategy with his news editor, Ross Hetherington.

'Can you tell me when you've got five minutes to spare, Ross?' Edwin asked. 'I could do with a word about how we're going to play this transplant story.'

'Let's do it now. What's the problem?'

Edwin knew that Ross liked short, succinct conversations without any unnecessary waffle. He always remembered him saying that if a reporter could not tell him the gist of a news story in ten seconds, there probably wasn't a story worth writing.

'In a nutshell, Ross, this Fisher guy sounds like a pretty nasty piece of work who has done a lot of people a lot of harm. But that's a side of the story we can't write while he is still in hospital – I've promised the surgeon that – and we could do with finding out who donated the heart. I think there's a hell of a piece to be written when we've got all our ducks in a row.'

'How do you know that someone else isn't going to publish it?' asked Ross.

'I don't – there's a risk, I know – but I think it's a very small one. Anyone else would have to do a lot of legwork to check everything out and we've got a massive head start.'

Ross drew on his cigarette and blew a cloud of smoke towards Edwin. 'When are you likely to get that bedside interview with this Fisher guy?'

'Very likely in the next few days. The surgeon said that they'd be happy for me to go along to interview him for a human-interest follow-up feature as soon as he's well enough. That's if he's agreeable, of course.'

'D'you think he will go along with it? If he gets a sniff that you know something of his background, he may refuse.'

'He might but I think he'll see it as a chance to promote his gym. As far as I can see he's not been in trouble with the law since he came over to Greater Manchester and I reckon he thinks people have forgotten all about his activities on Merseyside.'

'I hope you're right.'

'And, of course, I gather he wants to know the identity of his donor, and he'll very likely think I know.'

Ross took another drag on his cigarette, pausing in contemplation. 'OK, Edwin. Check out all these readers' allegations – we've probably got our own cuttings in the library – and, at the same time, see if you can find out the name of the donor. We can then take it from there.'

'Will do, fine, Ross.'

'I know you enjoy tracking people down, Edwin, so I've no doubt you'll find him. It's one of your fortes.'

'Well, to be honest, Ross, that should not be too difficult. The hospital would not be allowed to tell us but we know the donor's age, we know he was in intensive care for some weeks and we know he died in a North Manchester hospital. I'm sure we can track him down from that.'

'Fine, fine. I hope you're right. But we don't want to spend days on it.'

'I'll get on with it now, Ross – will keep you posted,' said Edwin, then added before heading off to the cuttings library, 'And I take it you want me to go along and see him in hospital when we get the go-ahead from the surgeon?'

'I do, yes. We want to get the measure of this guy, find out what makes him tick without giving any hint that we know all about his nasty activities.'

'I'm just planning a straight interview with him – nothing controversial. Not proposing to ask him anything about his run-ins with the law or anything like that. Will just be writing a feel-good human-interest story, as agreed with the hospital.'

'Great – that's all we want for the time being. Keep everything else up your sleeve.'

'Ross, even if I know the donor's name by the time I see him and he asks me if I know who it was, I'll simply tell him that he needs to go through the official procedure – by writing a letter addressed to the donor family and having it passed on via the transplant coordinators as intermediaries.'

'Fine, Edwin. Keep me up to speed.'

*

Edwin's first priority was to check out the allegations that had flooded in by letter and telephone. He grabbed a cup of tea in a plastic cup from the office vending machine and headed up a spiral staircase to the cuttings library.

'How was it then, watching a live heart transplant? Did you

16

feel that you might faint?' asked the chief librarian, Vicki, a tall, slim, dark-haired woman who was married to one of the newspaper's sports reporters.

'Surprisingly OK. No, I didn't feel faint at all. I was too busy to think about it, to be honest, and from the side of the operating theatre, you don't see a lot of the gory stuff. I could have gone out into the corridor if I felt I was going to pass out,' he said.

'What can I do for you anyway?' she asked.

'I want to know if we have a file on a guy called James Karl Fisher, who used to live in Liverpool but for the past few years has been in Lancashire. We're told he has a criminal record for racist attacks, stirring up race hatred, all that sort of thing.'

'Give me a minute – I'll have a look.'

Edwin made light conversation with the other librarians until Vicki returned a few minutes later, carrying a chunky buff-coloured file.

'That looks promising,' Edwin said.

'Yes, we seem to have a lot about him going back ten years or more.' Vicki handed over the portfolio.

Edwin signed the library register indicating that he had taken the file and returned to his desk in the newsroom.

*

It didn't take him long to establish that everything he had been told about Fisher was substantially right. There were a handful of minor discrepancies with respect to dates, precise locations and court sentences, but it was abundantly clear that Fisher was a serial offender with a track record for race-hate crimes dating back ten or more years.

All the clippings from his own newspaper and others, many of them with accompanying photographs, spanned Fisher's years in Liverpool, where he ran a haulage business with a fleet of trucks that travelled the length and breadth of the country. Several of the earliest cuttings referred to his ex-wife, Karen, a former glamour model, and drink-and-drug-fuelled parties he had had at his home in the affluent neighbourhood of Woolton.

Several of the accounts of Fisher's racist atrocities made Edwin feel sick in the pit of his stomach. One such account was about how, with the help of his henchmen, he bought a pig's head from a local butcher and drove several miles to toss it through the door of a newly-opened Jewish delicatessen. Another related how he had personally daubed swastikas on synagogues, desecrated Jewish graves with a sledgehammer and arranged to torch a yeshiva, a Jewish religious school.

One newspaper report of a court hearing, reported how he and three others had beaten up a young Jamaican, who he alleged had been having an affair with his wife which some six months later ended in their divorcing. The Jamaican was left with serious injuries.

In an interview later with a freelance journalist, Fisher was quoted as saying: "I could have maybe forgiven her if she had been fucked by a White man but not by a fucking nigger."

Edwin quickly came to one indisputable conclusion: that Fisher was a thoroughly unpleasant, ruthless white supremacist who hero-worshipped Adolf Hitler and denied that the Holocaust ever happened. He felt it was grossly unjust that a donor heart had been used to give the chance of a new lease of life to such an undeserving monster.

His trawl through the cuttings also revealed that after he was released from his last prison sentence in Liverpool, Fisher had moved to Greater Manchester where he opened his fitness club and kept a low profile, living a bachelor life in a secluded house in the Lancashire countryside.

For some seven years, he had been off the police radar and out of the public limelight. This, Edwin felt sure, was why no one in the Manchester newsroom had joined the dots when they were given his name by the hospital and invited to witness the transplant operation.

'It all stands up, Ross. Everything that we've been told about this guy is pretty accurate. He was – and probably still is – a pretty nasty character but seems to have kept his nose clean during the time he moved to his place in Rossendale,' Edwin told his news editor after perusing the file and making a few notes.

'So, what next? You now need to identify his donor.'

'I thought, at first, I would check what the *Manchester Evening News* and the Liverpool papers had on him, but I have had second thoughts, Ross. They would probably cotton on to the fact that we are working on a story about Fisher and they would likely start digging around.'

'You're right. Don't ring anyone. Keep it to ourselves. Just concentrate now on finding out the name of the donor.'

Edwin returned the cuttings file to the library, went back to his desk and picked up the phone to call the Greater Manchester Police press office. He was optimistic that they should be able to locate details of a serious RTA in which a forty-nine-year-old man had been admitted to the A&E and then transferred to the Intensive Care Unit, where he was on life support equipment until he died some three weeks after admission.

'I'm hoping he will be easy to identify,' Edwin told the press officer.

'We'll check it out and give you a call. It will probably be tomorrow now, is that OK?'

'Yes, tomorrow morning is just fine. Thanks.' Edwin rang off. He went home, content that news-wise everything was falling into place.

*

Almost before he could boot up his desktop PC the following morning, news editor Ross Hetherington, asked Edwin if he had been able to identify the heart donor.

'Hoping to hear any minute, Ross,' Edwin told him. 'I called the police press office yesterday and they promised to call me back this morning.'

'Chase them if you don't hear back soon. We need a name.'

'I certainly will,' Edwin said, deciding that he would call them if he had heard nothing in the next half-an-hour.

The thirty minutes passed and no one called him but, as luck had it, it did not matter. Around 10 a.m., one of the newsroom messenger boys brought Edwin his morning post. It contained a few more letters from readers about Fisher's nefarious activities, but also a more interesting-looking one in a neat handwriting with a fountain pen from an address in Prestwich. It was from a woman who described herself as the donor's widow.

Edwin read her name, then read it again His pulse quickened. Could what he was thinking be right? He read it for a third time: "Kindest regards, Mrs Leah Lieberman". Edwin could not believe that she was Jewish and that the anti-Semite James Karl Fisher had been given the heart of a Jew. What's more, as he read the full text of the letter, the heart of an Orthodox Jew who was an official at his synagogue.

His name was Marcus C. Lieberman, the synagogue cantor who led the congregation in song and prayer.

At first, Edwin thought that his coverage of the transplant operation had somehow caused offence to the donor's widow and that she was writing a letter of complaint. But it was nothing of the sort. She was writing, in fact, to ask if she and her children could be given the identity of the recipient and if, perhaps at some time in the future, it would be possible to meet him. It read:

Dear Mr Benn,

I hope that you can help. My dear late husband, Marcus Lieberman, recently passed away in hospital and my family and I gave permission for his heart to be donated for a transplant operation. I have read your report of the new heart given to Mr

James Fisher and in view of the fact that it took place just a few hours after Marcus died, I feel sure that Mr Fisher must have been the recipient. I would be most interested to know if you could confirm that this is the case and if, at some time in the future, it might be possible for my family and me to meet with Mr Fisher and his family.

Marcus was the cantor at our synagogue and so, when the doctors at the hospital asked my permission to donate his heart, I first called our rabbi, Nathan Goldbladt, to seek his guidance, as we only had a short time in which to make a decision.

Traditionally, the old Jewish religious laws dictated that the body of the deceased should not be desecrated in any way and should be buried intact – a belief that is part of what is known as Techiyat Hameitim *– but all that has now changed. The Jewish faith now takes the view that the saving of human life – something we call* Pikuach Nefesh *in Hebrew – overrides all other considerations and that, if a donor organ can save a life, it is not just permissible, but the right and proper thing to do. When the rabbi explained all this to us we consented right away to donate Marcus's heart – it is certainly what he would have wanted. It has already helped us to come to terms with our loss, to know that he has given new life to someone else.*

I expect that there is a formal hospital procedure for making contact with the recipient and their family and, if you are not able to confirm that Mr Fisher is the recipient, I will formally approach the hospital. I look forward to hearing from you.

Shalom and kindest regards,
Mrs Leah Lieberman

The letter presented Edwin with a raft of interwoven dilemmas. Even if he could be absolutely certain that Marcus Lieberman's heart was beating inside the chest of Jew-hater James Karl Fisher, he did not believe that it would ethically be right for him to act as an intermediary, passing on information between donor and recipient or vice-versa, unless he had the approval to do so from the hospital.

Edwin became increasingly aware that it was a highly delicate and potentially explosive situation.

He was on the point of seeking advice from his news editor when he took a call on his landline. It was from one of the press officers at police headquarters.

'Edwin, I've got a couple of names for you,' he began.

'Excellent, thanks.'

'There were two men who were involved in RTAs in North Manchester on and around that date, who were both admitted to hospital and ICU. Have you got a pen?'

'Yes, I've always got a pen. Fire away.'

'Well, one was a Jack Harding, aged fifty-five, from Crumpsall, who I gather has now been transferred from the ICU to a general ward, and the other was a Marcus Lieberman, aged forty-eight, who was on a life support machine until he was pronounced clinically dead and it had to be switched off. I am assuming that this Mr Lieberman must be the man who was the heart donor,' he said.

'Brilliant, many thanks. That's an amazing coincidence.'

Edwin went on to add that he had just received a letter from Mrs Lieberman, explaining that she had given permission for her husband's heart to be donated and that she had written to the paper seeking to make contact with the donor and family.

'Glad to help, Edwin. Sounds like an interesting piece you are going to write,' said the press officer.

'Possibly. Not sure yet. But, hopefully, yes.'

*

Everything was falling neatly into place, but Edwin still had to be one hundred percent sure that it was Marcus Lieberman's heart that was given to Fisher. And there was only one way to do that: he would have to call the transplant office and speak to his contacts there.

As luck had it, he managed to speak directly to James McCloud's PA, the heart surgeon who had recovered the heart.

'Would it be at all possible to speak with Mr McCloud?' he asked. 'It's Edwin Benn here from *The Informer*. You may know I was in theatre on the night of Mr Fisher's transplant.'

'He's not here at the moment but I can ask him if he will call you. I am hoping he'll be back within the hour,' she said in a secretarial manner.

'If you would, thanks. It is important.'

She was as good as her word. In little over half-an-hour the surgeon phoned.

'How can I help you, Edwin?' he asked.

'A somewhat delicate matter... I've had a letter from a Mrs Leah Lieberman, telling me that she gave permission for her husband's heart to be donated. She is asking me if I can confirm that it was the one given to Mr Fisher and if it might be possible for her to contact him in time.'

'It would be best if she wrote a letter to the transplant coordinators, asking them to pass her letter on to Mr Fisher – going through the usual formal procedure. But I can tell you off the record that it was Marcus Lieberman's heart that went to Mr Fisher.'

'I appreciate that. Rest assured we are planning to interview Mr Fisher before he leaves hospital and will be carrying a straight feature with nothing remotely controversial. I'm sure you know something of Mr Fisher's background.'

'I do, yes. I realise that you could consider writing a very different type of article knowing something of his background, but whilst Fisher is still in hospital and one of our patients, you cannot do that. I know that you will honour that.'

'We will, of course,' Edwin assured the surgeon, before thanking him and ending the conversation.

*

One overriding thought occupied his mind as he placed the receiver on the hook: a white supremacist anti-Semitic racist had been given the heart of an Orthodox Jew. There were still a number of important issues to resolve, but Edwin instantly recognised the fact that he was now sitting on a big news story.

Who, he thought, would be more distressed, sickened, even angered: James Karl Fisher, after being made aware that his life had been saved by an Orthodox Jew, or widow Mrs Lieberman, knowing that her husband and the father of her children had "given" his heart to a man who had a hatred of Jews?

Edwin threw his ballpoint pen down onto the desktop, swivelled round on his chair and walked over to the news desk.

'You're not going to believe this,' he told Ross.

'What won't I believe?' Ross responded bluntly.

'That our racist friend, James Fisher, who is now recovering in his hospital bed, received the heart of an Orthodox Jew – in fact, an officer at a synagogue.'

'Christ, bloody hell.' Ross blew another cloud of cigarette smoke into Edwin's face.

'Not Jesus Christ, but you're not far wrong. The heart came from an Orthodox Jew called Marcus Lieberman who was a cantor at his synagogue.'

'Can you be absolutely sure?' asked Ross.

'Absolutely, yes. The surgeon who carried out the op has just confirmed it off the record, and I also had a letter this morning from the donor's widow explaining how, after her husband's life support had been switched off, she had been counselled by their rabbi and he had advised her that donating the heart was the right thing to do. Then I managed to get hold of the surgeon and he confirmed that Marcus Lieberman was the donor.'

'Good story, Edwin. Well, a potentially good story. I know we cannot use it whilst this Fisher is in hospital but I can see a time when we will. In the meantime, just play everything by the book... what happens now?'

'Well, as soon as I get the nod from the hospital – and I am expecting that any day now – I'll be going down for that bedside interview with Fisher for a straight human-interest piece. That is the deal I have with the hospital. I will obviously have to stick to that. I suspect, like most of the patients I've seen before, he'll be asking me if I know the identity of the donor, but whilst he's in hospital, I'll just be advising him to go through the formal channels and write to the transplant coordinator's office.' Edwin paused. 'In her letter, Mrs Lieberman also asks me if I can tell her the identity of the man who received her husband's heart, so I am proposing to have a word with her rabbi and see what he suggests, bearing in mind how it could affect her. I am hoping that when Fisher is out of hospital, I can go along and see her at her home.'

'Sounds like a plan. I'll leave it to you to make contact. Just keep me posted.'

'Rest assured, I will,' said Edwin, realising, as he spoke, that it was the Jewish sabbath and that the rabbi was very unlikely to answer the phone.

Edwin checked out the synagogue's telephone number and decided that he would call the rabbi on Sunday morning from home. As a matter of courtesy, he thought that he needed to give Mrs Lieberman an answer as soon as possible.

He left the office at the end of his shift, satisfied that he had done all that he could.

CHAPTER 2

It was only just getting light on a typically dreary Sunday morning at the end of January, when Edwin's wife, Marion, who was always an early riser, called him from the foot of the stairs to tell him that she had made a cup of tea, signalling that it was time for him to get up.

Five minutes later, Edwin, who was not a good verbal communicator until he had showered and dressed, plodded his way zombie-fashion downstairs in a velour dressing gown and gave a mumbled good morning as he slumped onto the sofa. As usual, they sat silently watching the morning television news on the BBC until they had finished their tea and single digestive biscuit.

'Do you want a cooked bacon and egg breakfast today for a change?' Marion asked.

Normally they had cereal with raisins, followed by a round of toast with Marmite, but at the weekend, they would occasionally ring the changes, alternating between smoked salmon and scrambled eggs and traditional bacon and eggs.

Edwin gave her a thumbs-up sign and managed to utter the words, 'That would be nice'. Then, uncharacteristically, he added a whole sentence, 'Shouldn't really though; I've got to call that rabbi this morning so I shouldn't really be eating bacon sandwiches, being half Jewish.'

'You're being silly – it's too early in the day for that.'

'I'm only joking. Anyway, you know what I always say – I'll only eat half the sausages or bacon because I am only half Jewish.'

Marion seemed mildly irritated by the banal conversation so early in the day. 'You go and shower and get dressed, then after breakfast you can phone him. It's Sunday, you shouldn't be working on a Sunday anyway.'

'This is important and it won't take long. I couldn't phone him from the office. Right, I'm off for a shower.'

*

When he and Marion first met in their late 30s, Edwin's appearance was unmistakably Jewish. Despite this, on business trips to Lebanon, Kuwait and the United Arab Emirates, he had frequently been taken for an Arab. In those days, he sported a neatly trimmed black beard and thick, jet-black hair. But now, in his mid-50s, his hair had greyed, his facial features and his body shape had changed, and all the distinctive hallmarks of his Jewishness inherited from his late Jewish father, had all but disappeared.

For Edwin, it made little or no difference. Genealogically, he had always had a fascination with his Jewish ancestry, which he believed had its roots in Lodz in Poland, but at no time in his life had his Jewishness had any significant impact or influence.

He hardly ever gave it any thought and he could never recall a time when anyone had made reference to it.

In fact, when he was asked to state his religion on official forms, he would say to Marion: "do you think I could put 'devout journalist'?".

Certainly, he knew it would not be an issue when he conducted the bedside interview with James Karl Fisher, apart from the fact that it would augment his distaste for the man and his past activities.

*

After a stimulating hot shower and a streaky bacon sandwich with the bonus of some fried button mushrooms, Edwin sat down at his desk and phoned Rabbi Goldbladt.

'Good morning. Am I through to the synagogue's office?' he asked formally.

'You are, yes. How may I help you?' said a woman with a distinctly Eastern European accent.

'Thank you. Would it be possible to speak with Rabbi Goldbladt? My name is Edwin Benn. I am the health and medical correspondent of *The Informer*.'

'Could you tell me what you want to speak to him about?'

'I can, most certainly. I have received a letter from Mrs Lieberman, the widow of your late cantor who tragically died following his road accident. You may know that Mrs Lieberman and her family gave permission for her husband's heart to be used in a transplant operation, and she has written to ask me if I am able to put her in touch with the recipient's family.'

'Oh, I see. But why would she be writing to you?'

'Because I was invited by the hospital to be in the theatre to witness the operation, and she has read my report of the transplant in the newspaper in which we give the name of the recipient, a Mr James Karl Fisher,' he explained.

'I see.'

'Perhaps I could explain further. The reason I feel it is important for me to speak with your rabbi is because we have been made aware of the fact that Mr Fisher is a man with well-documented racist, anti-Semitic views and it could be very upsetting for Mrs Lieberman if I simply to put her in touch with him. It is obviously a very delicate situation and we would greatly welcome the rabbi's advice.'

'Yes, indeed, I can see that,' she said, adding, 'Unfortunately, Rabbi Goldbladt is not here at the moment but I am very happy to speak to him and ask him if he will contact you.'

'That would be most kind of you. Very helpful, thank you.'

'Leave it with me, Mr Benn. I hope to see him very shortly and I will ask him.'

'Much appreciated. Thank you,' said Edwin, ending the call.

*

Within the hour, the rabbi called Edwin back just before he and his wife, Betty, were about to take a walk along their local canal and surrounding countryside.

31

'Mr Benn, Nathan Goldbladt here. I gather you want to speak to me about Marcus Lieberman. You've had a letter from his wife, I understand,' said the rabbi. His voice was gentle, cultured.

'Yes, I do, thank you. It's very good of you to call me back so promptly.'

'Of course. I will help if I can.'

Edwin spent the next couple of minutes explaining his reason for seeking his advice, stressing that the decision to donate her husband's heart had clearly been difficult for Mrs Lieberman and it was important to ensure she was not distressed by learning that it had gone to a racist with a long history of anti-Semitism.

Rabbi Goldbladt asked bluntly, 'How can you be so sure that this man is what you say?'

'There's little doubt, I am sorry to say, Rabbi. The surgeon at the hospital told me that he and his colleagues suspected that he held these radical, racist views because of the way he treated the nursing staff and had specifically asked for his transplant to be carried out by one of the White surgeons. But since I wrote my report about the operation, I have spent a good deal of time going through the newspaper archives in our cuttings library, and there are countless articles about his neo-Nazi activities when he lived in Liverpool and his several court appearances and jail sentence. My overriding worry is just how she will react if and when we tell her the unvarnished truth about Mr Fisher and whether she will want him to know that he received Mr Lieberman's heart.'

Rabbi Goldbladt felt he needed time to absorb the information and took several seconds to respond.

'I can see why not knowing Leah Lieberman you would be concerned and I thank you for seeking my advice, Mr Benn,' he said. 'She is a sensible, level-headed lady and my first thought is that she should be told about this Mr Fisher, but that it would be entirely up to her whether she wanted him to know that her husband, a devout Jew, was the man who saved his life. My personal view is that she would want this Mr Fisher to know even though it is very likely that his first reaction is going to be one of disbelief, followed by real anger and outrage – we can only guess how illogically he might react.'

'Yes, I am sure you are right.'

'God, of course, works in mysterious ways and, through Mrs Lieberman, He may feel there is a real opportunity over time for Mr Fisher to undergo some psychological change of heart and come to realise that there is no good reason for him to hate Jews or Black people, or indeed any other minority group. She may feel that if Marcus could play a small part in helping to eradicate anti-Semitism even in just one person, it will all be worthwhile.'

Edwin concurred. 'That would most certainly be my view... but when I respond to Mrs Lieberman, I feel that I should tell her that I would like to give her the information in person and I am wondering if you would be prepared to be there at the time? I could simply pass on your view, but if you felt able to be there in person, I am sure that it would carry more impact.'

The rabbi's response was quite spontaneous. 'Yes, I would be more than happy to do that. If I can leave you to make contact and fix a date with her, that would be just fine by me.'

'I feel that she would take your advice, Rabbi, just as she did by donating her husband's heart in the first place. I will call her and see if I can arrange a meeting to see her, ideally after I have conducted a bedside interview with Mr Fisher for a follow-up article, as arranged with the hospital.'

'Just let me know the date and time.'

*

By the time he had finished his call, it was well after midday and Marion was keen to head off on their walk, starting from a country inn in Dunham village, a short drive from their Victorian home in Altrincham.

'Are you ready to go now, Edwin? If we leave it much later it'll be dark before we get back home. And it's looking like it's going to rain, too.'

'Would you mind if I just made one more quick call?' Edwin asked. 'I promise it shouldn't take more than a couple of minutes.'

'OK, I'll make us a coffee. Just make it quick.'

Edwin called Mrs Lieberman and, as luck had it, she answered almost immediately.

'Sorry to trouble you at the weekend, Mrs Lieberman. It's Edwin Benn here from *The Informer*. I've received your letter and would like to fix a time and date when I could come over and discuss it with you. It's better that we meet face-to-face rather than chat over the phone.'

'That would be fine, Mr Benn. You want to come here rather than discuss it over the phone?'

'If that's all right with you. It's just not quite straightforward. It's a little delicate and, if possible, I'd like Rabbi Goldbladt to come with me. I've already had a word with him.'

'Is there a major problem, Mr Benn? Has something happened to Mr Fisher?' she asked.

'No, nothing like that. As far as I know, Mr Fisher is doing well. It's just that there are certain things you should know and it would be preferable to see you in person.'

'That's just fine. When would you like to come? I'm a little busy next week, but the week after would suit very well.'

They compared their calendars and arranged to meet in another ten days in the late morning. By that time, Edwin was optimistic that he would have conducted his bedside interview with Fisher and that his follow-up feature article would have been published. It was even possible, he thought, that Fisher could be discharged and allowed to return home by the time he and the rabbi met Leah Lieberman. As the go-between, Edwin felt that chronologically this was the most satisfactory arrangement.

Content that he had everything tied up in a neat parcel, he drank his cup of coffee – by then only lukewarm – donned his red waterproof jacket, picked up his rucksack and headed off with Marion for their country walk. He looked forward to erasing all thoughts of Mr Fisher's heart transplant from his mind for the next three or four hours.

*

In the office the following morning, Edwin updated his news editor, checked his post, then settled down at his desk to make two important calls: the first to advise Rabbi Goldbladt of the time and date of their meeting with Mrs Lieberman and then to check with the transplant centre when Fisher was likely to be discharged.

Edwin called the centre's direct line and was put through to the coordinator, Anna Dickson, a slim woman in her late thirties, with a neat, boyish haircut. They knew each other well and he had always found her most helpful.

'Anna, good morning. Edwin Benn here. Just wondering if you know when Mr Fisher is likely to be going home. As you may know, I have arranged with Mr B to come down to interview him for a follow-up feature article.'

'He's being seen by Mr B and the team later this morning and, as far as I know, they are optimistic that he'll be allowed to go home in a couple of days. When I last heard, he was doing very well,' she replied.

'Excellent. That being the case, could I arrange with you to come with our photographer tomorrow to see him at any time that is convenient for the hospital and Mr Fisher himself? We'd probably need to be with him for around an hour, possibly a little less.'

Anna Dickson paused briefly before responding. 'I am sure that would be fine, probably sometime after lunch when Mr B and the team have done their ward round. Come around two o'clock on Tuesday, I suggest. If anything changes I will let you know, Edwin.'

'That's just perfect. We'll come along to your office and you could perhaps take us through and introduce us to Mr Fisher on the ward.'

'He has now been transferred to his own room – but, yes, I would be able to take you through.'

*

After a canteen lunch on the Tuesday, Edwin stepped into the passenger seat in photographer Mike Wolff's office car for the half-hour drive to the hospital. It was a still, bone-chillingly cold day but, at least, there was no biting wind and it was dry and crisp.

As they drove out of the newspaper's underground car park, Edwin opened the conversation. 'It's going to be a bizarre, bloody funny interview with this Fisher guy – but we'll just have to play it dead straight; treat him like any other transplant patient.'

'Can't see it being a problem for me,' Mike replied. 'I'll just do a few of the usual pics – perhaps a few shots with the surgeon or nurse, or both, if they're around – and that'll do for me.'

'As long as we don't give him the slightest idea that we know all about his obnoxious views and nasty activities, we

37

won't have a problem. In a way, I'm quite looking forward to it. I'm sure we'll get a pretty good idea as to what sort of guy he is without having to ask him any searching questions.'

'I suspect you're right, Edwin.'

Mike was an easy-going, softly spoken character with a more sensitive demeanour than many of the other brasher photographers. Edwin had always found him agreeable to work with.

'Of course, when he's out of hospital and back home, the gloves are off,' Edwin continued. 'We can run the neo-Nazi-gets-Jew's-heart story, assuming that it all goes according to plan when we see the donor's widow. I know the editor is quite keen on it, so anything we discover today that's relevant we need to keep on file.'

'Got you. You never know, I might be able to get some shots of those tattoos he's got,' Mike suggested.

'Not thought of that. Great idea. You know, in many ways I'm surprised that he has agreed to an interview at all considering it might have crossed his mind that we'd find out about his past, that someone may have tipped us off – as, of course, they have.'

'I'm guessing he's the sort of guy who just likes being in the limelight, good or bad. Reckon he's an egotist.'

'You could just be spot on there, Mike. Interesting though,' Edwin mused. 'Isn't it?'

*

On arrival at the hospital, Mike and Edwin were met by Transplant Coordinator Anna Dickson, who escorted them to Fisher's room. He was sitting up in his bed, propped on several pillows, looking through a health and fitness magazine with a muscle-rippled, square-jawed bodybuilder posing on the cover.

'Good afternoon, Mr Fisher – I believe you're expecting these gentlemen from *The Informer*,' said Anna.

'Gentlemen of the press! I'll take your word for it!' Fisher replied, expecting but failing to goad his guests into some defensive response.

Mike and Edwin ignored his barbed comment and sat down on two plain wooden chairs on each side of the bed.

'Good of you to see us, Mr Fisher. I'm Edwin Benn and this is my colleague, photographer Mike Wolff. You may know we were both in the theatre on the night of your transplant.'

'I've read your article – it was OK. What do you want from me now? What are you planning to write about? I can't promise you guys a good juicy story. Some of the nurses are a bit tasty but they haven't been hopping into my bed to test my new heart yet! Anyway, you just fire away.'

Edwin felt it necessary to explain precisely what he was now proposing. 'When we were here on the night of the transplant, that was for a news story – simply reporting that the transplant had taken place and how it had saved your life. We are now planning to run a feature article which will say more about you as a person – your hopes and plans; that sort of thing. All pretty straightforward really.'

'Was that the first time you'd seen a heart transplant? A bit gory, I reckon, was it? Mind you, you reporters like a story with a bit of blood and guts, don't you?'

Edwin decided not to enter into anything remotely controversial. 'Yes, it was the first time I had witnessed a heart transplant – in fact, any transplant, for that matter – but I have been in theatre for other operations. When you're working, you don't get time to feel queasy or anything.'

'Will I get to see this article before it's printed?' Fisher asked.

Edwin hesitated. 'I'm afraid that the editor wouldn't allow me to do that. It's something that we cannot do.'

'Guess I'll just have to trust you guys then.'

'You needn't worry, James – may I call you James? – it will just be a straightforward human-interest article with nothing remotely contentious. It's as much to illustrate the amazing work of the transplant centre as anything else. All positive stuff,' Edwin explained.

'You can call me Jim – everybody calls me Jim or Big Jim,' Fisher said, accepting the fact that he would have no control over the content of the article.

Having dispensed with the introductions, Edwin felt it was time to get on with the interview and produced his spiral-bound reporters notebook.

'OK, Jim – I must say that you look remarkably well, bearing in mind that it's only been such a short time since your op.'

'I feel well. Better than I have felt for a long time. It's bloody amazing.'

'I gather you've always been a healthy guy, and even run your own health and fitness gym?'

'Yes, Big Jim's Gym. Give it a plug, if you can. I need the business.'

'I should be able to give it a mention... do you think you will ever be able to get back to training, Jim?' Edwin asked.

'The doctors here say that I will be able to take exercise but, yes, I am planning to get back to some serious training in time. But it'll be just light stuff at first. Will have to work up gradually. I'll not be looking like him any day soon,' he said, pointing to the bodybuilder on the cover of his magazine. 'If I take it easy, I'll be just fine. My competition days are over, I know that, but I'll be happy just staying strong and fit enough to give the old John Thomas a workout again... but don't put that in your paper.'

Edwin did not think that he looked like a ladies' man. Apart from his acreage of tattoos, many of which were now more visible than in the operating theatre, he had a thick bulldog neck, a wrestler's belly and a skinhead haircut. He reminded Edwin of the statue of Bacchus he had seen as a teenager in the Boboli Gardens in Italy.

'Could you get the nurse to bring us a cup of tea or coffee?' asked Fisher, altering his position in the bed.

'Yes... what do you want, tea or coffee?' asked Edwin, getting up from his seat.

'Hang on.' Fisher peered through the door. 'Ask the nurse over there on the right, not the one with the big fat ass.'

Edwin and Mike could not help noticing that the nurse he did not want them to approach was a pleasant, attractive-looking Black woman. It was the first time that they had witnessed Fisher's racist behaviour. Neither of them remarked but noted it mentally for another day. The other nurse said she would see if could arrange to get them a pot of tea.

'I gather that you could be going home tomorrow, Jim,' Edwin said, continuing their previous conversation.

'So they tell me, but I'm not sure yet.'

'If they do, have you any immediate plans?'

'I'm hoping the quacks will allow me to have a bevvy or two with my mates and a Chinese takeaway. Whatever, I'll be having some sort of knees-up, to be sure, sooner or later.'

'Sounds reasonable enough to me.'

'Can you tell me something, Edwin – do you know if I can find out the name of my donor?'

'I think you can, Jim. There's an official procedure for recipients wanting to contact the donor family and vice versa. The transplant coordinator will give you the details,' said Edwin, making a note of Fisher's home address and telephone numbers.

'I don't want my full address in your paper either,' Fisher stated bluntly.

'Rest assured, that's just for me. We would never give the full address in this kind of article. Have no worries.'

'When I'm back to my old self, I might even see if I can arrange to meet the guy's widow – assuming that it was a bloke, of course, and he was married. Who knows, she might be a bit of all right and we might just hit it off. That would be a story for you guys, wouldn't it?'

Edwin and Mike smiled but said nothing, realising that each was fully aware of the absurdity of his suggestion.

A moment or two later, a young woman pushing a trolley arrived at the door of Fisher's room.

'Are you the gentlemen who wanted some tea?' she asked, placing three plastic cups on the bedside table along with some sachets of sugar and a plate of plain biscuits.

As they drank their tea, Edwin ploughed on with some more fundamental questions, studiously avoiding anything about Fisher's activities during his years on Merseyside.

'Do you have a message for the donor family?'

'A bloody big thank you. Sorry someone had to pop their clogs for me,' Fisher replied.

'Do you think this is going to affect the way you live from now on?'

'That's up to the doctors, mate. I'm looking forward to getting back in the gym but will be taking it easy for a while... and, if they let me, I'd quite like a holiday in Vegas with a few of my mates from the gym.'

'Do you have anything you'd like to say about the transplant team here at the hospital?'

'Bloody miracle workers. It's no good being given some poor bugger's heart unless you've got the right mechanics who know how it fits into the engine – and how to service it afterwards.'

'And, finally, Jim, can you just give me details of your family?'

'There's just me – never had any kids. I did have a wife but gave her the boot when I found out she was having it off with a bloody coon. Sorry if that offends you, but that's what I call them.'

Edwin closed his notebook and nodded to Mike. 'All yours, Mike,' he said.

'Jim, before we leave you in peace, we'd just like a couple of shots of you looking so fit and well. Perhaps a shot of you with all those get-well cards,' said Mike, gesturing toward a dozen or more cards on his bedside table.

'Fine, fire away.'

Mike removed some crockery and other sundry items from the table and re-arranged the cards. As he did so, he couldn't help noticing that one included the greeting "Heil, mein Fuhrer – get well, Stormtrooper Bill", and another with six or seven signatures who called themselves The Aryan Bodybuilders.

There were others with similar messages, too, but Mike felt that it would not have been prudent to scrutinise them. Satisfied that the messages would not be visible in the photographs, Mike walked around the bed and fired off half a dozen shots with Fisher in a thumbs-up pose and the cards in the background.

'Thanks, Jim, that's fine... do you think we could now have a shot of you with one of the nurses?' asked Mike.

'Fine by me, if she'll do it. Ask Chloë, the nurse who organised the tea,' Fisher said, making it clear, without actually saying so, that he would not have posed for photographs with any of the other nurses.

Chloë, who was quite oblivious to the circumstances, readily agreed and moved over to Fisher's bedside. Mike took several shots, remarking that she had a natural smile and instinctively knew how to present herself to the camera.

In several of the photographs, a number of Fisher's tattoos that they had not seen before were visible. But they were taken out of interest only and Mike knew they would not be used in the paper.

'Well, thanks Jim,' Edwin said. 'We can call it a day, I think. I'll be writing my piece later today and, with luck, it should be in the paper tomorrow or they could just hold it until the day after. Depends what's happening in the world.'

'I look forward to reading it.'

*

On their return to their car, Edwin and Mike called in at the transplant coordinator's office to say goodbye to Anna Dickson and thank her for her help.

'It all went well, Anna,' Edwin informed her. 'I gather you know something of his background when he was in Liverpool – but, suffice to say, we never mentioned anything about that and we won't be alluding to anything about his past in the article.'

'Yes, we do know that he has some pretty unpleasant racist views but, of course, whilst he is here, he is just simply a patient,' she said.

'Absolutely, we quite understand that,' Edwin assured her. 'But there is something you need to know. He has asked if he can make contact with the donor family. I have told him that there is a formal procedure and I have no doubt that he'll be in touch with you about that.'

'That's fine,' said Anna.

'Well, there could be a problem. The donor, as you will know, was a Marcus Lieberman, an Orthodox Jew who was the cantor at his local synagogue. His widow, Leah, wrote to me asking if we could confirm that Mr Fisher was the recipient and if it might be possible for her to make contact with him, even meet him. As we speak, she doesn't know anything about Fisher's background but I have spoken to her rabbi, Rabbi. Goldbladt, and he takes the view that she would want to know. We didn't think it was a good idea to tell her over the phone or by letter, so we have arranged to see her. If you like, I can contact you afterwards and let you know what she said.'

'I would appreciate that, thank you.'

'Meanwhile,' continued Edwin, 'I would suggest that if Fisher makes contact, you simply tell him you will go through the formal channels but it may take a little while or something like that. Does that make sense?'

'In the circumstances, yes, I agree that seems like the best plan. But, please, keep me informed.'

'I will, of course.'

They shook hands and said their goodbyes.

*

'Well, well, well – that was all very interesting, to say the least,' said Edwin as they pulled out of the hospital car park and headed back to the city centre.

'He's a nasty piece of work, that's for sure,' Mike agreed, 'and obviously still involved with the neo-Nazis. I don't think you saw all the messages from his racist pals in his get-well cards, did you?'

'No, I never saw them. What did they say?'

'I made sure they would not be able to be read on the photographs but I can remember some of them... addressing him as "Mein Fuhrer Jim" and another lot signing themselves "The Aryan Bodybuilders". All nasty stuff.'

'It's a wonder he put them up for everyone to see.'

'I don't suppose many of the staff would bother to read them and he probably wouldn't care if they did.'

'It's certainly going to be very interesting to see his reaction if and when he finds out the name of his donor. I reckon he'll be apoplectic – could even collapse with clinical apoplexy,' Edwin mused. 'Anyway, my immediate problem is to knock out a bland, straight up-and-down article that will rattle on about his rapid recovery and the miracle of heart transplants. We'll be doing it more for the hospital than for Fisher – by encouraging people to register as donors or to let their families know their wishes in the event they are killed or suffer a sudden death. But enough of that for today, I'm bloody starving. D'you fancy stopping off for a Big Mac?'

'Since you mention it, I could do with something to eat, too. Yes, great idea.'

Two or three minutes later, Mike pulled into the Drive Thru at a McDonalds he knew in Didsbury, one of the more affluent, buzzy districts south of the city. They ordered two Big Macs with regular fries, which they consumed whilst sitting in the car in one of the parking bays.

'You know, that was bloody difficult, being polite, shaking hands, asking all the normal questions, when you know the bloke's such a nasty racist pig,' Edwin said as he relished his burger. 'I kept thinking of the poor sod who died and whose heart went to someone who really did not deserve it. It's a damn good job he didn't know that my old dad was Jewish. I think we might have been given the boot – the jackboot in his case. All in a day's work, I suppose.'

'I've always said that in our job you can see saints and sinners, and just about everything in between on the same day.'

'You're right, Mike. At least it never gets boring.'

*

Back in the newsroom, Edwin bought himself a cup of coffee from the office vending machine and settled down at his desktop PC to write his article.

'Ross, I just had a thought,' he said, swivelling round in his chair to address the news editor. 'He's likely to be discharged and go home tomorrow, so if we are planning on holding the piece for twenty-four hours or more, we'll need to check that all is well.'

'We'll aim to use it tomorrow. You can then say that he is "due to be allowed home today". Keep it fairly tight.'

'Alright, will do.'

'How did it go anyway?' asked Ross.

'Pretty straightforward. It was just like interviewing any other patient. There's nothing that leaps out news-wise, but it will still make a nice piece and be good for our relationship with the transplant team. There's every chance that it might even encourage a few more people to become organ donors.'

'Did you find out anything especially interesting about Fisher himself?'

'I certainly discovered that he's not a very nice sort of bloke, definitely racist and crude to boot. After we'd been there a while, he asked me to ask the nurse for a drink but he said something like "don't ask her with the fat arse", pointing to one of the Jamaican nurses.'

'Was she aware of it?' asked Ross.

'I'm pretty sure she was – probably happened a time or two before – but she just ignored it. Bet she felt like dropping something lethal into his drink!'

'What a nasty bastard!'

Since the hospital's transplant programme had started, Edwin had formed a close working relationship with the surgeons and they had asked him if he would like to witness the procedure first-hand. They could not have known when they made the arrangements that a Jew hater's life would be saved by the heart of a Jew.

As he settled down at his PC, Edwin was well aware that the big story about Fisher and his donor heart was waiting in the wings to make its entrance on another day.

Three plastic cups of insipid coffee later, Edwin had, in journalistic terms, knocked out about fifteen hundred words. The next day, the article appeared accompanied by two of Mike's photographs, under the headline "I'll Be Celebrating with a Chinese Takeaway", and a strapline "Big Jim goes home today after lifesaving heart transplant".

It was inexplicable, even illogical, thought Edwin as he wrote his article, that Fisher's prejudice did not extend to the Chinese as well as Jews and Black people. But he did not dwell on it.

Within two or three days of its publication, the article generated a fresh influx of telephone calls and letters from readers who, in most cases, had not seen the original news report but knew of Fisher's past race-hate crimes. Collectively, they reinforced the litany of evidence of Fisher's vile past.

Edwin simply kept the letters on file and a note of the names and details of the readers who contacted him, knowing that he may be called upon to write a third article in which Fisher was exposed as the anti-Semite now alive and well with a Jewish heart pumping the blood through his body.

But before then, Edwin and the Rabbi Goldbladt had to keep their appointment with Leah Lieberman and, with delicacy and sensitivity, make it known to her that her husband's heart had saved the life of a despicable neo-Nazi Jew-hater.

*

On the day, Edwin and Rabbi Goldbladt arrived at Leah Lieberman's detached house in separate cars at almost exactly the same time. It was raining hard but unseasonably mild with just a moderate breeze.

'Rabbi Goldbladt? It's really good of you to come.' Edwin smiled as the two men stepped out of their cars and walked towards each other.

'It's my pleasure. Marcus was a very good friend and colleague. If I can be of help to Leah, his widow, it is my duty,' the rabbi replied as they walked along the short driveway to the front door.

Edwin rang the doorbell just below the mezuzah, the decorative parchment containing a Jewish prayer from the Torah affixed to the doorpost of religious Jewish households. Leah Lieberman, who had been expecting them, answered the door almost immediately and ushered them through the hallway into her sitting room. Edwin and the rabbi sat at opposite ends of a three-seater sofa.

Leah Lieberman was much as Edwin had anticipated: a neatly but soberly-dressed woman of medium build with short dark hair and wearing little or no make-up. Physically, she reminded him of the former MP, Edwina Currie, although he soon realised that their personalities were very different.

'Good morning, Mr Benn, Rabbi.'

'Good morning, Mrs Lieberman. My condolences for your loss,' Edwin said solemnly. 'May I wish you a long life.'

'Thank you, Mr Benn. Could I offer you a cup of tea or coffee?'

'Black tea for me, Leah, please,' said the rabbi.

'White with two sugars for me, if possible,' Edwin chimed in.

'Make yourselves comfortable. I'll be back in a few minutes,' she said, exiting the room for the kitchen.

Rabbi Goldbladt opened the conversation. 'Do you have medical qualifications, Mr Benn?'

'Edwin is just fine,' he replied, adding, 'No, in many ways it would be a handicap if I did. I simply have to ask the sort of questions that the public, the layman, would ask. If I were writing for a medical journal it would be different, of course. It would then probably be beneficial to have some medical qualification. I do, however, have a real interest in medicine. My late father was a GP and I have several close relatives in the medical profession.'

'It must be very interesting. Do you mind me asking, are you Jewish?'

'My father was Jewish but not my mother, although she was very much the Jewish mother in her ways and temperament.'

'Does this Mr Fisher know your father was Jewish,' the rabbi asked.

'No, he doesn't. He never asked me anything about my background and I never told him.'

Edwin looked around the sitting room and noted that it had the hallmarks of a Jewish household. The ornate sideboard that had probably been handed down through the family, provided a vantage point for a forest of framed photographs, which included a number of Marcus, and one which he assumed was his son at his bar mitzvah and another which Edwin took to be Leah and Marcus on their wedding day. There were also several of their two daughters and members of their extended family.

On the centre of the dining room table was a silver menorah, and two other tall silver candlesticks at each end of the fireplace. Several mirrors of differing styles hung from the walls, and over the mantelpiece was a framed print of Rembrandt's *Moses with the Ten Commandments*.

'Do you want me to tell her about Mr Fisher or would you prefer to tell her yourself, Rabbi?' Edwin asked.

'I'm more than happy to do it, but I really feel that it should come from you,' the rabbi replied.

'Fine by me.'

A few moments later, Mrs Lieberman returned with two floral china cups and a plate of plain biscuits on a tray, which she placed on a coffee table in front of the sofa.

'Help yourself to sugar, Mr Benn.'

Edwin put two teaspoons of white sugar in his tea. 'It was really a very wonderful thing you did in donating your husband's heart, Mrs Lieberman, and I can fully understand how you would now want to meet the recipient, Mr Fisher, and, yes, of course, it can be arranged but...'

Leah Lieberman interrupted, 'That would really please me; give me a lot of comfort, I think. I read your latest article in the paper the other day... it's marvellous to think that Mr Fisher is doing so well... it's a miracle really... I take it he has now been allowed to go home... is that where I would meet him?'

The rabbi stopped her in mid-flow. 'Leah, please let Edwin explain. There are things that you need to know about Mr Fisher.'

'Sorry, please carry on, Edwin – may I call you Edwin?' she asked, reaching out to take a drink of tea.

'Of course, you may. It's just that there are things you need to know and it's a little difficult to know where to start. It is certainly possible for donor families to meet recipients and vice versa, but the circumstances in this case are rather different and it is very likely that you will not want to meet Mr Fisher and, regrettably, even more likely that he would not want to meet you. It's something that I did not want to discuss with you over the phone. I felt that I needed to come and meet you, and Rabbi Goldbladt very kindly agreed to come with me for support.'

'My goodness, it all sounds very mysterious. You've got me very puzzled,' said Mrs Lieberman.

'Mrs Lieberman, I shall come straight to the point. The fact is, Mr Fisher is not a very pleasant man, to say the least. He is violently anti-Semitic and has served several prison sentences for racist crimes, defacing synagogues, Jewish businesses and the like. The surgeons and nursing staff in the transplant centre are aware of his racist views and some of them have experienced it personally,' Edwin explained as delicately as he could.

Leah Lieberman sat silently with her head slightly bowed for several seconds before responding. 'Does he know his new heart came from Marcus? Does he know he has a Jewish man's heart?'

'Are you all right, Leah?' the rabbi intervened.

'I'm shocked, but I'm fine,' she replied.

'In answer to your question, he doesn't know anything about his donor, Mrs Lieberman. But when I interviewed him in hospital for the article, he asked if he could be told who it was. Now that he has been discharged, I will be seeing him at his home shortly and, if you are happy for me to do so, I plan to tell him then. In the meantime, he will possibly go through the official hospital procedure, but they are aware of the situation and are happy to leave it to us to tell him.'

Mrs Lieberman looked for some moral support from Rabbi Goldbladt. 'Nathan, I don't know what you think but I feel that he should know who saved his life – I am sure that is what Marcus would have wanted. I don't see how he could hate him if he knew he'd saved his life and, who knows, he could become a changed man in time. Does that make sense, Nathan?'

Rabbi Goldbladt, a man in his sixties with a wife, Rebekah, and three children, was able to draw on his own experiences of anti-Semitism as well as his understanding of Jewish teachings. He stroked his short beard and adjusted his skullcap before giving a carefully considered response.

'I believe that makes perfect sense, Leah. Recently I read that "hatred of the enemy is the natural impulse of primitive peoples, but that a willingness to forgive is a mark of advanced moral development". And, of course, we also have the guidance of the *Book of Proverbs* – "if thine enemy be hungry give him bread to eat, and if he be thirsty give him water to drink. For thus shalt thou heap coals of fire upon his head, and the Lord shall reward thee". It is the right thing to do, Leah... but we must accept that it is unlikely that he would want to meet you.'

'I'd have to say I don't think that would be a very good idea,' Edwin advised, 'and I am sure you're right. I cannot see that he would want to arrange a meeting with Mrs Lieberman. He has a pretty nasty track record. I'm not sure how he'll react when we tell him it was your husband's heart but, having met him, I believe he could erupt with anger and say all manner of unpleasant things.'

'Edwin, you don't think that he is the sort of man who, even though he is known to be anti-Semitic, would simply regard Marcus as the human being who saved his life – and that would somehow temper his feelings?' asked the rabbi.

'I'd like to think so. But, no, I don't think it would make any difference, I'm sorry to say.'

'Will you convey his reaction to us, Edwin? I think I would like to know what he says. One day I may decide to write to him and ask him to tell me why he feels such hatred towards people of our faith,' said Mrs Lieberman.

'Yes, of course, I will,' Edwin replied. 'If you ever did write, I would love to know his response.'

Mrs Lieberman stood up, picked up a photograph of her husband from the dresser and passed it to Edwin.

'This is my husband. I don't think that you have seen him.'

'No, I haven't,' he replied. 'It's a lovely picture. He looks a really nice man.'

'He was the best, God rest his soul. I miss him so much and I know I always will. He was a wonderful father and husband, and he would dearly have loved to have seen our son and daughters get married and give him grandchildren. In the old days, Jewish people, you may know, would not have desecrated the body of the deceased, but Rabbi Goldbladt told me that if a donor organ can save someone else's life, it is now thought to be our duty to do so. Even though it has gone to this Mr Fisher, I still have no regrets. I know it was the right thing to do and it is what Marcus would have wanted.'

'That is right, Leah, I am sure,' the rabbi reassured her.

'Would you gentlemen like me to make another pot of tea? That one has probably gone cold by now,' she asked.

'Very kind of you, but not for me, thank you,' said Edwin.

'Not for me either, Leah,' the rabbi concurred. 'We must be on our way.'

'Edwin, if for any reason you would like to have a photograph of Marcus, I can send one to you. I can't take that one out of the frame but I have others like it. If you write any other articles you may like to use his photo,' said Mrs Lieberman, standing up as she spoke.

'Thank you.' Edwin handed her his business card. 'I would like to have a photograph, if possible. I am sure there will be future articles in which we could use it.'

The three slowly made their way through the hall to the front door.

'It's been lovely to meet you. I'm just sorry we could not bring you better news. But I know you have made the right decision,' said Edwin.

'Goodbye Leah.' The rabbi smiled warmly. 'I will no doubt see you in shul.'

Before heading to their cars, the two men stopped on the pavement outside Mrs Lieberman's house.

'I'm so glad that you could come today, Rabbi. I believe that it made everything so much easier.'

'I was very happy to do so. I have known the family for many years. As I am sure you realised, Leah is a very sensible woman who I knew would make the right decision. Clearly, it would be inappropriate – impossible – for her to meet with Mr Fisher, but in the future, who knows, he may want to meet her.'

'I will be arranging to see Fisher at his home soon and am not sure how that will go – it could be a bit fraught. He doesn't know yet that I want to go round to see him in person, but if there's anything significant to report, I will let you know, of course.'

'That would be good. Thank you, Edwin.'

With a handshake, they walked in opposite directions to their cars and drove off.

*

The following day – some six weeks after the transplant – Edwin phoned James Karl Fisher at his secluded rural hideaway in the Rossendale Valley in Lancashire to arrange a time when they could meet.

He answered with a blunt "hello" in a tone that suggested he did not welcome callers.

'James Fisher? It's Edwin Benn here from *The Informer.* How are you?'

'I'm great – getting better every day. Managed to do a few light weights yesterday. Have you something to tell me?'

'I have, yes. But first, can you tell me if you have contacted the hospital and whether they've got back to you yet?'

'No. I've been waiting to hear from you.'

'Right, well, I do have his name. Had a letter from his widow and since then I've been round to see her at her home. I'd like to do the same with you, James, if that is OK with you. I'd rather come over to chat face to face.' Edwin made sure to keep his tone of voice relaxed and friendly.

'You want to come here? Very mysterious. A bit unusual. But if that's what you want to do, it's fine by me.'

'Yes, James, I know it sounds a bit mysterious and all that, but it will all become clear when I see you.'

'OK then, when do you want to come over?'

They checked their diaries and were able to fix a date for the following week.

'You say that you've spoken to his widow, so I take it that it was a man's heart I received. Is that right?' asked Fisher.

'It was a man, yes, just a few years younger than you. A man with a wife and three children, one son and two daughters in their late teens and early twenties. I can tell you that,' said Edwin.

'Tell them that they have free membership in my gym.'

'I've not met them yet... don't know if they are the sporty type, but I'm sure they would welcome that. It's certainly not far from their home. I'll let them know.' Edwin knew full well that they would never want to go near the place.

'See you next week then. Goodbye for now,' said Fisher. Then, he simply hung up.

*

Edwin took himself off for a half-hour lunch break at his favourite hostelry a short walk from the office. When he returned to his desk, he briefed his news editor on the latest episode in the ongoing Fisher saga.

'I will be seeing Fisher at his home next week, Ross. He thought it was all a bit mysterious but said he was quite happy for me to go over. I reckon he'll go berserk when I tell him his donor was Marcus Lieberman.'

'If I were you, I'd have a word with the picture desk and see if Mike Wolff will be available to go along with you. I don't think you should go alone. We just can't be sure what his reaction will be and if anything untoward happens, I'd like you to have a witness,' said Ross.

'Makes sense. I'm not worried about it but I would certainly be happier if Mike could come along.'

Later that day, Edwin discussed the matter with the picture editor, William Royle – himself a former staff photographer, who was taken off the road and given the desk job after a freak fall down a lift shaft – who checked his diary and pencilled in the date for Mike Wolff to accompany him.

'Mike's in that day and there's nothing in the diary right now, so it should be OK. Remind me on the day, Edwin.'

'I will, Bill. Ross is right. We might well need a witness on this one.'

*

All went according to plan. The following Wednesday, Edwin and Mike met up for a mid-morning coffee in the canteen before setting off out of the city and through the rain-and-windswept Lancashire countryside. In under an hour, they pulled into Fisher's gravel drive leading to his converted two-storey barn apartment.

'Interesting place – it's a wonder that he didn't call it the Eagles Nest in deference to Adolf's hideaway in Berchtesgaden,' said Mike.

'The perfect hideaway, that's for sure,' replied Edwin. 'No one would know what the hell goes on in there. Could be the nerve centre of the neo-Nazi party in the UK, for all we know.'

'That's him on the doorstep, isn't it, Edwin?'

'It is, yes. He's obviously seen us arrive. It's the first time I've seen him standing up.'

Fisher's body took up almost the entire width of the old arch-shaped door. Despite the rain, he was wearing an open-necked plain white shirt and navy slacks, held up by a belt underneath his unattractive paunch.

'Good afternoon, gentlemen. Found it all right then,' he said as they walked towards him.

They shook hands and ambled through into a spacious hallway with a beamed ceiling and stone floor covered in several places with multi-coloured kilim rugs. Fisher ushered them into the sitting room that was dominated by an L-shaped leather sofa and an alcove that had been converted into a drinks bar complete with optic dispensers and upholstered bar stools.

'I didn't know you were coming with your cameraman, Edwin. I can tell you now I don't want any pictures here,' Fisher said bluntly.

Edwin had to think on his feet. 'No, we won't be doing any photos. It's just that we'd been on an earlier job together in the office car,' he lied, realising it would not have been prudent to tell him that Mike had come as a witness.

'Will you guys join me in a drink – tea, coffee or something stronger?' Fisher asked.

Edwin was surprised that he seemed to be drinking alcohol so soon after his transplant.

'Not for me, thanks. I've got to drive back,' said Mike.

'I'll just have a small brandy, if you have one,' Edwin conceded. He was keyed up and felt it might help him relax.

'I've got a three-year-old Asbach Uralt – the best,' said Fisher. 'Do you want ice?'

'No ice, thanks. Just straight. Sounds something special.'

Fisher poured the brandy and a bottle of Hofbräu Original beer for himself.

Edwin thought it was interesting that they were both German products.

'I quite liked your article by the way. I have always been a bit anti-press – some of you journalists just make up things to sell papers – but at least you stuck to the facts.'

'Thanks. Glad you liked it. We do try, you know, believe me.' Edwin chose his words carefully, politely defending the press.

Fisher took a drink from a tall glass bearing the Hofbräu logo and leaned back on his sofa. 'OK then, now who was this poor old guy who had to pop his clogs and gave me his heart? Reckon I owe his family a big thank you.'

There was a noticeable pause – almost an uncomfortable silence – during which Edwin took a slurp from his brandy and looked across at Mike before speaking.

'It's not as straightforward as you might expect, James,' Edwin explained. 'You see, the reason we wanted to come over rather than tell you over the phone is because we have seen some of the stories of the time you were in Liverpool and, well, the name may come as a bit of a shock to you.'

'A shock, why a shock? I'm not easily shocked, as you may well have gathered. Anyway, are you going to tell me his bloody name or not?'

'Jim, there's no easy way to tell you, but his name is Marcus Lieberman. He has a wife – his widow, Leah – and three children.'

'Say his name again, did I hear you right?' replied Fisher, drinking more beer.

'Marcus Lieberman, he was the cantor at the synagogue near his home in North Manchester.'

'You're telling me he was a Jew boy – that I've got the heart of a fucking Jew. You're fucking joking me, aren't you?'

'I can show you the letter from his wife if you'd like to see it, Jim,' said Edwin.

'I'm not interested in seeing any fucking letter from a fucking Jew... I don't believe this. Yes, I am fucking shocked. I'm not sure that I wouldn't prefer to be dead than have a Jew's heart. Christ Almighty, next you'll be telling me that he was a Jewish bloody nigger, like that one-eyed American singer Sammy Sambo Davis or whatever his name was.'

Edwin remained calm. 'You can see now, Jim, why we didn't feel it was right to tell you over the phone... having seen all the old newspaper stories we—'

Fisher interrupted. 'If you've seen all the stories then you know what I think about Jews and Blacks. I don't make any secret of it... the world doesn't need them. If you had the time, I'd tell you why we'd all be better off without them.' He paused, his expression of rage dulling to one of confusion. 'Tell me, if you knew all this stuff about my background why didn't you put that in your article? That would have been juicer material, wouldn't it?'

'Jim, I don't want to get into any ethical or moral discussions of that kind, but it was intrinsically a medical article about a heart transplant. The hospital wouldn't have been best pleased if they'd invited us to witness the operation and we had gone away and written something really controversial. We just stuck to the medical facts,' Edwin explained.

'OK, OK, I get that. But what are you going to do now?'

'Don't know, to be honest, Jim. That's a decision for the editor.' Then, changing the thrust of the conversation, he added, 'Jim, if I were you, I'd just think that you have been given a new healthy pump that doesn't have a religion.'

'A pump maybe, but one made from the flesh and blood of a fucking Jew. When they told me I was being listed for a transplant I was over the fucking moon, but now I think I'd have been better off dead. A Jew's heart – I just don't believe it!'

Edwin ignored his outpouring of vitriol and, in an attempt to restore some kind of equilibrium, asked Fisher if he had been in touch with the transplant coordinator's office and made an official request to see if it might be possible to meet his donor.

'I may have asked somebody something, I can't remember... but I can tell you now that if they do come back and tell me that they are hoping to fix it for me to meet his fucking family, they can take a running fucking jump. Why would I want to meet a fucking Jewish bitch just because her fucking husband was my donor!'

When Fisher had calmed down a little, Edwin felt that he had to tell him that now he was no longer a hospital inpatient, it was quite probable that his editor would ask him to write a new piece that would highlight the fact that he had received the heart of an Orthodox Jew.

'I'll bloody sue you if you publish anything like that,' said Fisher.

'We'd just be reporting the facts, Jim, not passing any comment on them. I think you will find that it would be a perfectly legitimate piece of reporting. I think you would find that any lawyer would confirm that,' Edwin responded cautiously.

'I wouldn't be so bloody sure,' replied Fisher, still clearly seething.

Edwin and Mike resisted the temptation to wade any further into what could have developed into a potentially explosive and contentious exchange. They realised that it was time to leave.

'Jim, thanks for the drink – I think we had better make a move. We just came to pass on the information – which we knew was likely to distress you – but we certainly don't want to have a major disagreement with you. Suffice to say, the editor may ask me to write something but it's by no means certain.'

'As you can tell, I'm not happy – not happy one little bit. But it's not your problem. Now, I suggest you bugger off and leave me to have a few more beers.'

Mike had planned to ask Fisher if he could photograph him relaxing at home but, in the light of his outburst and threats of legal action, decided it would be pointless and would almost certainly prompt a hostile response. Apart from that, they had told Fisher that he was only there because they had been together on a previous news story.

'Don't get up. We can find our own way out,' said Edwin as he and Mike made their way briskly to the front door and left.

It had stopped raining, there was the odd glimmer of winter sunshine and they felt relieved to have imparted the information without becoming embroiled in any physical violence.

'All rather predictable, eh?' Edwin commented as they fastened their seat belts for the drive back to Manchester.

'I guess so, but what an absolute nasty piece of work. How can anyone think like he does?'

'God only knows. I really would be interested to know where all that hate comes from. There has to be a root cause somewhere. But even if you managed to get him to talk quietly and rationally, he probably wouldn't know himself,' Edwin shrugged sadly. 'Anyway, all these threats about suing us if we carry a piece are just rubbish. As long as we just stick to the facts, no court in the land would ever find in his favour. It's a bloody good story but I'm honestly not sure we'd use it. It would certainly upset the Liebermans and I don't think the hospital would be best pleased either.'

He sighed, contemplating the situation as they paused for a moment at a set of traffic lights.

'I know the clinicians are only interested in ensuring that a donor's heart is a good match physically, but they may take the view that it would make them look a bit naive in the public eye – giving the heart of an Orthodox Jew to an anti-Semite, even though they probably would not have known that when he was first listed for a transplant.'

'I reckon he should be named and shamed. But that's just my personal view.'

'You're right, Mike. I'm all in favour of running it but I would want to give a heads up to Leah Lieberman first, just so that she isn't told about the article by family, friends or neighbours and is upset by it. If the editor does decide to run it, I'll give her a bell and warn her... and I'd also make sure we include a comment from the hospital making it clear that they knew nothing of Fisher's racist views when he was listed.'

'That's fair enough – you can't do more than that.'

'In my view, we should run it. There's no escaping the fact that it's one hell of a story. I think Ross and the editor will go for it.'

*

Edwin's prediction was right. On his return to the office, he was called into an impromptu conference with the editor and the news and picture editors. As briefly as he could, Edwin relayed the guts of the meeting with Fisher.

'I won't repeat his language but it was pretty colourful, to say the least, when I told him the name of his heart donor. It was just one expletive after another. He just lost it.'

'Did Mike manage to take pics of him at home?' asked the picture editor.

'There was not a cat in hell's chance of that, Bill. As soon as we told him the name of his donor, he started threatening us

68

– saying he would sue if we published anything about it and, shortly afterwards, we told him we had to make a move and we left.'

'Was there anyone else there in his house, apart from you and Mike?' asked Ross.

'No, just the two of us, and him. I'm pretty sure he lives alone.'

The news editor leaned back in his swivel chair, stroked his chin a couple of times, and then, a little like a judge in court, announced his verdict.

'We'll run it. He made the decision for us when he told us he'd sue if we publish anything. We cannot let him believe that we decided not to publish because of his threats. As long as we stick to the facts, it's legally watertight.'

'I think it's important that I speak to the donor's widow first,' said Edwin, 'and let her know what we are planning and hopefully get a quote from her. I also feel that I should let the transplant team at the hospital know.'

'Fine, fine. Just stick to the facts and we can't go wrong. I'm even happy if you use asterisks for his expletives, if it helps. Will leave that up to you. Good story, Edwin.'

'Thanks. I'll make a start.'

*

Back at his desk, Edwin switched on his desktop PC, glanced through his shorthand notes, flicked to a clean new sheet and then picked up the landline to call Leah Lieberman. She answered almost immediately.

'Apologies for disturbing you, Mrs Lieberman. It's Edwin Benn here at *The Informer*. Thanks again for seeing us the other day. Hope you're well.'

'Yes, I am quite well, thank you. How can I help you?' she replied.

'It's really just to tell you that I went to see Mr Fisher at his home and he now knows that it was Marcus who was his donor. My editor wants me to write a new article and I felt it was only fair I should let you know in advance.'

'Well, thank you... I expect that he was a bit shocked, wasn't he? From what you told me about him, I am assuming that he was not very pleased; probably upset him, I would imagine.'

'You're quite right, Mrs Lieberman. He did become very irrational, to say the least; used a lot of bad language... I just felt we ought to let you know that the editor is planning to publish a piece. I'll be working on it shortly. If there's any particular comment you would like to make, I would be happy to include it.'

'I think you know my feelings from our conversation when you were here with Rabbi Goldbladt. If you think it's relevant, I'm quite happy for you to refer to anything I said then... if you want, you can add that I am just sorry that he should think that my husband's heart is different from anyone else's. I don't really want to say much at all.'

'That just fine, Mrs Lieberman. I won't keep you. That's all I need really. If there are any developments, I will, of course, let you know.'

Almost immediately afterwards, Edwin called the transplant centre with the intention of speaking with the consultant, Mr Jonathan Barr-White. Anna Dickson, the senior coordinator, told him that he was not available but said she would ask him to call him back. Barely half an hour later, he called.

'Mr Barr-White here, how can I help? I gather you want to have a word,' he said.

'Thank you, yes. Good of you to call back.' Edwin explained the situation as succinctly as he could, stressing that he had already spoken to Mrs Lieberman and that she had no reason to object to an article being published.

'Edwin, we would obviously prefer not to see this kind of article in the national press, but I recognise that this is a most unusual state of affairs and one that your editor would quite understandably feel is newsworthy and, perhaps, in the public interest to publish. If you want a comment from myself, all I would be prepared to say is that Mr Fisher is no longer an inpatient, however, he is still under our care and it would be inappropriate for me to make any comment about his personal life or opinions. Would that suffice?'

'That would be absolutely fine. I could ask for no more,' Edwin replied earnestly.

'Off the record, you know my views and that of my colleagues, but they will have to remain off record, of course. Is that OK?'

'Of course, I just wanted to keep you up to speed. Many thanks as usual.'

*

71

Edwin was now ready to open up a blank page on his computer and start writing his article. He experimented with a number of introductory paragraphs, but ultimately opted for a simple but punchy sentence that read:

A self-confessed neo-Nazi white supremacist has received the heart of an Orthodox Jew in a life-saving transplant operation, The Informer *can exclusively reveal.*

James Karl Fisher, who served several prison sentences for racist hate crimes against Jews and Black people, was given the heart of a synagogue cantor declared brain dead after a road accident.

When 53-year-old Fisher was told the identity of his donor by The Informer *at his rural retreat in the Rossendale Valley in Lancashire, he launched into a verbal anti-Semitic tirade.*

It went on to include the comments from the donor's widow, Leah Lieberman, and the hospital consultant.

The article chronicled Fisher's racist crimes and court convictions over his ten years on Merseyside, referenced his racist attitudes toward staff in the transplant centre and the get-well cards sent to him in hospital that contained racist messages from his band of followers, many of them skinhead members of his fitness club, Jim's Gym.

It was given page one treatment, under the headline: DONOR HEART FROM ORTHODOX JEW SAVED LIFE OF NEO-NAZI – Exclusive Report by our Medical

Correspondent, Edwin Benn.

Almost as soon as the paper appeared on the news stands with accompanying billboards proclaiming NEO-NAZI GIVEN JEW'S HEART, it ignited a media frenzy. Within a matter of hours, reporters, photographers, as well as TV and radio crews descended on Fisher's home, parking their cars on the narrow country lanes on each side of his driveway.

Over a period of several hours, a steady stream of reporters knocked on the door which was opened by a muscular tee-shirted skinhead who, unceremoniously, told them to go away using a four-letter word expletive. Each time he opened the door, photographers with poised long lenses fired off a succession of shots hoping that they may snatch an image of Fisher.

One by one the journalists ambled up, gathering themselves into a cluster – the ubiquitous press pack – outside Fisher's gate. Several lit up cigarettes and folded and unfolded their arms to keep warm in a biting March wind. Others sat back in their cars to call their news or picture desks on mobile phones.

At one point, Fisher – who they recognised from the photographs in *The Informer* – was seen drawing the blinds in an upstairs window and two or three of the "snappers" succeeded in capturing a hazy image. But as the afternoon light began to fade, all agreed that there was little point in staking out the house much longer and, in unison, they drove for warmth and refreshments to the village hostelry about a mile away.

The following day, a miscellany of news stories appeared in the national press along with various reports on the TV and radio networks. They were dressed up with various emotive headlines and some with indistinct long-lens photographs – but all were essentially a re-hash of Edwin's original, exclusive article.

Several of the nationals approached the transplant centre but were simply given a polite "no comment" response. Others, in particular the local Greater Manchester media, carried photographs from both inside and outside Jim's Gym, along with inconsequential comments from members. Some of the reports carried quotes from Leah Lieberman's neighbours. Edwin had advised her that she could well be approached and she decided to stay with relatives until interest in the story waned. Rabbi Goldbladt gave instructions that anyone who approached the synagogue should be told simply that "we are unable to make any further comment".

'Fisher has obviously gone to ground. He's not saying anything to anybody and I cannot see him changing his mind,' Edwin informed his team as he and his colleagues scrutinised the coverage in the nationals the following day.

'Just keep tabs on it,' Ross requested. 'We cannot be sure what this Fisher character is going to do next.'

'He'll do something, I'm sure. Right now, I reckon, he'll be like the bear with the proverbial sore head. He was pretty angry when he realised his donor was Jewish and he won't be happy that, as a result of our piece, he's now being hounded by the press pack. I agree, he is likely to react in some way. My main worry is that he could send one of his heavies round, but most likely he'll just stay low and ride it out until everything begins to die down – as it always does. I've got the feeling that he really doesn't want any more run-ins with the law and that, right now, he'll be preoccupied with having to get used to the idea that he's a neo-Nazi with a Jewish heart. And there's really not a lot he can do about that unless he decides to top himself – and I'm sure that's not his style.'

'Just keep tabs on it.'

'The likelihood is that sometime in the next few weeks, he will have to go back to the hospital for a routine check-up, so there's a pretty good chance I will get some feedback from the transplant team,' Edwin reasoned.

'There's likely to be some more mileage in this story sooner or later. In the meantime, I'd like you to have a look at this one. We've just had a tip that a Manchester sailor who was bitten by a dog when he was recently in India, has died of rabies. Can you check it out?'

'I will, Ross,' replied Edwin, delighted to be working on a story with which he was not personally involved.

CHAPTER 3

When the national media interest in James Karl Fisher gradually petered out over the next few weeks and Edwin received no further letters or telephone calls about him, he convinced himself that the story had run its course.

But he could not have been more wrong.

One slow news day when Edwin was trawling through *The Lancet* and *The British Medical Journal* for potentially interesting stories to pursue, he took a phone call on his landline that was to boost the James Karl Fisher story back into the journalistic stratosphere.

'Good afternoon, Edwin Benn, news room here,' he said in an autopilot monotone.

'Hi. There's something that you need to know. I think you might be interested in it,' said a female voice with what Edwin determined was a Liverpudlian accent.

'May I ask who's speaking? How can I help you?' Edwin asked.

'I think it's more of a case of how I can help you... my name is Karen Passoa... you won't know me... I'm Jim Fisher's ex-wife. I've been reading your articles in the paper. Very interesting, but there is a lot you don't know,' she said.

'May I call you Karen?'

'Yeh, Karen's fine, luvvy.'

'Well, this all sounds very interesting, Karen. What's the big story, if I might ask?'

'Not over the phone if you don't mind, Edwin... but I promise you, you'll be more than interested. It's dynamite, I can tell you.'

'Well, you have certainly whetted my appetite, for sure. Can you just give me a hint of what it's about? Just a flavour...' asked Edwin.

'All I can tell you is that you don't know who he really is – or his background.'

'OK then, Karen, when would you like to meet and where?'

'Can you come over to my flat tomorrow? I'm in Speke, not far from the John Lennon Airport.'

Edwin had a quick look at his diary. 'Yes, around 11 a.m. tomorrow. If that's OK for you?'

'Fine for me, Edwin. You'll be shocked, I promise you.'

He wrote down her full address and mobile telephone number. 'See you tomorrow, then. I shall look forward to it.'

'You won't regret it.'

*

Experience, plus a sensitive nose for a good news story, convinced Edwin that Karen had something genuinely interesting to impart.

'I've just had an intriguing call out of the blue from Fisher's ex-wife saying she's got something to tell me about him that will be quite a shock… but she wasn't prepared to tell me over the phone, so I've arranged to see her tomorrow over at her home in Speke,' Edwin told Ross.

'Are you sure it's not some bloody ploy and you'll find Fisher and his henchmen there when you arrive? You can't be too careful.'

'Hadn't crossed my mind, to be honest. I'd have to say I think it all sounds genuine. I don't think she has any love for the guy,' Edwin replied.

'OK, but I suggest you don't go alone. Ask the picture desk if Mike is free and could go over there with you, just to be on the safe side.'

Ross Hetherington was a blunt-speaking, no-nonsense newsman who would sharply rap the knuckles of any journalist who failed to meet a deadline or whose work fell short of his high standards – but he was always fair and protective towards them. He would not let Edwin take any risks.

Edwin explained to Bill Royle on the picture desk that Ross thought it was best to double-up on the trip to Speke and, having checked his diary, he arranged for Mike to accompany him.

*

Around 9:30 a.m. the following day, Edwin met up with Mike in the photographers' restroom and they headed off for Speke in Mike's company car.

'Do you know anything about this woman, Edwin?' asked Mike as they headed out of the city.

'Not a lot, to be frank, Mike,' said Edwin. 'She's called Karen Passoa, so I reckon she must have married the guy she was having an affair with, which led to her getting kicked out by Fisher.'

'Well, we'll know soon enough.'

*

Within around an hour, they pulled into the forecourt of a modern block of flats a short distance from the Mersey Estuary and parked in a space marked "Visitor". Mike rang the bell for flat number 9 and a moment later they heard a woman's voice over the intercom.

'Come on up, first floor on the left,' she said.

They ignored the lift and walked up the stairs where Karen Passoa was waiting in the corridor outside her flat.

'Hi, Karen. This is my colleague, Mike. We've been out on an early job in the office car so came straight here,' Edwin explained convincingly. Mike nodded. Edwin did not feel that it would have been prudent to tell her the real reason they came as a twosome.

'That's OK. Come in and sit down,' she said.

They walked through to an uncluttered, clinical-looking sitting room where they sat down at opposite ends of a cream leather sofa. Apart from a massive TV with a sixty or sixty-five-inch screen, a stereo unit and a tall glass-and-chrome unit displaying photographs, a pile of CDs and some sundry ornamental cylindrical ceramic bowls, there was little else in the room.

'Thanks for coming over... anyway, can I get you guys a drink: tea, coffee or something stronger?' Karen asked.

'Coffee would be just great for me,' said Edwin.

'For me too,' said Mike.

From their brief telephone conversation, Edwin had visualised that as a former glamour model now in her fifties, she would be a busty but no longer shapely blonde, wearing excessive make-up and dressed in a style of a much younger woman. Except for the fact that she had black, dyed hair, he was uncannily accurate. Her short white mini-dress left little to the imagination.

'Well, you've certainly got us intrigued, Karen,' said Edwin stirring two spoons of sugar into a mug of coffee sporting the Liverpool FC logo. 'Do you mind if I take a few notes?'

'Whatever, fine by me,' she replied. Then, after taking a deep breath and crossing her legs, she began. 'I guess the first thing you need to know is that he was not born James Karl Fisher. His real name is Karl Fischer – with the German spelling F-I-S-C-H-E-R.'

'So, he was born in Germany, you're saying. I thought I detected some slight accent when I went to interview him at the hospital but it was predominantly a Liverpool accent,' mused Edwin.

'Yes, I am pretty sure he was but he has dual nationality... and he's gradually lost his German accent, you're right. As far as I know, he first came over here when he was in his early twenties to take part in some international bodybuilding contest – and that's where I first met him. I used to earn a bob or two as a cheerleader at some of the events around the country,' Karen explained. 'When his father died in Germany, he decided to stay here and with money that his father left in his will, he started a small haulage business which he grew into quite a big company.'

'Did you know his father?' asked Edwin.

'No, I never met him. All I know is that he was called Herman Fischer. I don't think that he liked his father much and I don't think he ever really knew his mother. I think she was divorced from his father not long after Jim was born and he lost touch with her. His grandfather was called Otto, I think.'

'Like Otto von Bismarck, the German Chancellor?'

'I don't know. I've never heard of him. Guess it could be.' Karen shrugged.

'So, where did the name "James" come from?'

'He just decided to call himself James so he could call his fitness club Jim's Gym, or as I call it, Jim's Whites-Only Gym. I know it's now over near Rochdale but he had a smaller place over here in Liverpool at the same time he was running the haulage business. They were both called Jim's Gym.'

'That certainly explains a lot.' Edwin glanced at Mike as he spoke.

'Yes, he came from a big Kraut family, but, if you're sitting comfortably, I'll tell you the real reason why he is such a horrible, violent, nasty racist pig,' Karen said excitedly.

'I'm sitting comfortably – go on.' Edwin gestured for her to continue.

'You'll have to check out all the dates and details for yourself – you'll be better than me at all the research stuff being a journalist – but his late father, Herman, always told him that they were related to a Nazi professor called Eugen Fischer who wrote a book about weeding out the so-called misfits and mental cases, which Adolf-bloody-Hitler read when he was in prison and which gave him the idea of his Master Race.

'I know that Jim's father was obsessed with this Nazi guy and he brainwashed Jim, or Karl as he have would been then, from when he was just a little lad and lived somewhere in Germany – somewhere I think near where the mad professor himself was born, in Baden something or other... I'm not sure exactly where. You might be able to find out.'

Edwin looked over at Mike, raised his eyebrows and took a sharp intake of breath. 'That is quite a story. Dynamite, I'd say. You say that Jim's father died?'

'Yes, I'm pretty sure he died around twenty years or more ago when Jim would have been in his late teens, early twenties. I think he would have been about the same age as Jim is now and I think that he died of some heart condition. Must run in the family,' said Karen.

Edwin was bursting with questions. 'Were they both living together for some years in Germany then?'

'That's all a bit hazy but if he brainwashed Jim they must have been living together for quite some years, I reckon. When Jim came over to Liverpool to take part in some bodybuilding

82

contest in his early twenties, I think he stayed here. His father stayed in Germany, I think, and was there until he died. I think he had some admin job with the public transport authority in Germany. Jim had an elder brother who he told me went to America, but I don't know any more than that.'

'What about Jim's mother? Do you know anything about her?'

'No, nothing really. He never spoke much about his mother. I'm pretty sure that his parents got divorced soon after Jim was born and he stayed with his father. I don't know where his mother went and I don't think Jim knew either. I think he may even have thought she was dead. If I'd stayed with Jim for longer I may have found out more about these things, but we were only together for less than three years.'

'I gather you split up and got divorced when he found out you were having a relationship with someone else? I read something about it in a newspaper cutting,' said Edwin.

'That's right. I met Fitzroy during one of the times that Jim was in prison and one thing just led to another. When he came out and found out my new man was from Jamaica, he went bloody crazy and physically threw me out. To be honest, I'd have left him anyway because his neo-Nazi activities were getting out of hand. He had the bloody cheek to say that if I'd been having a fling with a White guy he might have understood and been able to forgive me, but when he discovered Fitzroy was Jamaican, he just went bloody wild.

'When we first met, he just used to say he did not like Jews and Blacks and I used to tell him he had no reason to say things like that, but it got worse and worse with rallies and marches, damaging synagogues, violence; and I wouldn't have put up with that for much longer and he knew it. He was definitely brainwashed by his father who convinced him he was related to this professor who was one of Hitler's cronies.'

'Are you and Fitzroy now married?' Edwin asked.

'We are, yes, luvvy. It's coming up to our fifth wedding anniversary soon.'

'Congratulations.'

'Thanks.'

Edwin finished his mug of coffee and readjusted his position on the sofa. It had all been rather intense and the three needed a short emotional breather.

He reopened the conversation with another question, 'Do you know anything more about Jim's grandfather, Otto – Herman's father?'

'Not a lot, to be honest. But from what I did pick up from Jim, his father was also brainwashed by his father, Otto. I think he was one of Fischer's big followers and claimed they were related. Whether they were or not, God only knows. Jim certainly never had anything to prove that they were. Again, that's something you might want to check out.

'It was like father like son, like son. Before we got divorced, Jim was attracting all the racists and deadbeats from all over Merseyside like flies round a pile of shit – excuse my language. He really hated everybody who did not fit into the Master Race mould – Jews, Blacks, homosexuals, Romany gypsies, even people who were disabled or mentally ill. It got really extreme.

If he'd have had his way, he would have had them all sterilised, used for medical experiments or just exterminated.'

'Just as a matter of interest, Karen, what does Fitzroy do?' Edwin asked.

'He's a parks gardener. Keeps us well supplied with flowers for the flat in the spring and summer... all this is strictly off the record, you realise? If Jim thought I'd been talking to the press, he would probably send some of his heavies round. He won't have changed... so no names, addresses or photos, sorry.' She looked directly at Mike when she referred to photographs.

'Absolutely, fully understand. Don't worry about that. I'm just the driver today. Won't be doing any photos,' said Mike.

Edwin interposed, 'To be honest, Karen, we couldn't run a story in the paper anyway until everything had been carefully checked out. But I'm pretty sure that the editor will want to pursue it. We would obviously not attribute anything to you, and we'd almost certainly have to get back to Jim and he's not likely to make any comment or confirm anything. The hospital may also take the view that as a patient still under their care, we would be hounding him and that it could affect his health. But what you've told us does explain a lot.'

As they prepared to leave the flat, Fitzroy returned home from work. Karen made the introductions and Edwin and Mike shook his hand.

'Good to meet you,' they said in unison. Then, after a few other inconsequential pleasantries, they said their goodbyes and left.

*

85

Even before he had reached his desk back in the newsroom, news editor Ross Hetherington broke off from a conversation with his PA.

'Edwin, how did you get on?'

Edwin knew he only had ten seconds to "sell" the story.

'Very good, Ross... his real name is Fischer, spelled the German way. He was brainwashed by his father who told him he was related to the Nazi professor whose book inspired Hitler's Master Race ideology. That's the guts of it.'

'Bloody hell. You're saying he's one of Hitler's disciples!'

'Yes, you could say that. He was – and still is, as far as I know. But all this is strictly off the record. She made it very clear that we cannot quote her, that she would be really worried Fisher would take some sort of revenge if he discovered she had been talking to the press,' Edwin explained.

'We'd have to check it out anyway. We couldn't take her word for it. We need to check out this Nazi professor – see if what she says all stacks up and if he was related to him.'

'I shall enjoy that. Will make a start asap.'

*

Searching for nuggets of information either through the Internet, library archives or direct contact with individuals, was for Edwin the journalistic equivalent of digging for gold. His inquisitiveness was boundless and he never lost the thrill of discovering or unearthing hidden treasure – tracking down the facts that could convert the mundane into a page one story.

He had never heard of Eugen Fischer, but couldn't wait to find out who he was and if he did play such a crucial and influential role in implanting the concept of the Aryan Master Race in the mind of Adolf Hitler. Quite apart from his innate journalistic curiosity, Edwin had his own personal interest in the persecution of the Jews throughout history, primarily because many of his late father's Jewish ancestors had fled their native Poland during the pogroms of the late 19th century, and also because he had a few years earlier ghost-written a Holocaust memoir about a man who had witnessed the extermination of thirty-seven members of his family at the hands of the Nazis.

Neither Edwin nor his late father, a former single-handed family doctor, were practising Jews, but as he grew older, Edwin became increasingly interested in tracing his Eastern European roots and the origins of anti-Semitism, and why it was possible for one man to brainwash his fellow countrymen into believing that Jews were somehow sub-human beings who should be wiped off the face of the earth.

As he trawled through the Internet, it did not take him long to discover that Fisher's ex-wife was right. Prof. Eugen Fischer – a tall, thin-faced man with cold staring eyes – was, indeed, the university academic who formulated the blueprint for the implementation of Hitler's Master Race. He was the undisputed father of Nazi eugenics – the misguided, scientifically-flawed theory that the human race could be improved through selective, planned breeding of populations.

Eugen Fischer, Edwin established, was a German professor of medicine, anthropology and eugenics and a highly-influential member of the Nazi Party. Edwin's first thought was that he had given his name to the theory of eugenics but, as he delved deeper, it became clear that the concept had its origins in the very early 1800s, some seventy or more years before Fischer was born in July 1874 in Karlsruhe, Germany. Possibly his parents had given him the name Eugen because they were blinkered followers of the principles of eugenics – or it could simply have been an uncanny coincidence.

In 1908, when he was only thirty-four years old, Fischer founded the Society for Race Hygiene in Freiburg im Breisgau and served as a judge for Berlin's Hereditary Court , where he worked with an American eugenicist, Charles Davenport, on what were disturbingly known as "bastard studies" at the International Federation of Eugenics Organizations.

But Edwin was especially fascinated and intrigued to learn that it was Fischer's textbook – *Principles of Human Heredity and Race Hygiene* – that was read by Adolf Hitler when he was in Landsberg prison and, more importantly, informed his later theories and policies on the creation of a "pure" Aryan Master Race. Fischer's principles of racial hygiene found fertile territory in Hitler's mind, who believed that the German nation had become weak and corrupted by the infusion of "degenerate elements not in its bloodstream".

Fischer's academic treatise became what, in effect, was the blueprint for the Holocaust – perhaps the greatest stain on the history of mankind but one which James Karl Fisher denied ever happened. Ironically, after the war, when Eugen Fischer completed his memoirs, he played down his role in the genocidal programme of Nazi Germany, probably to save his own skin. He died in Freiburg im Breisgau, in July 1967, aged ninety-three.

As Edwin continued to research Fischer's cancerous legacy, it became abundantly clear why James Karl Fisher had also been brainwashed by his father – and probably grandfather, too – to hate Jews, Blacks and other minority groups whom Fischer claimed corrupted the purity of German blood. Fischer, he learned, was also infamous for authoring a study of mixed-race children, mostly the offspring of Hottentot women and Dutchmen who came from German-run African states. In his 1913 study of the "Mischlinge", Fischer predicted that these mixed-race children would "bring about the demise of European culture".

Under the leadership of Hitler, Eugen Fischer's insane selective breeding ideology was even more widely interpreted to include anyone whom the Nazis identified as *Lebensunwertes Leben* – people regarded as "life unworthy of life". They included prisoners, degenerates, dissidents, those with congenital and physical disabilities and even those considered to be *Schwachsinn* – the term used at the time for the feebleminded.

Edwin could not bring himself to forgive Fisher for his decade or more of anti-Semitic and racist crimes, but knowing that he had been schooled since childhood in the teachings of the Nazi professor, he understood why he held such radical views and had behaved so violently in the past to those he hated.

According to Karen Passoa, Fisher's father, Herman Fischer, and his father before him were German patriots who slavishly believed that if the professor's policies on racial hygiene – *Russenhygiene* – were being implemented by the Fuehrer, then they were clearly in the best interests of the nation and should not be challenged.

As such, Herman Fischer accepted without question that Jews, Negroes and other minority groups were racially inferior and that inter-breeding with people of Aryan stock would destroy European culture.

It was clear to Edwin that the young brain of James Karl Fisher, or Karl Fischer as he would have been when he was born in Baden-Württemberg, would have been indoctrinated with these philosophies and he would have been too young to question them – to decide for himself whether they were right or wrong.

Fisher had also been brought up in the belief that he was related to the "great" Professor Fischer, but his ex-wife told Edwin when they met at her home on Merseyside that he had never been able to find the familial link and he had never been able to establish if he was related or not.

Edwin, who was a member of a number of family history websites for his own purposes, decided that, whilst it was not an immediate priority, he would be interested in conducting his own research. If heart transplant recipient James Karl Fisher was, related to the father of Nazi eugenics, it would most certainly be newsworthy.

After several hours of research on the Internet, Edwin was satisfied that what he had been told by Karen Passoa was almost certainly correct. He copied and pasted all the relevant information into a single Word document which he saved to his computer under the heading "Eugen Fischer – research info". He did not believe that Fisher was related to the mad Nazi professor, but there were still doubts that he knew only a professional genealogist would be able to resolve.

He wasn't quite sure how or if he would make use of all the information. Without question, it would make yet another interesting follow-up article with the specific news angle that Fisher had been brainwashed into believing the "racial hygiene" lunacy of the German professor.

But, for the time being, all he wanted was a strong coffee, something to eat and a breath of fresh air.

*

When Edwin returned to his desk after an hour's break, news editor Ross Hetherington called him over for a short briefing.

'Did it all stack up? Did you find out anything about this Nazi professor?' Ross asked.

'Yes, it's all there in black and white. Chapter and verse,' confirmed Edwin. 'Fisher's wife was right, but we don't know yet whether Fisher was related to the professor or whether his father just believed or wanted to believe that they were.

'If, of course, we do eventually find out that he was related to Adolf's academic pal, then that would be one hell of a story – but that may prove difficult without professional help. But to be honest, Ross, it doesn't really matter in one sense. The fact that Fisher's father and grandfather believed that the professor's philosophy was right and that they brainwashed the young Fisher is all that really matters.'

'It's all strong stuff,' said Ross. 'But without some attribution – someone who's prepared to go on record and say he was brainwashed and believed he was related or we can prove he was related – we really couldn't run it. We need a strong news peg to hang it on and it falls just that crucial bit short of that, as it stands. Just keep everything on file for the time being. I'm sure we'll be able to run it before too long.'

'You're right. I could knock out a piece claiming this and alleging that with all the colourful hard facts about Eugen Fischer and eugenics but we'd just be flying a bit of a kite.'

When he sat down at his PC, he opened the Eugen Fischer file, ran off a hard copy and consigned it to a safe place in a buff-coloured file in his top drawer. For several weeks, the story with its various twists and turns had occupied most of Edwin's working hours – and it was frequently the last thing on his mind as he put his head on his pillow at night before falling asleep.

In the weeks ahead, Edwin planned to use his amateur genealogical skills – restricted largely to researching his own family tree – to see if he could find any conclusive familial links between James Karl Fisher and the champion of Nazi eugenics.

Journalistically, he knew it would be yet another big news story if he could establish any blood relationship with Eugen Fischer but, having met Fisher, Edwin had also developed a keen personal interest in the people who had influenced him in his early years. And he knew he would not be satisfied until he knew more.

Instinctively, whether he could unearth any startling revelations about his ancestry or not, he knew that the Fisher saga would resurface in some shape or form before long. But, for the time being, it was in the pending file.

CHAPTER 4

Several weeks had elapsed since Edwin and photographer Mike Wolff had witnessed first-hand surgeon Jonathan Barr-White and his team stitch the donor heart into the gaping chest cavity of transplant recipient James Karl Fisher.

As his newspaper's health and medical correspondent, Edwin had been invited to be there because it was the 25th anniversary of the launch of the hospital's heart transplant programme, launched not long after the late Prof. Christiaan Barnard performed the world's first at the Groote Schuur Hospital in South Africa.

Clinically, there was nothing especially significant about the operation itself, and Edwin had expected that he would simply be required to write a blow-by-blow report of the transplant and a follow-up article a week or so later based on a bedside interview with the recipient. But when it became known that James Karl Fisher was an anti-Semitic racist with a long criminal history who had received the heart of an Orthodox Jew, it was instantly elevated to a running news story that attracted international coverage.

But as the winter morphed slowly into spring and the story gradually slipped out of the headlines, Edwin found himself increasingly devoting his working hours reporting a range of sundry health and medical stories of a more mundane, run-of-the-mill nature.

News, he had learned over the years, was an ephemeral commodity. One day a story could be attracting banner national, even international, headlines, the next it could be relegated to a mere paragraph or two or even disappear altogether, with something else stepping up into the spotlight.

It meant that the life of a newspaper reporter, be it in the medical arena or any other, was almost never the same on two or more consecutive days, and certainly never boring. As a health and medical affairs reporter, Edwin could on the same day be called upon to report a breakthrough that had the potential to save countless lives, to an individual's survival against all the odds or the tragedy of a rare and unexpected death.

At other times – on what were recognised as quiet news days – Edwin would trawl through medical journals such as *The Lancet* and *The British Medical Journal*, as well as government and health authority reports, in the hope of finding a "hidden" gem that could be fashioned into a news story or feature article with wide public appeal. It was on such slow news days that Edwin would also spend an hour or two accessing the family history websites to see if he could establish if James Karl Fisher had anything in his genetic profile in common with the professor of Nazi eugenics.

When he had initially spent time researching the life of Eugen Fischer, he had not found anything to suggest that they could be related, even though geographically transplant recipient Fisher and his father and grandfather came from the same region of Germany. Fisher's ex-wife, Karen Passoa, he recalled, had also told him that Fisher did not have any documentary evidence to prove any familial relationship. It was beginning to look less and less likely.

After perhaps a day or two of further searches, Edwin informed his news editor that he had not been able to establish any link and that because all the relevant information was probably buried away in German archives, coupled with the language problem, he would require the services of a professional genealogist if he was going to make any real progress.

'Just forget it – just kick it into touch. You are probably wasting your time and I doubt very much if the editor would authorise spending any money to hire a professional to research it for us,' said Ross.

'It's just that it really fascinates me,' Edwin replied. 'I'd really love to know if they were related.'

'If you hear anything new from anywhere – the hospital or his ex – or anyone else and the story rears its head, then maybe I can persuade the editor that we need to spend a few quid on a professional researcher. But, for now, just leave it.'

'OK, will do,' said Edwin, knowing that he would nonetheless carry on researching it in his own time out of personal interest.

*

A few days later, on what promised to be an uneventful day in the office, Edwin was perusing through the agenda of a forthcoming health authority meeting, when he took a phone call that would propel James Karl Fisher back into the headlines.

'Hello, Edwin Benn, *The Informer*. Can I help you?' he said automatically.

'I think perhaps that I can help you. It's Anna Dickson here, the transplant coordinator. We have not spoken for a little while. How are you?'

'Well, thanks. And you?'

'I am well, too... now, let me tell you, Mr Fisher was in the unit yesterday for one of his routine check-ups and, having read your earlier article, I think that you really ought to know that he now has a swastika tattooed over his new heart and the words "One Jew Less" written underneath in German. We think that he must have had it done since he learned the identity of his donor some weeks ago.'

'Anna, I do really appreciate you letting me know. I'm not sure what to say, to be honest. It's unthinkable that anyone could do such a thing, especially knowing that you would see it at the hospital. It really is a shocking thing to do. And who would have been prepared to do it for him?' asked Edwin.

'The nurse noticed it right away but, of course, couldn't really say anything to him. He is first and foremost a patient and, as such, our only interest is in the health of his heart. But,

97

of course, privately, we have our own views, as you well know,' she added.

'Of course, I appreciate that.'

'Much as we might loathe what he stands for and the man himself, it's not our job to comment – unless, of course, it were directly to affect our staff or other patients. The surgeons, by the way, Edwin, know that I am calling you... they felt that it would be wrong to keep this from you.'

'Thank them, will you, Anna,' said Edwin, adding, 'As a matter of interest, did Fisher remark about the tattoo to anyone?'

'I gather he said to one of the nurses something like "You probably don't approve of it but it had to be done – I want my new heart to feel that it belongs to me". The nurse replied that she couldn't possibly comment and just got on with her job.'

'It must be very difficult for you not to say anything to him – to show your disgust.'

'Yes, it is but we simply have to remain impartial and say nothing. Between ourselves, of course, we have all been saying a man like him didn't deserve to be given a new heart but we cannot say that to his face.'

'Could you simply refuse to see him?' asked Edwin.

'We could, I suppose, but if anything happened to him – if he died – we could find ourselves in serious trouble with claims for medical negligence and the like,' she replied.

'Difficult, I can see that.'

'Just one important matter: I know that you could have heard this from other sources but we would prefer it if this were not published – and certainly not attributed to us – if that's all right with you.'

Edwin paused before responding, 'Anna, it is newsworthy, as I am sure you understand, but if we simply published a non-attributable story, I am pretty sure that Fisher would know that the information came from the hospital. I suspect there is no one else outside the hospital who knows about this tattoo except perhaps one or two of his followers and they are certainly not going to broadcast it.

'I suspect that there could well come a time in the future when we might be able to use it without it relating back to the hospital, but for the present, I will explain to the editor that we should keep it under wraps.'

'Thank you,' replied Anna. 'I appreciate that.'

*

Both Anna and Edwin had their own professional codes. For Anna, it was the sacrosanct code of medical ethics and patient confidentiality. For Edwin, it was the unwritten rules of responsible journalism coupled with press freedom and, in this particular case, the need to maintain an amicable working relationship with the hospital.

Journalistic ethics aside, Edwin knew that he had to relay this new and shocking piece of information to his news editor.

'Christ almighty. A swastika tattoo, you say. Bloody hell. Great story,' said Ross, using, as he often did, the name of the Lord Jesus as an expression of surprise with no intent of religious offence.

'It is a good story, I know, but we cannot attribute it to the hospital and they have asked me not to use it at all, if possible – at least not yet.'

'Can we not just attribute it to a hospital spokesman?' asked Ross.

Edwin explained, 'They wouldn't be happy with that, Ross. There's only a handful of people who would have seen the tattoo and Fisher would know who they are. And, of course, he will have to go back there again for another check-up before too long. Ross, they do recognise that it is newsworthy but have specifically asked us to keep it on file until such time as it emerges from another source... as I am sure it will before long.'

'OK, but don't kick it into the long grass. I'd like to think that we will be able to carry a piece about it before too long. Keep me posted.'

'I will, yes.'

*

That opportunity came quite unexpectedly only a few weeks later. It was a bright October day with the midday temperature in the upper teens, and Edwin was about to go out to buy a birthday card for his wife during his lunch break, when his office phone rang.

'Newsroom, can I help you?' he said cheerily.

'Am I speaking to Edwin Benn?' asked a woman with a Lancashire accent.

'You are, yes.'

'You don't know me, Mr Benn, but I felt I had to call you. My name's Sylvia Hartshorne. I'm the licensee at The Kettledrum Tavern, Jim Fisher's local – you're the reporter who has been writing all these stories about his heart swap, aren't you?' she began.

'Yes, you are right. That's me,' said Edwin, pricking up his ears in anticipation. 'I think I know your pub... I seem to remember I once came in to warm up after I'd been covering a story about a blizzard that blocked the roads, leaving drivers stranded. Anyway, how can I help you?'

When he picked up the handset, Edwin had expected it would be something of little consequence that would take only a minute or so of his time, but when he realised that it was about James Karl Fisher, he sat down at his desk, flicked open his spiral notebook and prepared to give his caller his full and undivided attention. Lunch and the greeting card would have to wait.

'May I ask how you know him?' asked Edwin directly, half expecting that as the landlady of Fisher's local, she could well be a sympathiser with his odious racist views and would be ringing to complain about something he had written.

But he couldn't have been more wrong.

'I've known Jim Fisher for donkey's years, ever since he moved over here from Liverpool,' she said. 'But I never really knew anything about his past or what sort of a bloke he was until I read those articles you wrote in the paper after he had his heart transplant.

'He used to come in the pub several nights a week and one night, after I had read your article about his crimes and prison sentences, I plucked up the courage to tell him what I thought of him. When he'd had a few pints, he used to tell me that he fancied me and say that my late husband was a really lucky guy. I never felt that he would threaten me or get nasty, especially as there were always lots of other people around.

'I suppose I noticed things over the years that made me think he was a bit of a racist, but he never really caused any bother so I just tended to ignore it.'

Edwin interjected, 'What sort of things did you notice, Sylvia – is it OK to call you Sylvia?'

'Yes, no problem. What did I notice? Well, I always noticed that he would move away if any Black people ever came in – which, to be honest, was not very often. Then there was one occasion I remember in particular when a Jewish couple from Rochdale had their wedding reception at the pub and he just got up and buggered off home.

'When he next came in I had a big row with him. I told him that I'd prefer anyone to a horrible neo-Nazi like him and his cronies and, for a time after that, he just stopped coming in and I thought that I had seen the last of him.'

Edwin sensed there was a big news story waiting in the wings and felt a number of questions queuing up to be asked.

'Do I take it then that he has now come back and is one of your regulars again?' he asked.

'Yes, I suppose you could say that. He started coming in on the odd occasion but he's now in the pub two or three nights a week – and during the day as well – mostly on his own but sometimes with some of his old mates from the gym.'

Edwin asked another direct question. 'Do they ever cause you any problems?'

'Not really. There's been the odd time when I have had to tell them I'd have to ban them if they didn't stop making racist comments but for a long time now he's behaved himself – most noticeably since my husband, Laurie, died about eighteen months ago.'

'Why do you think that is – I mean since your husband died?'

'Well, he always told me he fancied me when Laurie was alive, but after he died he must have thought that he was in with a real chance and I did go out with him for a meal on a couple of occasions. He also took me to the Grand National at Aintree and once to the races at York. He could be quite good company and was certainly always very generous.'

Edwin was intrigued by her anecdotes but was not sure why she had called him. 'So, you obviously got to know him pretty well. But has something now happened that—'

Sylvia interrupted. 'I know what you're going to say – you want to know why I called you. Well, let me tell you. I think you will find it very interesting.'

'Go on, I am most interested,' said Edwin, his ballpoint poised to record her comments in shorthand. He had abandoned the idea of finding a birthday card for his wife.

Sylvia took a deep breath before continuing, 'May I call you Edwin?'

'Yes, of course, you can.'

'Well, Edwin, he's now just not the same bloke. Since his transplant, he has been a completely changed man. I don't really know how to describe it. He's like one of those people who go off on pilgrimages to Lourdes and say they have seen a vision. I'm not a religious person but it's like he had some sort of revelation, seen the light. He's certainly not the same person he was, that's for sure.'

'Sounds like you're describing some sort of biblical epiphany,' said Edwin.

'I don't know what that is but, without any exaggeration, it's like the nasty old devil I remember of old has walked back into the pub and become some sort of saint, certainly a Mr Nice Guy. It's almost like he has had a new brain as well as a new heart.'

'What sort of changes have you noticed, Sylvia?'

'It's difficult to know where to start, to be honest – he just behaves differently, even looks different, less aggressive, less angry. He's altogether more relaxed, more tolerant of people, never makes any racist comments and he now doesn't seem to hang about with all his hangers-on any longer. In fact, I'm told that he's sold the gym where they all used to hang out.'

'That is all certainly very interesting – quite an amazing, miraculous transformation from the Jim Fisher of old. What do you think has brought about this dramatic change in him?' Edwin asked.

Sylvia paused to consider her answer. 'In my mind, I have no doubt that it was the transplant. I'm sure of it. It just cannot be anything else. I'm not a medical expert but it just has to be his new heart. It's changed him into a new person.'

Journalistically, Edwin realised that this was potential dynamite. James Karl Fisher, it seemed, had not only had a change of heart anatomically but had also undergone a change of heart psychologically and emotionally. This was big news.

He quizzed Sylvia for more details. 'Are there any particular, practical changes that you have noticed?'

'There are, yes. For a start, he's having all his tattoos removed – it's costing him a fortune by all accounts. I don't know whether you know or not but when he first heard that his heart donor was a Jewish person, he had a swastika tattooed over his heart – which I had to tell him was a bloody stupid, horrible thing to do.'

'As it happened, I did know about the swastika... but you say it's now gone as well as the rest of his racist tattoos. Obviously, something has dramatically changed the way he thinks and you could well be right, that it was having someone else's heart. I'll be checking that out with the medics, for sure, in due course.'

'What do you think, Edwin? Do you think that someone's whole personality can change after they've had a heart transplant? Would it just be a physical thing or psychological, or maybe a combination of both?'

'To be honest, I just don't know. It's something that I have never come across before but I can well believe that it's a very real possibility. I will most certainly find out.'

Edwin glanced up at the office wall clock and realised that he would have to be content with a sandwich lunch from the canteen and that the birthday card for his wife would have to wait until the following day.

'Is there anything else, Sylvia, you've noticed in particular about the way he's changed?' he asked.

'Well, apart from the fact that I no longer hear him slagging off "Blacks, Jews and Pakis", as he used to call them, he seems to have taken on some new interests – things that he never really had an interest in before.'

'Such as?'

'He regularly plays chess with one of our regulars who comes in two or times a week, on a couple or more occasions he's joined in on our karaoke night which he never did before his transplant and he told me that he's started tracing his family history on the Internet. He didn't do any of those things before his transplant,' said Sylvia.

'Fascinating, really fascinating. I'm going to be looking into all this. There's every possibility that the transplant team at the hospital may have come across this type of phenomenon before. I'll certainly be asking them about that – and if they've noticed any changes in Fisher, of course.'

Sylvia added, 'At first I thought that it was probably my imagination but it definitely isn't. He just isn't the same person as he was. In fact, I have never seen such a big change in anyone as I have with Jim Fisher.'

Edwin took note of her contact details and promised to make contact with her again should he glean any relevant medical information. They agreed to keep in touch and then said their goodbyes.

'Sounded like an interesting one. It's about our neo-Nazi transplant friend, I gather,' said a newsroom colleague, Niall, who was sitting only a few feet away and had picked up the thread of the conversation.

'It was, yes,' confirmed Edwin. 'It could be very interesting, to say the least. Could be a case of sinner turns saint after heart swap... but right now I'm interested in something to eat and a mug of sweet tea.'

He had planned to go to the office canteen but instead started thumbing through his notes, marking key sections with asterisks in the margin. As he did so, he beckoned one of the messenger boys and gave him some coins.

'Can you go and get me a chicken mayo sandwich, a bag of plain crisps and a mug of tea,' he asked.

Had Marcus Lieberman's donor heart given Fisher much more than a new lease of life? Was it possible that psychosomatically he had also been given a completely new personality? Could he even have acquired some of the traits and characteristics of his donor? Was it a phenomenon known to medical science?

It opened up an exciting and fascinating area of research for Edwin and he could not wait to get started.

As a medical journalist, he knew that anatomically the heart was simply a four-chambered pump that circulated blood around the body. But he also knew that since the dawn of civilisation, it was regarded as the seat of mankind's emotions, his psyche, his spirituality – his very heart and soul.

Be it in the classical literature of Ancient Greece or Rome, the works of the great poets, romantic Victorian novels or even the language of contemporary pop culture and music, the heart is seen as the barometer of human emotion that had given rise to a lexicon of idioms and phrases in everyday common English usage.

People, for example, could "find it in their heart", they could "follow one's heart" or "speak from the heart". Someone who was well-intended had "their heart in the right place". People could "get to the heart of the matter" or wish for something or someone "with their heart's desire".

They could express their true feelings in their "heart of hearts" or their "heart could sink" if they became discouraged or disappointed. They could "open their hearts", act out of the "goodness of their hearts", "put their heart into something" or, at times of despair and distress, "pour out their heart and soul".

James Karl Fisher, it seemed, was having a change of heart. Surgically, it was an anatomical fact. Another man's heart was now beating inside his chest. Psychologically and emotionally, it now seemed that he was also undergoing an equally impactful personality change.

An initial trawl through the wealth of academic research papers on the subject confirmed that it was a well-recognised, well-documented phenomenon. References to clinical studies around the globe confirmed that a heart transplant could lead to significant, permanent changes in a recipient's personality caused not only by emotional triggers but also by real physiological changes.

Edwin was fascinated to see that reports published in academic journals around the world, referred to the role of "cellular memory", of "intracardiac neurological memory" and "memory transfer" – of memory transmitted from one individual to another through the heart nerve cells.

His many years as a medical journalist had taught him to recognise the difference between serious peer-reviewed reports and fanciful, unsubstantiated claims written by cranks and charlatans. The ones he was now seeing with respect to heart transplantation were not in the dangerous kite-flying category but authoritative papers based on balanced research conducted by health professionals. They stressed that whilst the majority of heart transplant recipients did not experience any personality change post-surgery, one in five reported that they did experience changes and a percentage of those reported "drastic changes".

It seemed clear to Edwin, based on all the information he had been given about Fisher's "reincarnation", that he was one of those for whom the transplant had, indeed, resulted in radical changes. But it was certainly not without precedent.

According to the wealth of authenticated medical and scientific research that Edwin was able to identify via the Internet, Fisher was far from unique.

One of the largest studies of heart transplant recipients, conducted by Paul Pearsall, Gary Schwartz and Linda Russek at the University of Hawaii and published in the journal of Integrative Medicine, noted post-operative changes in their preference for certain foods, music, art, career choices, sensory experiences and even changes in their sexual and recreational preferences.

It highlighted the case of one patient who received the heart of a man killed by a gunshot to the face who, post-operatively, reported having persistent dreams in which he saw hot flashes of light directly on his face.

The researchers also documented what they described a case of "cell memory" in a woman – a former professional dancer – who received the heart of an eighteen-year-old male who died in a motorcycle accident. They reported that sometime after the transplant, the woman developed cravings for beer and chicken nuggets and had recurring dreams about a man she named "Tim L".

She subsequently discovered, after searching through obituaries and eventually tracking down his family, that her donor was, in fact, called Tim and that he had a passion for the same food and drink that she craved following her transplant. Reportedly, her daughter even told her that she began to walk more like a man.

Yet another authoritative report "Heart Transplant, Personality Transplants", by clinical psychiatrist Thomas R Verny, the author of the book *Mysteries of Cellular Memory, Consciousness and Our Bodies*, stated: "The heart is not only a pump but a centre of feeling, memory and personality". Key phrases in the report jumped off the page at Edwin, each reinforcing his conviction that following his transplant, Fisher was no longer the racist pariah.

Some of the key sentences and phrases were: "the heart, like the nervous system, possesses the properties of memory and adaptation", "the heart acts as a synchronisation force within the body, a key carrier of emotional information as well as other personality keys" and "sensitive transplant patients may evidence personality changes that parallel the experiences, likes, dislikes and temperament of their donors".

In all his many years of reporting advances and developments in the world of health and medicine, Edwin learned that it was always prudent to be sceptical and questioning. He had come across several unscrupulous practitioners, cranks and charlatans who claimed so-called miracle cures for everything from cancer to alopecia, arthritis to erectile dysfunction. They were, at best, simply worthless claims that could be dismissed but, at worst, they could be dangerous and life-threatening.

For Edwin, the concept of cell memory transference following a heart transplant was entirely logical and supported by orthodox scientific research. In Fisher's case, he felt that it was perfectly reasonable and rational to conclude that his new heart had obliterated all the hateful and malignant thoughts from his mind that had been implanted by his father – leaving him with the untarnished brain with which he was born.

So, armed with this wealth of convincing data and the anecdotal "evidence" from Sylvia Hartshorne, Edwin felt ready to approach the hospital transplant team for a comment.

His contact, Jonathan Barr-White, the consultant who carried out the transplant, was attending an international conference in the United States, but his colleague, James McCloud, who recovered the donor's heart, was available. They knew each other well so there was no need for any introduction, any formalities.

'How can I help, Edwin?' the surgeon asked.

'You'll not be surprised to hear that it's about our old friend, James Fisher.'

'Our patient with all the unpleasant tattoos and equally unpalatable views – to say the least,' said the surgeon in his softy-spoken Scottish accent.

'Precisely so... but I take it that you haven't had contact with him of late?'

'That's right. I've not seen him personally for some months.'

'Well, I'm told on good authority that he is a completely changed man in every way, physically, emotionally, politically... no longer the rabid racist anymore,' said Edwin.

'That's very interesting. I have heard the odd bit of feedback from staff who have seen him when he has been back for routine assessments in outpatients that would seem to confirm what you are saying.'

'Let me tell you what I've heard. I would then welcome your professional opinion,' continued Edwin. 'I had a call from the landlady at his local, Sylvia Hartshorne, who sees him regularly and knows him well. She says that she hardly recognises him as the same person. It seems he has even had all his neo-Nazi tattoos removed.'

'Really? That I didn't know.'

'She said there were times in the past when he was in the pub with some of his skinhead supporters and they would storm out if ever a Black person came in, and on several occasions he would shout out obscenities at them. But in recent months she says he's been a totally different person in every way.'

'In what way "different",' asked the surgeon.

'Well, he no longer seems to associate with any of the loud-mouthed racists and he's closed down his gym where they all used to meet. She says that he now often sits quietly in a corner of the pub playing chess with one of the old regulars and sometimes he will get up to sing at one of the karaoke nights. She says that he also spends a lot of his time now tracing his family history.'

'It certainly doesn't sound like the Fisher we knew before and directly after his transplant and when he first started coming back for his assessments – all very interesting. Quite amazing, to be honest.'

'James, let me get to the point – I've been conducting some research on the Internet and it appears that the phenomenon of post-operative personality change is well established. It has been researched and documented at various centres around the world. Apart from the emotional changes, which to me seem very understandable, they also describe how what they call cell memory can play a significant role – and they give several examples of it.'

'Interesting, most interesting.'

'Is that something you or your colleagues have observed among your own patients?' Edwin asked.

'Small changes, yes, but I cannot say we have noticed any really radical personality changes in a patient. Lifestyle, diet and leisure activities changes, yes, but that would be expected in anyone who has undergone a heart transplant or, indeed, any form of major surgery,' the surgeon replied.

'But no complete personality changes?'

'In all honesty, it is not the sort of thing that we would routinely look for. When our patients return for their assessments, we are interested only in how their new heart is functioning, in their physical health. We are not looking in particular for any changes in a patient's personality traits – that is not part of our remit, although I am sure if there is a major change like you describe for Fisher, we would almost certainly be aware of it.'

'Yes, I can see that.'

'However, I would say that from a clinical perspective, it would seem entirely reasonable that there would be both physiological and psychological changes in a patient who had received a new heart.'

'That would certainly seem to be the case with Fisher. Do you know if your staff noticed changes in him when he last came back to outpatients?' asked Edwin.

'By all accounts, he made a point of apologising to one of our nurses, telling her he was sorry for "ignoring" her when he was on the recovery ward. Apparently, he said something like he was "not a very nice guy then" but was now "a changed man". There were odd comments like that which would support what you are saying.'

*

Later that same day, Edwin managed to speak to the transplant coordinator, Anna Dickson, who confirmed the consultant's story.

'The last time we saw him, we couldn't get over how much he had changed; he was so much gentler and kinder. It was really quite remarkable. We all noticed it. And, of course, all those horrible, offensive tattoos had gone.'

*

Armed with this new information about Fisher, Edwin felt that he needed to speak with Leah Lieberman, the heart donor's widow. It had been some considerable time since he and the rabbi had been to her home, and he was reluctant to raise an issue that would inevitably remind her of her husband's tragic, untimely death. But he felt that he had little choice.

He called her from the office the following day. She answered almost immediately.

'Leah Lieberman here. How may I help you?' she said.

'It's Edwin Benn here, Mrs Lieberman. My apologies for troubling you again. Are you well?' he asked.

'You are not troubling me in the least and I am well, thank you. And you?'

'I'm just fine, thanks. I was a little reluctant to call you after all this time but I feel that what I have to tell you may be of interest.'

'Oh, what might that be, then? Sounds very mysterious.'

'It's just that when I last spoke to the transplant team at the hospital, they told me that on James Fisher's most recent visit to outpatients for his check-up, they had noticed some pretty dramatic changes in him – not just physically, but more importantly in terms of his whole personality and his extremist views. You may know about it?'

'No, no one has informed me or told me anything. And I don't know, to be honest, whether I am interested to know any more about Mr Fisher.'

'I can fully understand that Mrs Lieberman, but you may well be interested to hear that he's just not the same man since he received Marcus's heart. He is, by all accounts, not a racist any longer and is apologising to staff for the way he used to behave and the things he used to do and say. It's quite remarkable,' said Edwin.

There was a long silence.

'Are you still there, Mrs Lieberman?' he asked.

'Still here, yes. Just shocked. I'm not sure what to say. How can it be that he has suddenly changed? I don't understand how that could happen.'

'Well, I gather it's not a sudden, overnight change. It seems it has taken place slowly over the past few weeks, months. It's been very obvious to the doctors and nurses but, most interestingly, to Fisher himself. He keeps telling people that he is a reformed character and has apologised to many of the nurses for the way he behaved when he was recovering from his operation. I've been researching this sort of phenomenon and there is a wealth of medical evidence to show that in a number of cases, this sort of thing can and does happen.'

'Well, of course, I am very pleased to hear this, but I have to say, I still find it very hard to believe that someone can just change like that, don't you?'

'In a way, I do, yes. It is, I must admit, quite amazing. But I've been reading all the literature and it's clear from studies around the world that this sort of thing does happen when patients have undergone transplant surgery and, in particular, heart transplant surgery.'

'Has he mentioned Marcus or me as far as you know, Edwin?' she asked.

'That I don't know but I might well be able to find out and let you know. But from what they tell me at the hospital, I think it's safe to assume that he now thinks of Marcus in an entirely new light.'

'Why would he think that?'

'Well, first of all, he had all his nasty tattoos removed and I was told by the landlady at his local pub in the Rossendale Valley that he now plays chess with one of the regulars, joins in the karaoke nights but never sang a note before, devotes a lot of time tracing his family history and he no longer sees any of his old racist supporters,' Edwin explained.

There was an even longer silence from Mrs Lieberman.

'Are you OK there, Mrs Lieberman?'

'Yes, yes. It's just all a little bit unsettling really. I'm not sure what to make of it.'

'I'm sorry to hear that. I hope that I have not—'

'No, it's just some of the specific things that you mentioned would also have applied to Marcus. It's very difficult to get my head round that.'

'Would you like me to leave it for today and call you back on another day? That would not be a problem.'

'No, there's no need for that...' She took a long, deep breath and continued, 'It's just that Marcus was a very keen chess player and used to play online against people in Israel and was also very keen on tracing our family history. He had a close friend who was a member of the Jewish Genealogical Society of Great Britain.'

'Yes, I can see how that could be disturbing.'

'And you mentioned about him taking part in karaoke at his pub. Marcus never took part in any karaoke or anything like that, but, of course, he did lead the singing in the synagogue and you said that Fisher never sang in public before his transplant. It gives me a strange, odd feeling – a bit scary, I suppose.'

Edwin attempted to change the tenor of the conversation. 'I'm no expert, of course, but all the research does suggest that heart transplant patients can and do have complete personality changes and have often been known to take on the traits of their donor. I honestly believe that this is what has happened in Fisher's case. It's sort of wiped the slate clean.'

Leah Lieberman thought for a few moments and then responded, 'All I would say is that if having Marcus's heart has stopped him being anti-Semitic and a racist, then it has to be a good thing. Marcus, I know, would feel the same.'

'That's a very charitable, noble sentiment, Mrs Lieberman.'

'Thank you...' she said, then, after a few moments continued, '... what really puzzles and concerns me is how someone like Fisher could ever have felt so hostile towards Jews and people of colour in the first place. I just cannot understand where and how all that hatred could have started.'

'Mrs Lieberman, I think we do know the answer to that in Fisher's case but I did not feel that you would be greatly interested, especially now that he no longer thinks and behaves as he did.'

'No. I would still be interested to know why – to be honest, anybody would ever think like that.'

'It is, in fact, very interesting in Fisher's case. His ex-wife contacted me when she read about his transplant in our paper and I went over to see her at her home because she said that there was a lot that we did not know about Fisher,' Edwin explained. 'She told me that he was born in Germany, his birth name was Karl Fischer, spelt the German way F-I-S-C-H-E-R, and that his father and grandfather had brainwashed him ever since he was a small boy into believing that the Jews – as well as other minority groups – were a malignant cancer in society and needed to be cut out and destroyed.

'What is really fascinating is that his father and his father before him claimed that they were related to the Nazi professor, Eugen Fischer, whose book about what he called racial hygiene was read by Hitler when he was in prison and it inspired him to draw up his plan for the Master Race. You can see that the younger Fisher was indoctrinated – that he really didn't have a chance.'

The explanation made Leah Lieberman feel considerably less uneasy. 'I am so glad you explained that to me, Edwin. I can understand now that he never stood a chance of ever being able to form views of his own. It makes me feel much more charitable towards him – certainly, now that you say he is a reformed man anyway.'

'By all accounts, Fisher is now in the process of tracing his family ancestry and I am now proposing to contact him and offer him some help and support with his research.

Journalistically, we are now interested to find out more about his background. I've been researching my wife's and my own family history for many years and I would like to think that I might be able to speed up the process for him... although I know from my own experience that you can come up against brick walls that can make it difficult,' said Edwin.

'Yes, you are right. I know that Marcus often ran into problems tracing people in Eastern Europe, especially as a lot of Jewish records were destroyed by the Nazis. But if you do find out anything of real interest about Fisher, I would be most interested to hear it.'

'Of course, I will let you know. If you would be good enough to relay our conversation to your rabbi, I would be most grateful. I will keep in touch.'

Edwin ended his telephone conversation feeling pleased that they had established such a harmonious rapport.

CHAPTER 5

Edwin realised that he was sitting on another big news story. He had first-hand testimony from both the hospital and Sylvia Hartshorne at Fisher's local that Fisher was no longer the tattoo-emblazoned racist – that by some psychosomatic metamorphosis, evil had changed into good and Mr Nasty had become Mr Nice Guy.

There was also abundant scientific evidence to show that transplant recipients and especially those who had been given new hearts, could adopt through cell memory the traits and characteristics of their donor. And, in Fisher's case, his donor's widow disclosed that his sudden interest in chess, genealogy and music had been three of her late husband's greatest passions.

But, convincing though it was, it was still all largely anecdotal. Before he could be sure that Fisher was now a new man who had cast aside all his neo-Nazi views and bodily hallmarks for good, he would first have to speak to the man himself again. He needed Fisher himself to tell him that he had changed. Only then would he be able to sit down at his desktop PC and write about his cathartic body-and-soul cleansing.

Edwin's first thought was simply to pick up the phone and call him, but after a few moments of reflection, he decided it would be prudent to seek the guidance of his news editor.

'What do you think, Ross? Should I give him a call and see if he'll agree to meet me, bearing in mind that the last time I saw him he was in a wild rage turning the air blue – and virtually threw Mike Wolff and me out of the door.'

He knew that he would get a succinct, straight answer.

'Just ring him – you've nothing to lose. If he won't talk, so be it, but if he's the changed character you say he is then he should want you to know – and everyone else, for that matter.'

'True,' said Edwin. 'I hoped that's what you'd say. If I arrange a meeting with him and he confirms everything I've been told, I reckon it'll make one hell of a good piece.'

'Give him a call and let me know what he says.'

'Just one thought, Ross. If he refuses to see me, I think there would be a pretty good chance that Sylvia Hartshorne at the pub could persuade him that it would be a good idea to talk to us. But, yes, I'm optimistic that he'll agree to see me.'

'I'm sure you'll persuade him... and, if you can, tell him you will be coming along with a photographer. Good luck.'

*

With some trepidation, Edwin returned to his desk, located Fisher's number in his contacts book and dialled. Despite what he had been told about his new clean-cut persona, he expected a rude response, possibly even a blunt two-word expletive. But he couldn't have been more wrong.

'Is that Jim Fisher?' asked Edwin boldly.

'Who's that, who's speaking?'

'We've not spoken for a while – it's Edwin Benn here from *The Informer*. I was just—'

Fisher cut him short in mid-sentence. 'That's a coincidence. I was planning to give you a call.' His tone was mellow; placatory.

'How are you anyway, Jim? Is everything going well? It must be six or seven months now since your transplant.'

'Yes, I guess so. I'm just bloody great. I feel as fit as the old butcher's dog. The doctors are letting me do some light jogging round the country lanes and that keeps me in pretty good shape.'

'Wonderful. That's good to hear,' said Edwin, disguising the fact that he could hardly believe he had been given such an instantly friendly reception.

'I don't know whether you know or not but I've sold the gym and no longer see anything of the old gang that used to go in there. They think I've gone a bit soft since my transplant, and I suppose they're right. Glad to see the back of them, to be honest.'

'Sounds like a good move, Jim,' said Edwin.

'It was. In fact, there have been a whole lot of changes in my life since I got my new heart. I'm not the person I used to be, I'm pleased to say, and that's what I was going to call you about. I wanted to apologise for everything I said when you came over to my place with your photographer.'

'Accepted. That's all right, Jim. That's all in the past now.' Edwin was finding it hard to believe that this was the same man who erupted volcanically when he learned for the first time that he had been given the heart of an Orthodox Jew.'

'Is there something that you particularly wanted to know, Edwin – I can call you Edwin, can't I?' Fisher asked.

'Of course, yes.'

'I'm sure that you've called me a few names in the past, not all of them repeatable!' he joked.

'You may know, Jim, that your good friend, Sylvia, has told me about how your lifestyle and views have changed, and I know that the staff at the hospital have also noticed the changes in you when you've been back for check-ups. Now, if you're happy about it, I'd like to come over and go into it in a bit more detail. It's a really uplifting, heartwarming story, if you'll pardon the pun, Jim.' He gritted his teeth as he waited for Fisher's reply.

'I don't know how interesting it is but that's OK by me. I suppose it's high time that I got rid of my old image and gave myself a bit of a makeover. You say you'll come over here to see me?'

'Wherever you like, Jim. It's entirely up to you. We just need an hour or so.'

'Are you happy to meet me at The Kettledrum, Sylvia's pub, in a couple of weeks?'

'That would be just perfect. I can buy you a pint.'

'No, I think I owe you one by way of an apology. Anyway, it couldn't be any sooner than the week after next because Sylvia and I will be away next week for a short break in Spain.'

'Very nice... it should still be nice and warm there at this time of the year.'

'Yes, I reckon so. You could call it a bit of a trial honeymoon really. We've had our ups and downs over the years, but since my transplant, we've been getting on famously and I am pleased to say that she's agreed to become the next Mrs Fisher. We are hoping to fix a date pretty soon.'

'Congratulations, Jim. I suppose you could say that you've been given a new heart and now you're planning to give it away!' Edwin joked.

'I like that. I'll tell her that next time I see her; it'll give her a chuckle,' said Fisher. 'So, is the week after next OK with you?'

'Absolutely, I shall look forward to it.'

They agreed on a date and time, exchanged a few pleasantries and then ended what had been a calm-as-a-duck-pond conversation compared with the angry, stormy seas of their last encounter.

Edwin found it hard to believe that he had been speaking with the same man. The tone of his voice, his language, his whole demeanour – everything had changed. When the time came to write the article about his psychosomatic change, Edwin could see himself alluding to the man who not only had a heart transplant but also a personality transplant. He found it hard to comprehend the totality of his reincarnation.

*

Two weeks later, Edwin and photographer Mike Wolff headed off for a lunchtime meeting with Jim Fisher at the Kettledrum Tavern. They felt none of the stress and apprehension of their last meeting with him at his home when they had to tell him that his donor was an Orthodox Jew and a synagogue cantor to boot.

'I think you'll be amazed to see just how he has changed – all the anger and hate that Jim Fisher the racist had seems to have gone. It's like the old Jim just never existed,' said Edwin as they headed out of the city for the open countryside of the Rossendale Valley.

'Is this all the result of the transplant?' asked Mike.

'I've never come across anything like it before, but according to all the scientific and medical literature, it is a recognised phenomenon, yes. I read a lot of the papers online and they refer to what they call cell memory, and the medics and staff at the transplant centre accept that it makes medical sense.'

'Is it permanent? Can they revert back to their old ways over time?'

'That's a good question and I don't know the answer. But I suspect it would be permanent. New heart, new personality – I suppose it works as simply as that,' Edwin suggested.

'I hope you're right. When I first heard that we would be going to meet him again today, I thought we could end up getting beaten up by some of his heavies. I was quite worried about it. I thought that I might need my tin hat,' said Mike.

'By all accounts, he no longer associates with any of his old neo-Nazi gang. He's sold his gym where they all used to meet up and they have all drifted away from the pub. No, I don't think there's any risk we're going to get knocked about.'

'That's a relief...' Mike paused, continuing in a more contemplative tone, 'This cell memory thing presumably would also work the other way round. I mean, if it were the Jewish guy who had the transplant and he'd been given Fisher's heart... could he have become a neo-Nazi? Just a thought.'

'Logically, scientifically, it makes sense but it seems that the old grey matter reverts to its default setting, so to speak – the way it was at birth. But yours is an interesting theory. It's quite a thought. You could end up with people or families suing doctors for turning their loved ones into monsters,' mused Edwin.

*

Just a few minutes before one o'clock on the day of their meeting, Edwin and Mike pulled into The Kettledrum's car park. The tavern was in an exposed location and as they stepped outside they were instantly aware that it was an overcoat colder compared with the fairly balmy temperature in the city centre.

'Very picturesque and all that but I'm not sure I'd like to live up here in the winter,' said Edwin.

'You'd soon get used to it, I'm sure,' replied Mike, who was very much the all-weathers outdoor type.

'Maybe you're right. Great for long country walks if you're well wrapped up, but living here, not so sure.'

'Would suit me. I'm a bit of a sky-at-night enthusiast and there would hardly be any light pollution around here. Would be great for astronomical photography.'

Mike lifted the heavy metal latch on what looked like the tavern's original front door, which led to a short stone-paved passageway, off which there were a number of individual small rooms all with their own unique names. Unlike many other old inns throughout the county and elsewhere, The Kettledrum had seen structurally little changed since it was built in the 17th century.

Jim Fisher was sitting at a corner table in the main parlour a few yards from a blazing log fire that cast an inviting and welcoming blanket of warmth over the whole room. He was playing chess with an older man who Edwin and Mike later learned was a retired schoolteacher and now served as a local magistrate. They were both drinking beer from tall pint glasses.

Although it had been some months since they had met – and under very different circumstances – Fisher instantly recognised Edwin and his colleague. He stood up and gave a thumbs-up sign as Edwin and Mike walked towards them. Edwin and Mike stretched out their arms and they all shook hands.

'This is my chess-playing mate, Bernard Haworth – I should really say my checkmate because he always beats me!' Jim jested.

'Pleased to meet you,' said Edwin and Mike almost simultaneously.

'Likewise,' said Bernard, a man in his early seventies with a ruddy complexion, a shock of wavy white hair and a sizable paunch underneath a thick woolly sweater.

Edwin and Mike sat down on the two empty seats at the same table, being careful not to disturb the chess board and the few remaining pieces, suggesting that their game was coming close to its end.

'Can I get you gentlemen a drink?' asked Bernard.

'No, you finish your game with Jim. We'll get the drinks,' Edwin assured him.

'That's kind of you.' Bernard moved his bishop across the board as he spoke. 'Same again for me. Sylvia knows what we have.'

'And for me, too,' said Jim contemplating his next move.

Edwin walked over to the small bar, introduced himself formally to Sylvia and ordered the drinks.

'Mike and I will have the same,' said Edwin.

'I think I'm buggered again, Mr Haworth,' sighed Jim, 'but one of these days I'll beat you. I'm still a learner, remember.'

Sylvia placed a tray of four pints on the table and Jim, having resigned himself to another defeat, removed the chess board and put all the pieces back in their box.

'Right, gentlemen, I know you've not come all this way to watch me get another hammering from Bernard here. What is it you want to ask me?'

'Well, a few things really about the way you now feel after your transplant and how it's given you a new lease of life in more ways than one,' said Edwin. 'Are you OK here or would you prefer to go somewhere and chat privately?'

'Here's just fine. Bernard knows all about the old Jim Fisher. In fact, as a magistrate, he's often told me how tough he would have been with me in my bad old days if I'd ever come before him. No, feel free to ask me anything you like in front of Bernard.'

Edwin took a swig from his pint, opened his spiral reporters' notebook and took a ballpoint pen from the inside pocket of his blazer.

'Just fine by me, Jim. But the first thing I must ask you is did you and Sylvia have a good break in Spain? You certainly look as though you caught the sun.'

'It was bloody marvellous – best holiday I've had for many a year... wall-to-wall sunshine every day, great hotel with great food and, well, suffice to say, that lady there and I had a terrific time,' he said, nodding towards Sylvia serving behind the bar.

'Where was it you went? Did you tell me on the phone?' asked Edwin.

'We went to Nerja on the Costa del Sol. Loved it... now, gentlemen, what do want from me?'

Edwin felt that a short introductory preamble was necessary before asking him any personal, direct questions. He could see from Jim's whole body language, his genuinely affable demeanour and tone of voice that he was no longer the James Karl Fisher wracked with hate and irrational prejudice, but he still could not help feeling that he needed to tread carefully.

'Jim, I gather from Sylvia and the hospital that things have changed in many ways for you since your transplant. Are you able to say in what ways you feel that you have changed and if you feel that it is as a direct result of the transplant?'

'OK, fair enough. Well, first of all, I would say that I have most certainly changed and that I believe that it can only be as a result of having a new heart. I'm not a medic or any kind of expert but I just can't see how it could be anything else.'

'So what changes have you noticed?' Edwin continued.

'I just don't hate Jews any longer, or anyone else, for that matter. As you know – you've read about my past – I used to hate minority groups with a vengeance and felt that the world would have been a better place without any of them. But I just don't feel like that anymore. In fact, the only person I hate now is myself and that's because I cannot believe that I ever did all those horrible things years back.'

Jim took another long swig from his beer.

'Do you feel that you've changed permanently? Do you actually feel any differences in yourself, in how you respond to people?'

'I'm happier, I know that, get less angry about things, generally much more relaxed about things. I suppose I enjoy life now much more than I can ever remember. You could say my old dicky heart was full of all sorts of rubbish and nonsense but this new one is, well, how can I put it, full of sunshine and happiness. Does that sound a bit soppy?'

'No, not at all, Anything but. It's just great to hear that you are not only physically now in good shape but that you feel that you're also in a better, happier place mentally,' said Edwin.

'Yes, that's true. I do. And I'm sure it's permanent. All that hatred and violence was really never the real me. It was drummed into me when I was a child. My mind just soaked it all up like a sponge and I couldn't do anything about it. I can still remember my father telling me that the Jews – and others minorities as well – were *Untermensch*, sub-human.' Then, turning to his friend, Bernard, said, 'You'd agree that I've changed for the better, wouldn't you?'

'Absolutely. I know from my time in court when people have changed their lives for the better, and that's certainly true in your case, Jim. I remember you telling me that in your bad old days, you wouldn't even have played with the black pieces on the chess board but you now realise that there's no place in your life for any kind of prejudice like that,' said Bernard.

'You're right. The old Jim Fisher went into the incinerator with the old heart.' Jim chuckled. 'I expect you newspaper guys find it hard to believe that I'm no longer that nasty racist bastard. To be honest, I sometimes find it hard to believe myself. What you need to know is that my father and my grandfather, too, brainwashed me as a child growing up. I never stood a chance of believing anything else. They told me that we were related to Eugen Fischer, the German professor... I don't know whether you know anything about him.'

'Yes, a little,' said Edwin, deciding it was the right time to tell him that he had been told about him and was aware of the connection.

'Well, he was the Nazi who wrote the book that gave Hitler the idea of the Master Race... that Jews, Black people and others were a sort of cancer in society that had to be cut out... and I was brought up to believe all that rubbish.

'I was even called Karl because we lived near Karlsruhe where Fischer came from, but since my transplant, I've been doing some research online and I haven't come across anything to suggest that we were related to Eugen Fischer. I think my father and his father just wanted to think we were. I guess my father was brainwashed by his father.'

Edwin thought it was the right time to tell him a little about his donor, Marcus Lieberman.

'Jim, it's interesting that you've started trying to trace your family history. You probably won't know this but your donor was a keen amateur genealogist – and also a very keen chess player. It certainly looks like you have adopted at least two of his traits.'

'I'm thinking there's probably a third one as well. Bernard will tell you that he has to put up with me getting up when they have a karaoke night, yet before my transplant, I wouldn't have dreamed of doing that. But, of course, you told me my donor was also a singer at his local synagogue... that just has to be more than a coincidence; taking up family history, chess and karaoke just a few weeks after I got my new heart.'

'He's not got a bad voice either,' said Bernard.

'Do have a favourite song, Jim?' asked Mike.

'There's a few... but the top of the list is probably Frank Sinatra's *My Way*.'

After this short light interlude of laddish banter, Edwin got back on track with a further question. 'What was it that brought you over to the UK?'

'It wasn't until I was in my early twenties. I used to do a lot of weight training and keep fit in Germany and came over to Liverpool to take part in a bodybuilding contest, where I met an English lad who was also taking part and later became my partner in the haulage business I had over on Merseyside,' Jim explained.

'Did your father come over with you?'

'No. He divorced my mother when I was only a year old and I think he had met someone else. I didn't get on all that well with him and I think he was glad to get rid of me so he could move in with his new lady-friend. But he did send me a fair chunk of money to help me set up the old business. It did well; gave me a good living over here.'

'What happened to your mother? Did you have much contact with her?'

'No, after my parents got divorced, I went to live with my father and my elder brother in Ulm and I lost contact with my mother altogether and then, after a while, Uwe emigrated to America and I lost contact with him as well. I was too young to remember my mother and, sadly, don't have any photos of her. I never knew what happened to her but would love to know now. Perhaps you can help me find out one of these days,

Edwin? I'm not very expert at this ancestry tracing but I'd love to know.'

'We might need to hire a professional – but, yes, I would be delighted to help. With a bit of luck, I think that I could persuade my editor to cover the cost of hiring someone. I'll check it out and let you know, Jim,' said Edwin.

'Would appreciate that... now, there's something else I'd like to ask you...'

'What's that, Jim? Fire away.'

'Well, I've been thinking about all the things I did in the past that I'm not proud of and would like to try and find some way of putting things right... what do they call it, atonement? I'm not a millionaire, but I still have a bob or two in the bank and would be happy to find some way of giving something back to all those poor sods who got hurt. I reckon now that it wasn't the real me who behaved like that but some bloody demon that burrowed into my brain. Anyway, I'd like to do something to try and mend some of the damage I caused over all those years. What do you think, Edwin?'

'Let me give it some thought. I'm sure there would be many things you could do. Meanwhile, I'll also have a word with my editor to see if the paper will pay for a professional genealogist. We could try on our own, but since it would involve records kept in Europe, I think we will need expert help.'

'That would be good,' said Jim, getting up from his seat to order another round of drinks at the bar from his lady friend, Sylvia. When he returned to his seat carrying three pints and a double tomato juice for Mike who would be driving, Sylvia came round from her side of the bar to join him.

'Let me introduce you to Sylvia properly, gentlemen. We used to fight like cat and dog when the old Jim Fisher was in here with some of his old supporters but we now get on famously. Has she told you that we are planning on getting married after Christmas – ideally in January, exactly a year after my transplant? It'll be a double celebration.'

'If I mention that to my news editor, he'll want us back here to cover the wedding, Jim!' said Edwin.

'That would be OK with me and I don't expect Syl would have any objections, would you, Syl? But don't mention anything in your article about us getting married or we'll have the world's press here. If you want, you can write a story for your paper afterwards. That wouldn't be a problem.'

'No, we don't want dozens of reporters but, yes, I'd be happy for you guys to come,' said Sylvia. 'We'll put you both on the official guest list then – you can bring your partners, of course, if you like.'

'Thanks,' said Mike and Edwin in unison.

'OK, gentlemen, if I've answered all your questions, Bernard and I will have another game of chess – and I'll see if, for the first time, I can beat him!'

'Could I just take a couple of shots before we leave you in peace, Jim?' asked Mike.

'Do you want me on my own and with Syl?'

'I think with Sylvia would be nice, if that's all right with you – and maybe one of you playing chess with Bernard. I just need a few minutes.'

Five minutes later, Mike had half a dozen or more shots in the "can" and, after a flurry of handshakes, he and Edwin said their farewells and headed to the car park.

Throughout the interview – albeit in a relaxed and informal environment – Edwin could not entirely dismiss from his mind their last encounter, fearing that at any given moment, Jim Fisher would relapse into his former unpleasantly aggressive self. But it never happened.

'Well, that all went very smoothly. I couldn't help thinking that there would be a bit of friction – some flashes of the old Jim Fisher breaking through. But happily, I was quite wrong,' said Edwin as they set off on the drive back to Manchester.

'Anyone meeting him for the first time would have thought what a really nice bloke he is. Amazing, just amazing,' exclaimed Mike.

'It'll certainly make a good piece with good pics.'

'Would you go with Marion to the wedding?' asked Mike.

'Yes, I think so. What about you?'

'I might possibly take someone. Not sure yet.'

*

As they approached the outskirts of the city, Edwin began thinking about the way he would approach the article he would be writing about Jim's emotional and psychological change of heart. Journalistically, he knew that the juxtaposition of the old criminal, racist Jim Fisher with the new genuine Mr Nice Guy he had just met would require a delicate touch.

He would have to demonstrate to his readers that Jim's transformation was a rare but recognised phenomenon supported by authoritative medical and scientific evidence and that it did not read like the story of Dr Jekyll and Mr Hyde in reverse.

Sooner or later, too, he knew that he would also have to convince his editor that it would be in the best interests of *The Informer* to hire the services of a professional genealogist – that the James Karl Fisher story still almost certainly had many more newsworthy twists and turns to come.

'How did you get on, Edwin?' asked Ross in his usual direct manner as Edwin headed towards his desk in the newsroom.

'Couldn't have gone any better – just great,' Edwin replied, feeling a sense of déjà vu.

'Do you reckon it's all genuine or is he just faking it?'

'It's genuine all right, Ross. He's even asked me how he could make reparation – what he can do to say sorry to all those people he hurt mentally and physically when he was over in Liverpool. It's one hell of a story.'

'Have we got pics this time?'

'We have, yes. We got pics of him playing chess with his magistrate friend and also with his lady friend, Sylvia, the landlady at the pub – and in January around the anniversary of his transplant, they are planning to get married and we will be getting an invitation.'

'Sounds like this Fisher story is going to run and run – just make sure that we get the first bite of the apple every time there's something new.'

'That's not a problem, Ross. I'm not going to mention the wedding in this next piece and so, no one else is likely to know about it. He's told me that he doesn't want any other papers there, so we will have it to ourselves on the day,' Edwin reassured his news editor.

'Great, great, let me have this new piece as soon as you can... no more than fifteen hundred words.'

'There's just one more thing I need to raise with you. Do you think the editor would agree to hire a professional to trace Jim's family history? He tells me that he's been dabbling at it himself but he's not really making much progress and I've come to a bit of a brick wall myself. It appears that his immediate ancestors are from Germany and he seems to think there could be a Polish link as well. It would need an expert to get to the bottom of it.'

'How's it going to benefit us?'

'I'm pretty sure it would uncover a real treasure trove of fascinating information that would keep the story going well into next year. It would tell us if he is related to Eugen Fischer or not. Jim himself now thinks it's very unlikely but that his father either thought they were or wanted to believe they were – and that's why he was brainwashed from being a small child.

'It would also be interesting to find out why his father divorced his mother when Jim was just a year old, and why he never really had contact with her again. He says he's always wanted to know what happened to her and, by all accounts, he also has an older brother and would like to know what happened to him as well.'

'Edwin, I'll not ask the editor. Just find out how much it is likely to cost and let me know. If it's not a fortune, you can arrange it,' said Ross, true to his reputation for making quick editorial decisions.

'Thanks. I'm pretty sure it will pay dividends in the long run. I'm off now but will make a start on this new piece early tomorrow.'

'OK, as soon as you can.'

*

Five minutes later, Edwin started up the engine of his Saab parked in the newspaper's underground car park and drove out into the city centre rush-hour traffic for the forty-minute drive back to his Cheshire home.

He tried to concentrate on a news programme on *Radio 4*, but his mind was preoccupied with the interview with Jim and how he was going to angle his article when he was next in the office. He knew he would have to steer a tricky middle course between an approach that was not sensational – and acceptable to medical professionals – but which, at the same time, was impactful and believable to the layman.

'Hi, honey. Had a good day?' he asked as he walked into his elegantly furnished sitting room with its original, arched Victorian window frames, heavy pine doors and high skirting boards.

'Much the same. You?' she responded.

Marion, a petite woman in her mid-forties with black hair styled in a bob, worked as a PA for the controller in the Highways Agency in Manchester's city centre and had already been back at home for more than an hour when Edwin returned.

'Very interesting, that's for sure. I've been thinking about it all the way home. I just cannot believe that this was the same Jim Fisher I saw ranting and raving when – at his request – we told him the identity of his donor. It's nothing less than a miracle – a medical, not a religious one, that is.'

'Are we going for a curry?' Marion asked.

'We are, yes – have been looking forward to it... and, by the way, it looks like we'll be going to a wedding in the New Year.'

'A wedding, whose wedding?'

'Mr Fisher and his bride-to-be, the landlady at his pub. We were officially introduced to her this afternoon – she seems very pleasant, a bit on the brassy, buxom blonde side but very nice and seemingly quite sensible.'

'Do you know when it will be?'

'It'll be on the closest Saturday in January to the anniversary of his transplant at some licensed wedding venue in an old hall somewhere in Todmorden – not too far from his place in Rossendale.'

'Will you have to write a piece? And what about a present – will we have to take them a present?'

'We'll be getting an official invitation like all his other guests but, yes, I will have to write a piece afterwards. Mike

Wolff is also invited and he might be taking someone with him… I don't think a present will be necessary… he knows that I'll have to write a piece afterwards, so he'll assume that it's a job for Mike and me.'

'I think that's right. I know you say he's a changed man but I'd still have felt a bit uneasy about buying a present for someone with his track record.'

'What I might do is arrange for the picture desk to send them a really nice framed wedding pic afterwards. Are you ready to go, by the way?'

'Yes, I just want to comb my hair, put some lippy on and I'll be ready. Are you going to change?'

'I think I should. I don't like going to the Bombay Palace in my office suit. I'll just have a quick wash, change my shirt and find a sweater. Give me five minutes and I'll be with you.'

Half an hour later, one of the restaurant's old retainers, a waiter in his late sixties whom they had known for the best part of twenty years, ushered them to their favourite corner table.

'Are you both keeping well?' he asked.

'We are both well, thanks. And you?' they asked politely.

'I am good, thank you… do you need a menu or are you having your usual?'

'It's the usual, please,' Edwin confirmed. 'Not very adventurous, are we?'

'So, that's an onion bhaji and sharmi kebab to share for starters, one prawn bhuna with pilau rice and chicken tandoori for the lady and some poppadoms – and two Coca-Colas,' said the waiter without pausing to think.

'I just don't know how you can remember all that. Very impressive, if I might say so. Do you remember when we also used to have a portion of Bombay duck?' said Edwin.

'I remember. The boss told us that we couldn't serve it any longer because several customers used to complain about its strong smell.'

'I remember that,' chuckled Edwin. 'I agree, it didn't smell very enticing but it was good to eat. Of course, it was called Bombay duck but it was some kind of fish, wasn't it? Very moreish.'

Until the starters arrived, Edwin and Marion nibbled mouthfuls of spicy finely-chopped onion, sweet mango chutney and bitter lime pickle on poppadoms. It was a culinary ritual they had experienced on countless occasions over the years – often in the company of friends – but the enjoyment never waned. Over the years, they had dined in several other Indian restaurants, both in Manchester and elsewhere around the country, but the Bombay Palace never disappointed and was always special.

They returned home just in time to watch the BBC ten o'clock news, after which Edwin printed off his favourite cryptic crossword from the Internet, which he endeavoured to complete in bed whilst listening to *Classic FM* playing low in the background. As he put his head on the pillow that night, his thoughts turned once again to the feature piece he would need to write the following day about James Karl Fisher.

*

Something must have distilled in his mind overnight, because when he sat down at his office desk the following afternoon, the words began to flow freely, and within a couple of hours he felt he had succeeded in finding the right balance and was happy overall with the way his article read.

'Here's the latest Jim Fisher piece, Ross,' he said, handing over three folios of A4 of double-spaced type.

'Great, all being well, we'll use it tomorrow. What have you got on now?'

'Three things really: first a quick call to the donor's widow to give her a run down of my meeting with Jim as promised, then I'm planning to ring the rabbi to ask him how he suggests that Jim could atone and then I'm going to contact a pro genealogist.'

'OK, keep me posted.'

*

Edwin called Leah Lieberman first. As was often the case, she was at home and answered almost immediately.

'Mrs Lieberman, Edwin Benn here, *The Informer*. How are you?' he asked.

'I am all right thanks, you? I still have good days and bad. The loss of Marcus is still very raw, you understand.'

'It must be. I can fully understand that. I just wanted to keep my promise and tell you about my latest meeting with Mr Fisher,' Edwin explained.

'Oh, thank you. How did it go?'

'It's difficult to know where to start... it was just remarkable, quite amazing,' he said, going on to explain as succinctly as possible how as a result of the phenomenon of cell memory – of psychosomatic change precipitated by his new heart – he had shed all the years of hate, prejudice and bigotry and become a new man with normal, healthy attitudes. 'What's more,' Edwin continued, '... he has asked me how he can best atone for his sins – or, as he put it, how he can make amends and put things right.'

'This is wonderful news. If that is so, I am sure that God is working through Marcus. It makes me very proud to think that Marcus, with God's help, has been able to bring about such a miraculous change. Do you think that it will last, that it is permanent?'

'I do, yes. I am sure that the old Mr Fisher has gone for good. I believe that as long as he has Marcus's heart, nothing will change.'

'That is so comforting to hear,' she said.

'You may also be interested to know that around the anniversary of his transplant, he will be getting married to the widowed landlady at his local pub. My wife and I are going to be invited to the wedding and also our photographer and his lady. We'll be reporting the wedding in the paper.'

'Who knows, one day I may also meet him now. That's, of course, if he would want to meet me.'

'I am sure that he would. In fact, there's every possibility that you will receive an official invitation to the wedding.'

'I would probably go, all being well.'

'If and when I next speak with him, I will tell him that,' said Edwin. 'As I said, he also asked me if he can say sorry for everything that happened in the past and I am planning to have a word with Rabbi Goldbladt about that. I am sure he will have some useful, practical suggestions to make.'

'Atonement, as you probably know, has a special significance in the Jewish faith and I am sure that Nathan – Rabbi Goldbladt – will be able to advise you.'

'Thank you, Mrs Lieberman. I will call him shortly.'

*

Edwin wasn't sure whether it was his wife or his secretary who answered the phone, but she was able to put him through to the rabbi right away.

'Rabbi Goldbladt, apologies for troubling you. Edwin Benn here from *The Informer*.'

'It's really no trouble. How can I be of help?' the rabbi asked in a cheery, avuncular way.

'I've just been talking to Leah Lieberman about my last meeting with James Karl Fisher. I told her about his quite remarkable character change since his transplant and the fact that he now regrets all the hurt he caused in the past and wants to make reparation. He asked me how he should go about it, and I thought that it would be prudent for me to ask you for your advice,' Edwin explained.

'I appreciate that, thank you. My goodness, that is quite a question, especially as he is not Jewish. We must presume his racist crimes were not only directed at Jews but, by all accounts, at many other minority groups.'

'I can see the difficulty.'

'You will know of Yom Kippur, the Day of Atonement, I am sure... this is the most solemn and most holy day in the Jewish calendar, the day when we strive to remove the obstacles from our lives and seek reconciliation with God, for God to forgive us for our sins against Him. But for our transgressions against a fellow man, it is necessary to make restitution and be forgiven.

'Now, I would have to say that none of this would seem to be either appropriate or practical in the case of Mr Fisher. It would be impossible for him to repay – to make restitution to – all the many people he has hurt either emotionally or physically in the past, and there would be no mechanism now after all these years to ask for their individual forgiveness – in any event, he would not know who they are and, sadly, many of them will no doubt not be with us any longer.'

'Yes, I can see the problem,' said Edwin.

'He could, I suppose, and if he has the funds, make donations to Jewish and Afro-Caribbean charities and synagogues, and he could perhaps write an open letter of apology that your newspaper as well as others may be willing to publish,' the rabbi continued.

'That would certainly be a possibility. I was also thinking, Rabbi, that I might be able to persuade him to travel to Yad Vashem in Israel and see, first hand, the evidence of the Holocaust that he denied ever happened, or even visit one of the concentration camps he once claimed never existed. It might even be possible for me to go with him.'

'That would certainly demonstrate his seriousness. Atonement, in fact, simply means being "at-one-ment", so if Mr Fisher, as a non-Jew, makes reparation in kind, then I would suggest that would suffice in the circumstances. The mere fact that he feels the need to atone for his sins is already a significant step towards satisfying God he has serious intent. I hope that this has been helpful.'

'It has, Rabbi. Whatever he does, it's not likely to be until the New Year because he will be getting married again in January – around the anniversary of his transplant – and my wife and I will be on the guest list, he tells me. I will try and speak with him before then but I think it's very unlikely that he would do anything before his wedding,' Edwin explained.

'That sounds reasonable enough. Perhaps you would let me know what he decides.'

'I will, of course. I also have to find a professional who can delve into his family history, so you'll appreciate that journalistically, Mr Fisher is currently occupying a large slice of my time and it looks like it will continue for the foreseeable future.'

'That should prove fascinating. I would be most interested to know what it reveals.'

'I will most certainly let you know and Leah Lieberman, too, of course,' said Edwin. 'We will speak again, soon, no doubt. Thanks once again for all your advice.'

*

Before he left the office that evening, Edwin succeeded, after several telephone calls to a miscellany of genealogical associations, in identifying a professional whom he believed was well qualified to fill in the blanks in Jim's European ancestry. His name was Dr Konrad Jäger, a German-born retired history lecturer, now living in London, who had written books and academic papers on how the "cancer of the Nazis" had been allowed to spread across his native country. He also had particular expertise and an enviable track record for finding ways through and around genealogical brick walls in those parts of Europe where records had either been lost or destroyed and where individuals had changes of name.

Edwin also noted that by happy coincidence, his surname translated as "hunter" or "huntsman" in English – it promised to be a good omen. He would surely be the right man to track down Jim's family roots in his native Germany and any movement of his immediate family to neighbouring countries. And the fact that he spoke perfect English was an added bonus.

In view of the fact that Edwin was commissioning his services on behalf of a third party, he felt it necessary to explain his professional involvement and provide Dr Jäger with an outline of Jim's unsavoury past, his lifesaving transplant with the heart of an Orthodox Jew, his remarkable attitudinal change of heart and his desire to atone for his crimes.

'I will send you copies of the articles that we have carried in *The Informer* that may just provide a little more information and give you some useful leads that could be helpful in your research.

'Over the past few months, Mr Fisher and I have independently been carrying out our own research using the Internet family history sites and, whilst we have made some reasonable progress, we have reached the point where we don't think we can take it any further. We really need professional help,' Edwin told Dr Jäger.

'That will be most helpful, I am sure. It is always good in these cases if I have a framework on which I can build.'

'I will draw up his family tree as it currently exists and, if that's all right with you, email it to you as an attachment along with a bullet-point letter listing all the key gaps in our information. May I ask roughly how long it's likely to take?'

'I could never say precisely but would aim to send you an interim report in three to four months, after which you can decide if that is sufficient or you would like to take it any further,' Dr Jäger replied.

'That would be perfect. I will send over all the relevant information in the next twenty-four hours.'

'I look forward to receiving it. It sounds like a most interesting project.'

*

As promised, Edwin emailed the information to Dr Jäger the following day, along with an electronically signed note from Jim giving permission for him to carry out the research into his family roots. He also included Jim's contact telephone number should Dr Jäger feel it necessary to confirm that he had given his authorisation.

On a family tree chart that Edwin had downloaded from the Internet, he inserted all the principal ancestors, some with dates of birth and death, that he and Jim had together been able to find through their own amateur research before they realised that they required professional expertise to find some of the most significant, but elusive, pieces of missing information.

The family-tree framework he provided noted that James Karl Fisher was born Karl Fischer in 1964 in Karlsruhe, Germany, that his father was Herman Fischer (1929-1983) who was born in Ulm, Baden-Württemberg and that his father, Otto Fischer, was born in 1896 also in Ulm. It also showed that Jim had an elder brother, Uwe Wilhelm, with whom he had lost touch and had not seen since Uwe had moved to live and work overseas after what they believed was an altercation with his father in his early twenties.

They were only able to provide very sparse information about Uwe and even less about Jim's mother, ironically the one person he was most keen to learn more about and to discover why, as Jim put it, "she suddenly seemed to disappear a year or so after I was born".

In the information he provided to Edwin to pass on, there was simply a rather sad list of haphazard and uncoordinated morsels of information that collectively he and Edwin hoped might just provide useful clues to assist Jäger's research. Jim remembered that her name was "Susanna" but did not know how it was spelt, that she had long dark hair, that he was as certain as he could be that she breastfed him and that on several occasions she sang him a lullaby as he lay in his bed as a baby.

Jim added a personal footnote that Edwin also passed on to Dr Jäger. It read: "It may be my imagination but there are times when I think that I can remember her smell and the warmth of being close to her. If nothing else, I would like to know more about my mother. I want to know what happened to her."

In a covering letter, Edwin stressed that Jim had always been told by his father – and grandfather, too – that the family was related to the Nazi professor, Eugen Fischer (1874-1976), but neither he nor Jim had been able to find anything in their research to support it. Edwin had spent several hours searching to try and establish if this could be true but had eventually concluded that it was simply something that Jim's father and grandfather wanted to believe but had no basis in fact.

It was nothing more than speculation built on a foundation of logic, that at a time in Germany when it was fashionable, patriotic, almost obligatory, to support the Nazi ideology, Herman and Otto Fischer felt that it would somehow enhance their social status and standing to claim kinship with the academic who had been instrumental in moulding the Fuhrer's plans for the Master Race.

They needed the expertise of a professional genealogist to confirm it conclusively one way or the other.

Edwin ended his working day feeling content and satisfied. He had updated Leah Lieberman, sought the advice of Rabbi Goldbladt on the best way that Jim could make reparation and briefed Dr Jäger in respect of the gaps in Jim's tree they were anxious to fill.

He also felt that he had given himself some welcome breathing space. It would be another three months or so before Jim and Sylvia became man and wife, and until then, Edwin felt it unlikely there would be any surprise developments in what had become a news story saga.

For a short time at least, Edwin looked forward to more run-of-the-mill days in the newsroom, reporting one-off news stories, socialising with his colleagues and contacts at office parties on the run-up to Christmas, and especially enjoying Christmas dinner with his wife and family. He drove home feeling that all was well with the world.

CHAPTER 6

THREE MONTHS LATER

It was just before midday on a cold but thankfully dry January day, when Edwin and his wife, Marion, drove into the car park of a former Grade II Victorian school building in Todmorden – now converted into an elegant wedding venue – to attend the marriage of James Karl Fisher and the landlady at his pub, Sylvia Hartshorne.

Twelve months had elapsed since he and photographer Mike Wolff had first set eyes on Jim Fisher, lying prostrate and anaesthetised in the operating theatre in the Transplant Centre at Roundthorn Hospital. One year on, after receiving the heart of an Orthodox Jew and experiencing the metamorphosis brought about by the phenomenon of cell memory, the former obnoxious neo-Nazi racist was now totally reformed, with not a vestige of hate in his heart for anyone.

As Edwin and his wife walked towards the entrance, he spotted Mike Wolff, accompanied by a lady he did not recognise, walking from another direction. Although they and their partners had been invited as guests, Edwin would also be filing a story for *The Informer* accompanied by at least one of Mike's photographs.

'Happy New Year to you,' said Mike, offering his outstretched arm to Edwin and his wife. 'Can I introduce you to my friend, Paula.'

'Nice to meet you, Paula – and a very Happy New Year to you, too. You know my wife, Marion, don't you?' said Edwin.

Mike had taken a week's holiday since New Year and although they had both been in the office, their paths had not crossed. It was the first opportunity they had to wish each other New Year greetings.

'The weather's pretty much the same as it was when we witnessed Jim's heart swap a year ago, but the venue and the circumstance are a whole lot different – it's amazing what's happened over the past twelve months,' said Edwin.

'Hard to believe, to be honest,' agreed Mike as the foursome were greeted by the warmth inside the building.

Inside, a young woman in a white blouse, black skirt and a tartan waistcoat offered to take their coats and another young woman, wearing a similar uniform, came forward and offered them a glass of Prosecco in a fluted glass. There were no more than another twenty or so guests in the room, all of them standing and chatting in small groups in spite of the fact that there were serried ranks of cloth-covered chairs laid out in front of a raised area beneath a round ornate window where the wedding ceremony would take place.

Jim and his bride were standing on the far side of the room talking with a middle-aged Filipino woman, a professional celebrant, who would be conducting the civil, non-denominational marriage ceremony. Edwin and Jim caught

155

each other's eye and broke off their conversations to greet each other.

'Good of you to come. I take it this lady is yours,' said Jim, looking in the direction of Marion.

'She is, yes... Marion, this is Jim Fisher who had the new heart exactly a year ago. And you will remember our photographer, Mike, who's here with his partner, Paula,' said Edwin.

'Good to meet you all. Glad you could make it,' said Jim.

'It was kind of you to send us an invitation, Jim. As you know, we have also got to file a story about your wedding for the paper... this time, a nice happy story with a nice happy photo,' said Edwin. 'If I might ask, did you invite Leah Lieberman and is anyone coming from the hospital?'

'Yes and yes. I sent an invite to Mrs Lieberman and said she could bring someone with her. James McCloud, the surgeon who collected my heart, is already here, along with Anna Dickson, the transplant coordinator. They are over there.'

'Oh, yes, I see them now,' said Edwin. 'What about your surgeon, Mr Barr-White, is he coming?'

'No, he couldn't make it but sent us his very best wishes.'

As they chatted, Leah Lieberman entered the room accompanied by a tall young man, who they later learned was Daniel, her son. She was wearing a black silk blouse, a black below-the-knee skirt and a tailored dusty pink jacket with a cameo brooch on the lapel.

Jim was acutely aware of the significance of her presence, excused himself from Edwin and his party and went immediately over to greet her.

'It's Leah Lieberman, isn't it? Jim Fisher, so glad you felt that you could come. I would have understood if you hadn't.'

'There was a time when I would not have come but I know that everything has changed. I'm really very pleased to be here now. How are you now? You look well,' she said.

'I'm really very well now, thanks – thanks to your Marcus. I am so sorry that you lost him. I know that must be very hard for you. But, how can I put it, he was obviously a man with a good heart in every way and it's now keeping me alive. And, as you know, it's changed me, thank God. I'm no longer the nasty bad beggar that I used to be. All that's gone with my rotten old heart, I'm pleased to say,' said Jim with a slight tremor and hint of nervousness in his voice.

'You must introduce us to your lady, Jim. It would be nice to meet her,' said Mrs Lieberman.

'I will, of course. She's keen to meet you, I know. We'll talk again later,' said Jim, offering her his arm and shaking her hand.

Mike realised immediately that this was a photograph he would have to re-stage at the appropriate time: the former neo-Nazi, far-right white supremacist shaking hands with the widow of the Orthodox Jew who saved his life. This was an image that expressed the whole essence and spirit of the occasion. It was one of those photographs that is, as they say, worth a thousand words.

When Jim returned to his bride, Edwin and Mike made a

point of speaking with Mrs Lieberman themselves.

'This is my colleague, our photographer, Mike Wolff... good to see you here. It can't have been an easy decision to make,' said Edwin.

'It's what Marcus would have wanted and I know it was the right thing to do,' she replied. 'This, by the way, is my son, Daniel. He drove me over.'

'When we first met at your home with Rabbi Goldbladt, I never thought that we'd see the day when you would meet Jim Fisher, let alone shake his hand. It was really one of those landmark moments.'

'It was, yes,' confirmed Mike. 'After the ceremony, if it's OK with both you and Jim, we would like to re-stage that handshake moment for a photo.'

'I would have no objection. If Jim agrees, it is just fine by me,' said Mrs Lieberman.

*

The young lady with a tray of Prosecco offered drinks to a trickle of latecomers and topped up the glasses for those who had already consumed or partially consumed their first. For the next twenty minutes or so, the guests continued to mingle, among them Jim's gardener and handyman, several of the regulars and bar staff at his local and a local farmer who supplied him with eggs, chicken, meat and vegetables.

Present, too, was Jim's best man, his chess-playing tutor, Bernard Haworth, and Sylvia's younger married sister, Evelyn, who was her matron of honour. Both Bernard and Evelyn were there with their own partners.

*

On the dot of twelve-thirty, the venue's master of ceremonies, a middle-aged man impeccably dressed in a black, tailed morning suit, grey waistcoat, white shirt and a pastel-blue tie, stepped onto the raised platform and tapped one of the fluted glasses several times with a spoon. Slowly, the chatter ceased and the room fell silent.

'Ladies and gentlemen, kindly be seated. The wedding ceremony is about to begin,' he said.

Gradually, over the next minute or so, the gathered assembly shuffled along the rows collecting their Order of Service programmes placed on each seat before sitting down. It was all very informal, with no numbered seating plan or areas designed for relatives and friends of the bride or the groom.

When everyone was seated and settled, the Filipino celebrant took up her position on the dais beneath the circular window, followed by the bride and groom and their attendants. Knowing their background and lifestyle, Edwin had anticipated that it might be a somewhat flashy affair, reminiscent of some of the weddings he had seen on TV in the popular soaps such as Coronation Street and Eastenders.

But he had to admit that he was entirely wrong.

The bride was wearing an elegant French navy suit over a white silk blouse and a navy and white fascinator in her hair. Her high-heeled shoes were also in matching navy and white leather. Jim, who seemed to have shed a noticeable amount of weight since his transplant and had grown his hair, was wearing a dark grey lounge suit with a light blue shirt and a tie in a slightly darker blue. He was also wearing matching blue leather shoes with white leather ornamentation.

'Welcome and good afternoon, ladies and gentlemen. My name is Evangelista dela Rosa and it is my pleasant duty today to officiate at the marriage of James and Sylvia, who chose a humanist ceremony because they wanted to celebrate their union in a manner that is inclusive of all beliefs,' she began.

Edwin could not help thinking that it was not a sentiment that Jim would have shared when he and Mike first saw him on the day of his transplant a year earlier. But he kept the thought to himself.

The celebrant, an attractive young woman with a comforting voice, open face and infectious smile, went on to talk about the sanctity and significance of marriage.

'Marriage is always a special event to be cherished. It is outside the routine of our everyday lives – an extraordinary and pivotal event in people's lives. But, in a way, marriage is, at the same time, also an ordinary event because it is about everyday life. It holds special, heightened moments as well as the ordinary and the routine.

'In the case of James and Sylvia, it is especially significant because, as James's family and friends, you will be aware that were it not for one of the great advances, even a miracle, in modern medicine, our groom and his bride would not be here today to exchange their vows.

'Almost exactly one year ago, James was given a new healthy heart in a transplant operation that saved his life and today he is figuratively, emotionally and selflessly giving his heart away to the woman with whom he will spend the rest of his life.'

There was a ripple of applause across the room.

'... We are especially honoured that among our special guests here today is Leah Lieberman, who gave consent for the heart of her late husband, Marcus, to be donated and used in the transplant that saved James's life. She is here with her son, Daniel.'

The celebrant, who had been briefed in advance about her presence, gestured towards Mrs Lieberman and her son, who smiled and mouthed a semi-silent thank you.

She then called upon Magistrate Bernard Haworth to say a few words. As best man, he felt that it was obligatory and his duty to say something laddish and humorous.

'As some of you will know, I have been teaching Jim to play chess for the past few months. So far, he hasn't beaten me, although he's getting better all the time and reckons it will not be too long now, because he says, "I think that's checkmate", but he's already got his own back by capturing our very own queen, the lovely Sylvia. They make a super couple and, of course we are all really delighted for them.'

Celebrant Evangelista then continued with the service.

'Bernard has just mentioned his local tavern which I believe is at Rossendale. Well, we all know that it can be pretty wet and cold in that part of the world in the winter, so I thought it might be appropriate if I read to you a popularised adaptation

161

of a Native American, Apache, wedding blessing: *Now you will feel no rain, for each of you will be shelter for the other. Now you will feel no cold, for each of you will be warmth to the other.* I'm sure we all hope this blessing will apply to every aspect of your lives together – including the inclement weather!'

Jim and Sylvia, who had been holding hands as they listened to the celebrant, were then asked to exchange their "I do" vows, exchange rings and sign a certificate.

'I now present you all with our newlyweds, James and Sylvia,' she said joyously.

The couple kissed, prompting another wave of applause, before everyone was invited to move through to an adjacent room for a cold buffet lunch with the addition of two hot dishes – a chicken curry with rice and a hotpot with red cabbage and beetroot.

Edwin had the curry. Mike the hotpot. They consumed them quickly before excusing themselves from their ladies and slipping into work mode. Mike managed to set up a photograph of Jim shaking hands with Leah Lieberman, and Edwin interviewed several of the guests as well as the newlyweds themselves.

*

Just as it was beginning to get dark and some of the guests had already left for home, Jim and Sylvia decided that it was time that they, too, drove back to Rossendale, where they were planning to spend the night before setting off the following morning for a week's honeymoon in Palma, Majorca.

'Would you like one of our young men to bring your car to the door so that you and your bride can get in together and everyone can wave you off?' asked the master of ceremonies.

'Yes, thank you. That would be nice. Good idea,' said Jim, taking the ignition key from his pocket and handing it to him. 'I'm parked just on the left going to the main gate. It's a silver Mercedes with a personal plate – my initials JKF.'

'Are you ready to go now?'

'Yes.'

A young man, who had been helping out behind the bar at the buffet, was handed the keys and dispatched to drive the car up to the front entrance.

He returned a few minutes later, clearly distressed and visibly shocked.

'What's the matter? Is something wrong?'

'I've had to leave the car where it is. It's been vandalised. Someone's scrawled slogans all over it in white paint. I couldn't see through the windscreen to drive it,' said the young man.

The master of ceremonies went straight over to Jim Fisher and his bride and relayed the news.

'Some bad news, Mr Fisher, I am afraid. The lad has just told me that someone has painted slogans on your car.'

'Bloody hell. We could do without that sort of thing. Better go and see, I guess,' he said striding out purposefully accompanied by Sylvia, the MC and the young man who still had the car keys. Edwin and Mike realised that there was some kind of problem and followed them.

What confronted them was worse than they had anticipated.

Daubed across the windscreen were the words: "Turncoat – Jew lover" and along the whole of one side "Nigger lover". There was also a swastika daubed on the bonnet and another on the rear window.

Mike reacted instinctively, taking photographs of the car and of the newlyweds, venue staff and other guests who had ambled over to see what was wrong. But Jim's reaction was surprisingly unpredictable. The master of ceremonies said he would call the police immediately, but Jim told him that he did not want them involved.

'Under different circumstances, I can see that would be the right thing to do. I'm pretty sure I know who has done this and I don't want the police involved,' he said. walking around the vandalised vehicle as he spoke.

'What are you going to do then, Jim?' asked his bride, who had a slight tremor in her voice and looked tearful.

'I'm just going to ring my garage and arrange for them to come out, tow it in and get it all cleaned up. I know it's going to cost me a bob or two but I've got my reasons for doing it that way,' he said.

'I'm not so sure that the garage would tow it through the street looking like that,' said Sylvia.

'You're right, they probably wouldn't. I'll explain what the problem is and tell them they need to bring some sort of dust cover or sheeting,' said Jim. Then, turning to Mike and Edwin, he asked, 'Are you guys planning to report this in your paper? I know it's newsworthy and I can't stop you, but I'd rather you didn't.'

Edwin had already given the matter some thought, although he had not had the time to discuss it with his colleague, Mike. A complex matrix of thoughts was swirling around in his head. The shiny Mercedes being daubed with racist slogans and swastikas was undeniably a news story, but was the story and photograph of ex-neo-Nazi Jim shaking hands with the widow of the Jew whose heart saved his life a better, stronger one? Certainly, it had more human-interest appeal.

Quite apart from that, any news coverage they gave to the daubing of Jim's car along with an accompanying picture, would simply give oxygen to the racist perpetrators.

'I'll have to mention it to the news editor, Jim, but I'm pretty sure that I can persuade him that we won't give it any coverage. If we have to do something at some later date for whatever reason, I'll let you know.'

'I appreciate that, Edwin,' said Jim as he and his bride headed back into the venue.

'I hope the desk agrees to that,' said Mike.

'I know there's a risk they won't and, of course, there's also a risk that someone, perhaps even the perpetrators themselves, may tip off one of the other nationals but I think that's unlikely. We'll have to take a chance.'

It was the first time in his long journalistic career that he was proposing to suppress a news story, but he felt that it was both morally and journalistically justified. He could certainly not be accused of being pressurised or influenced by anyone else. He genuinely believed that it was the right thing to do.

*

A good hour later, a breakdown truck from the garage where Jim regularly had his car serviced pulled into the venue's car park, its orange flashing lights attracting Jim's attention. He went out alone to meet them and twenty minutes later after covering the car with a tarpaulin that hid the daubed slogans from view, they began towing the Mercedes back to the garage.

By this time, all the guests had departed except for the best man, Bernard, Sylvia's matron of honour and Edwin and Mike, who felt that they should wait until the car had been removed.

'You say you're pretty sure you know who it was, Jim,' asked Edwin boldly.

'Yes, I think so. It'll be one or more of the guys who used to follow me around in the old days, who used to come down to the gym and until we sort of fell out, used to come in the pub. Pardon my French, but they all got a bit pissed off when I told them I'd given up all the stuff I used to get up to in the old days on Merseyside.'

'But why would they do such a thing, Jim?

'Because that's the sort of thing they do... the sort of thing they've always done... the sort of thing that I used to do myself at one time... so that's why I don't want the police involved. It could be any one of half a dozen people I know, but I'm not interested in knowing who exactly... it wouldn't do any good... it won't change them if they're caught... in fact, it would probably just make them worse. I think we should have a drink and just try and forget about it.'

Hand in hand with Sylvia, Jim walked over to the bar and

ordered himself a large brandy.

'Sorry about all this, sweetheart. It's not important and we're not going to let it spoil our wedding day. What are you going to have to drink?' he asked her.

'Not for me, Jim. I'm just going to have another coffee. How are we going to get back home now?'

'I'm sure that Bernard and his wife will take us. He'll be going back that way. If not, we'll just call a taxi. It's no big deal, Syl.'

But in less time than it took the barman to serve the brandy and coffee, the problem resolved itself.

'Whenever you guys are ready, I'll run you back home,' said the best man, Bernard, ambling over to the bar.

'Are you sure? That's very kind of you,' said Sylvia.

Jim put his arm round Bernard's shoulder and gave him a hug.

'Thanks a lot, pal, appreciate it,' said Jim.

Edwin and Mike realised it was high time they said their farewells and headed back to the office.

*

In the car park before picking up their cars and heading back towards Manchester, Mike posed the question, 'D'you think that Ross will agree not to publish the car daubing story? As far as the pic goes, I'm not so sure that we'd carry one clearly showing those racist slogans anyway. It's a difficult one.'

'You're right. It is.'

'Of course, we could just not mention it at all.'

'I thought of that, too. But we really don't have much choice. If we don't mention it and the story gets out somewhere else, we'll be in big, big trouble. And that is a possibility, even though Jim has told people that he wants to keep a lid on it all, it could still leak out.'

'Well, we'll know soon enough.'

'We will. See you tomorrow in the office,' said Edwin, as he opened the passenger door of his car for his wife, moved round to the driver's seat and headed out onto the road for the journey back.

*

In the office the following day, news editor Ross and the picture editor had an impromptu conference with the editor and, much to Edwin and Mike's relief, they decided not to publish the car-daubing story on the basis that, as no other media were there, it would give oxygen to the perpetrators and possibly fuel other similar incidents, the photographs of the slogans on the car would have to be radically edited and it detracted from the human-interest story of a former neo-Nazi shaking hands with the Jewish widow of his Jewish heart donor.

'Just keep your fingers crossed, Mike, that there is nothing in the other nationals tomorrow or even in the weeklies when they come out, for that matter,' said the picture editor.

'Someone would have to tip them off and I can't see that happening, but only time will tell,' said Mike.

'My worry is that one of the culprits themselves will make an anonymous call to one of the papers, but that I reckon would alert the police and increase their risk of getting pulled in and charged,' said Edwin.

*

Fortunately, there wasn't a line about the wedding in any of the nationals the following morning.

'Looks like we're in the clear,' said Edwin.

'So far so good. Let's hope it stays that way,' replied Ross, as Edwin settled down at his computer to draft his report. 'If we carry it tomorrow, will Fisher see it?'

'I don't think so. They are flying to Palma from Manchester early this evening, so I reckon they won't see it until they come home next week, unless they pick up the English papers in Palma.'

'Have you thought that the same villains who daubed the car may also read the piece and start calling the newsroom saying God knows what?'

'It had crossed my mind, but I think it's unlikely, to be honest, Ross. If we ask them who is calling and say we would need to have their full names and addresses, they would probably just ring off.'

'Just put them through to me, if there's any kind of problem or unpleasantness.'

'Thanks, Ross. I'm sure it won't be necessary.'

*

Three cups of coffee later, Edwin was satisfied that he had struck just the right emotional note with his interpretation of

Jim and Sylvia's wedding, and with one click of a button on his PC, he sent his piece electronically to the news desk.

'Nice piece, Edwin,' said Ross as he skimmed through it quickly before ambling over to the picture desk to take a look at the photographs that had been selected to marry up with it. There were three: the handshake, the bride and groom exchanging their vows and one of them sharing a kiss afterwards, which was decided to be used as an inset.

The following day, the article occupied the whole of page three of the tabloid under the heading: "THE HANDSHAKE THAT SAID: I'M NO LONGER A RACIST".

Back at home that evening, Edwin and his wife decided to go out to their local Italian restaurant for their evening meal. Edwin knew he would have the spaghetti carbonara and Marion the crab ravioli, accompanied by two glasses of Chianti. It was a modest, unpretentious bistro they had visited on countless occasions but where they always had an enjoyable meal.

Edwin felt the need for some relaxation and he knew of no better way to do so than at one of his favourite eateries in the company of his wife.

'Looks like I might have a Jim Fisher-free week next week,' he said, taking a sip of Chianti.

'What's next then?' asked Marion.

'The report from the genealogist. Exactly what that will reveal, I have no idea. I just hope that it produces something interesting.'

'It will. I'm sure.'

'I hope you're right. It's cost the paper a fair old sum of money.'

CHAPTER 7

Edwin's hopes of a week-long respite from the ongoing James Karl Fisher saga, in fact, only lasted three days. Whilst Jim and his bride were presumably still enjoying the winter warmth of the Balearics, Edwin returned from a sandwich lunch to find a large brown envelope lying on his desk.

'It just arrived in the second delivery, Mr Benn,' said one of the teenage messenger boys.

'Thanks,' said Edwin, as he began to open it and remove the contents.

His suspicions were right. It was from Dr Jäger, the genealogist whom he had commissioned to see if he could throw any light on the dim and dark areas of Jim's family history.

Ever since he had enlisted his professional help, Edwin had been concerned that it would not reveal anything of any great significance and that he would be unable to justify to the news desk the three thousand pounds-plus they had spent on Dr Jäger's services.

But he need not have worried.

The package contained a brief covering letter, a one A4-

page summary and a longer, more detailed report that itemised all the new and incontrovertible hard facts in bold type and also what Dr Jäger called "reasonable assumptions and suppositions" in italics.

Edwin glanced at the summary and immediately one line jumped off the page and hit him between the eyes. He had to read it a second time just to make sure that he had not misread the first.

It referred to Jim's mother and read:

His mother was Zuzanna Perla Zederbaum, born in Lodz, Poland, in 1959, and died in Vienna, Austria, in 2010. Both her parents were Jewish. She became a celebrated pianist and composer.

Edwin had expected the research could produce some fascinating and surprising results, but nothing on this seismic scale. It took him a little time to appreciate the full, almost unbelievable implications: that James Karl Fisher, the former neo-Nazi who desecrated Jewish graves and synagogues and who denied that the Holocaust ever happened, was, in fact, a Jew.

He had a Jewish mother – a famous one to boot – and in the Jewish faith, this made him irrevocably Jewish. Surely, thought Edwin, he could never have known he was Jewish. And if he did, why did he harbour such hate in his old heart for his fellow Jews? Why was he indoctrinated by his father and grandfather to believe that Jews were a cancer to be excised when his father had married a Jewish woman? Did his father know that the woman he married was Jewish? When he had recovered his composure, he settled down to read the report in full in the hope that it would answer the many questions that were racing through his mind.

Slowly, a clearer picture began to emerge. Two key facts in Jäger's report were especially significant and answered some of Edwin's most perplexing and pressing questions. The first was that Zuzanna Zederbaum's mother, Ida Rachela Bermann, who was born in Lodz in 1915, had died in childbirth in 1939 and Zuzanna, whose father, Hans Zederbaum, had died in an accident when Ida was pregnant, had been taken in and brought up by nuns who ran a former Catholic children's home in a rural area about an hour's drive from the city.

Jäger added a note to the effect that the home had been closed for almost twenty years but his research to date suggested that the building was still standing and had been converted into a residential care home for the elderly.

The other most telling fact was that Jim's father, Herman Fischer, who was born in Ulm in Germany in 1929, was divorced from Zuzanna in 1965, approximately one year after Jim – then Karl Fischer – was born in 1964. Dr Jäger added that he could only presume that Fischer had not known that Zuzanna was Jewish when they married in 1958 and divorced her when he discovered, after Jim's birth, that she was.

Jäger stressed in his report that whilst it was pure speculation, it was possible that Zuzanna had not been aware of her husband's anti-Semitic views – that he had hidden them from her – and that the conflict between them arose when Zuzanna raised the question of her son's bris, the covenant of circumcision, the traditional religious ceremony for Jewish male babies.

But the fact that Jim had an elder brother, Uwe, who was born in 1959 when his mother Zuzanna was only twenty – a year after she and Herman Fischer were married – "lessened the likelihood" said Jäger that any discussions about Jim's circumcision was a factor.

He stressed: "It is reasonable to surmise that if Zuzanna raised the question of circumcision for Jim, she would also have done so for her firstborn son, Uwe, and Herman Fischer would have become aware that she was Jewish many years earlier. It cannot be ruled out, however, that as a young twenty-year-old woman who had been raised by Catholics, she did not have the courage or indeed the knowledge to discuss circumcision with her husband in respect of her firstborn son. We might never know if Herman Fischer discovered that his wife was Jewish or if this was the reason for their divorce. It is also plausible to surmise that she was brought up in the Roman Catholic faith and did not know herself that she was Jewish until she left the home and became curious about her family background."

As for Uwe Fischer, the elder brother, Jäger reported that he had to date only been able to establish his date of birth in Ulm, Germany, but "there was sketchy evidence to suggest that as a young man, he had emigrated to the United States of America". If requested, he would carry out further research.

Edwin found it especially interesting to learn that Jim had

an elder brother who would have known his mother and could be alive in his early sixties with a family of his own. But would he, too, have been brainwashed with Nazi ideology by his father and grandfather? Would he have grown up to be a racist who hated Jews, Black people and other minority groups? Did he maintain contact with his mother after she and his father were divorced? He felt confident that given time, he would be able to discover more about Uwe, and perhaps even make contact with him, without any further professional assistance.

The fulsome information that Jäger was able to supply about Zuzanna's life after her divorce and up to the death from a fall in Vienna in 2010, made it clear to Edwin that Uwe would have almost certainly been able to keep track of her whereabouts and keep in contact with her. Jim, he had already established, had only the most ephemeral of memories of his mother and had never sought to find her, assuming that when he lived with his father in Germany, his mother must have died or deliberately disappeared from his life.

Dr Jäger's research into the life of Zuzanna Zederbaum had been considerably facilitated by the fact that in her later years after she and her husband divorced, she became a celebrated concert pianist and composer who had given solo recitals at many of the leading concert halls in Europe. Reviews and articles that he was able to find in the archives of local newspapers in Germany, Hungary and Austria – some with black-and-white photographs of her – made it possible, not only to follow her career and put a face to the name but also retrospectively to form a picture of her upbringing and teenage years in the Catholic children's home.

He wrote in his report: "From the reviews that I have read in the local newspapers (some of which I have printed off, copied and included with this report), it is evident that Zuzanna Zederbaum had an illustrious and acclaimed career, using the professional stage name of Perla Bermann, her mother's maiden name and her own middle given name.

"In interviews that she gave to journalists, usually after her concert recitals, she refers to the fact that she was taught to play the piano at the Catholic children's home and that as a young girl, she gave concerts at the home and other local venues, often playing the works of Karl Tausig (1841-1871), the Polish virtuoso pianist and composer who was regarded as the most accomplished pupil of Franz Liszt. Tausig was born to Jewish parents in Warsaw."

It was on the basis of the reports of Zuzanna's burgeoning reputation as both pianist and composer, that Dr Jäger came to certain conclusions about how she and Herman Fischer had first met. In a census document for Ulm, Jäger noted that Fischer gave his occupation as "piano tuner" – only later was he shown also as a "public transport manager" – and from this, he made the assumption that sometime before her twentieth birthday, Fischer had been called upon to tune a piano at a venue where she was due to give a recital. "This is nothing more than supposition, but I would suggest there is a good probability that this is how they first met," he wrote.

Edwin was greatly impressed by Jäger's genealogical sleuthing.

His report went on to show that at the height of her career in her sixties and seventies, she was acclaimed as one of the great exponents of the works of both Liszt and her fellow countryman, Frederic Chopin, and that she had given masterclasses at the Franz Liszt Academy of Music and music university in Budapest, a city where she lived in the old Jewish Quarter for many years.

Dr Jäger also established, by marrying up newspaper accounts with obituary notices, that Perla Bermann, as she was known, died in 2010, aged 71, from head injuries sustained in a fall after giving a recital at the Wien Konzerthaus in Vienna. His report went on to note that in a ceremony that attracted a large crowd of fellow classical musicians and local politicians, she was buried in the Jewish section of the Zentralfriedhof Cemetery in Vienna, where an ornate headstone was erected some eight months later. "In death, she is in the company of Beethoven, Brahms, Strauss, Gluck and many other luminaries from the world of classical music who lie at rest in the cemetery."

Who paid for the headstone? Did she, perhaps, have siblings? But, more importantly, how would Jim – and now also his wife – react to learning that he was Jewish and had a famous Jewish mother? Would he be satisfied with Dr Jäger's findings or would he want to know more? Would he, in particular, want to know if there was any way of establishing if his mother had ever tried to find him? Would he perhaps suggest making a pilgrimage in her memory, tracing her steps through Europe and ending with a vigil at her grave?

Such questions and many others, flooded into Edwin's

head, but it would be several more days and probably longer before he would be able to arrange a meeting with Jim to pass on Dr Jäger's interim report. His first job was to appraise news editor Ross Hetherington of the guts of the report and convince him that the fee they had agreed for the research had been worth every penny.

'We've had the interim report from the genealogist, Ross. Absolutely fascinating stuff. It will make a great story. I'll let you have a photocopy. You'll be amazed,' said Edwin, reeling with enthusiasm.

'I won't have time to plough through any reports today. Just tell me, what's so interesting. What's the story?' Ross asked.

'In a word, it turns out that Jim is Jewish. He had a Jewish mother who was brought up in a Catholic children's home but who became a celebrated concert pianist playing all over Europe. She's buried in Vienna and has a big, monumental headstone.'

'Where did he manage to dig up all that?'

'Mostly from newspaper archives. He was able to locate several reviews of her recitals and concerts in various local newspapers, as well as articles based on interviews that she gave.'

'And what about the family link to the Nazi professor? Did he look into that?'

'He did, yes, and he is pretty sure there is no blood link. He thinks that Jim's father and grandfather claimed they were related to Eugen Fischer because it simply gave them more street cred when it was fashionable in Germany to support Hitler's plans for the so-called Master Race.'

'Just kick that bit of the story into the long grass then. Fisher, at least, should now be pleased to hear that he's not related to any mad and misguided Kraut academic!' said Ross.

'He should be, yes,' agreed Edwin. 'But, of course, he is still sunning himself on honeymoon in Majorca, so it'll be a little while before I get to see him, I expect. I'll have to call him when he gets back and tell him there's some really interesting stuff in the expert's report. I'm sure he'll then want to see me as soon as he can.'

'OK. Keep me posted. I'm not sure how we'll play this story yet but it is a good one, for sure. Ex-Nazi finds out he's Jewish... that's quite a headline.'

*

Just to make sure that Jim and his wife were back home and had time to settle into their normal day-to-day routine, Edwin did not call him for another full week. He called him mid-morning and he answered after just three rings on his mobile.

'Hello, Edwin. Jim speaking,' he said, obviously having logged Edwin's contact details into his phone and seen his name come up on the screen.

'Jim, hello. How are you? How's Sylvia? Did you have a good time in Palma? I think you had pretty good weather.'

'The weather was just great. Warm and sunny during the best part of the day and a bit chilly in the evenings, but still pleasant enough to stroll out if you were wearing a sweater or a jacket.'

'Glad you enjoyed it. How did you get on with your car? Did the garage manage to clean it up?'

'I got it back yesterday and, yes, they have done a terrific job. There was no actual damage and I gather the paint was some kind of emulsion, which they managed to clean off without affecting the paintwork. It looks back to normal now.'

'That's good news. Mike and I were worried that it would need a complete respray.'

'I have to say though that it cost a bloody fortune which I decided to pay out of my pocket. I just felt that I didn't want to try and put it through the insurance company. They would probably have asked me a lot of questions and, as you know, I decided not to contact the police at the time. I would not have felt inclined to answer. Anyway, it's all done and dusted now. Anyhow, how are you guys? Did you and the ladies enjoy the wedding?'

'We're, happily, all fine, and we did. We thought it was a lovely ceremony and the curry was great. And Mike, I know, enjoyed his hotpot. Did you manage to see the article in the paper?'

'I did, yes. They kept a copy of the paper for us at the pub. Yes, we were both happy with it and thanks for not making any reference to the incident with the car. Now, are you ringing me for anything in particular, Edwin?'

'I am, indeed, Jim. We have had the genealogical report from Dr Jäger and it's fascinating, to say the least. He says it is what he calls an interim report and that there is still probably a lot more to discover. He says he'll happily carry on the research if you want to take things further. But, to be honest, I think that we have probably got all the key information we need already. I just need to fix up a time and place we can meet up and you can see it. I'll print off a copy.'

'You've got me intrigued. What's the big discovery? Can you tell me now or give me a clue?'

'I don't think it would be right over the phone, Jim. All I can say is that he's found some pretty amazing information about your mother who died in Vienna in 2010, not really that long ago. We need to fix a meeting.'

'In Vienna, well, that's a surprise already,' Jim replied in a somewhat puzzled, bemused tone. 'I don't know whether it helps or not, but I've got a routine check-up at the hospital at midday on Wednesday next week, so I could see you after that either in the hospital café or somewhere in South Manchester. I'm usually there for an hour or two, so if we say around five o'clock. How does that sound?'

'Perfect. I'll see you in the restaurant and, if you fancy it, we can go for a drink somewhere local. Don't worry if you haven't had your check-up by five – I'll get myself a coffee and wait until you arrive.'

'I'm hoping that you can give me a bit of advice at the same time, Edwin. Sylvia and I are thinking of selling up at Rossendale and moving over to South Manchester as soon as we can. It'll make sense for a couple of reasons.'

'Obviously, you'll be nearer to the hospital.'

'Yes, that's one of the reasons. I have a check-up every couple of weeks and in the winter, it can be a nightmare driving from Rossendale. But apart from that, Sylvia doesn't feel safe in the house any longer and she's probably right.

'Those so-called old pals of mine who gave my motor a paint job that cost me a small fortune, are very likely to be back and maybe go for the house next time. I know what they are like. It's just that you may be able to tell me which areas we should be looking at that are not too far from the hospital.'

'Yes, I could do that, with pleasure. I'm sure you could find a really nice place within four or five miles of the hospital. But what about Sylvia, would she still keep the pub?' asked Edwin.

'No, she'd find someone else to take it over. It's long hours and she says she'd welcome the rest. We'd probably go back now and again, but just as visitors and to see some of the locals Anyway, to get back to the report you've got – I can't wait to see it,' said Jim.

'I don't think you'll be disappointed. Surprised, even amazed but not disappointed, I'm sure. Next Wednesday then. Five o'clock at the hospital.'

'I'll be there. I'll be on my own. Sylvia will have to be at the pub.'

*

The first thing that Edwin noticed when Jim walked into the hospital café the following week was just how well he looked. Apart from the suntan – a legacy of his week in Majorca – he exhibited none of the stress and strain that was evident when he first interviewed him at the hospital after his transplant. He had also shed several pounds of surplus fat and looked fitter and slimmer. The former racist skinhead looked quite the gentleman.

'Hi, Jim, you're looking well. You obviously had a good holiday,' said Edwin.

'Thanks, yes, it was great. Nice hotel, good food, hot sunny days, interesting place – we enjoyed every minute of it.'

'How did today's check-up go,' Edwin asked.

'All is normal, they tell me. I don't have to come back now for a couple of weeks. That Marcus Lieberman gave me a good one. Now, are you going to show me the report from our ancestry friend?'

'First of all, let me get you a tea or coffee, Jim – and d'you want anything to eat with it?'

'No thanks. A tea would be good with just one sugar.'

A couple of minutes later, Edwin returned with a tea in a white mug and removed Dr Jäger's report from a blue wallet folder.

'That's it then, is it, Edwin?' asked Jim.

'Yes, this is Dr Jäger's report... and very interesting it is.'

'Go on then, tell me what you think I need to know. I don't think anything will really shock me anymore.'

'Well, this just might, Jim. I'll give you a copy of the report to take home, but let me tell you what I'm sure is the most interesting, most remarkable discovery... are you ready for it?' Edwin did his best to prepare him for the finding he was about to reveal.

'Yes, go on. Just tell me, please,' said Jim, impatiently.

Edwin took a deep breath and paused for a few seconds, then said, 'Dr Jäger concentrated on your mother as we asked him to and he discovered that although she was brought up in a Catholic children's home, she was, in fact, Jewish and that both her parents were Jewish. There's a lot more about her, Jim, but that's the finding that will come as the biggest surprise, the biggest shock, I suppose.'

Jim's jaw literally dropped open and he stared at Edwin, his eyes blinking uncontrollably. It was several seconds before he spoke.

'Can I see where he says that? Let me see it please,' he said.

Edwin placed the report in front of him and pointed to the relevant section. Jim read it, then read it again.

'I can't believe this. I'm bloody gobsmacked, pardon my French... my mother was Jewish! I never really thought about what she was but I would never in a million years have thought that she could be Jewish. It's going to take a while for that to sink in.' There was a noticeable tremor in Jim's voice.

'I'm sure it will; that's quite understandable. Of course, if your mother was Jewish that means that you are also Jewish. Jewish people take the religion of their mother,' said Edwin.

'I know I've got a Jewish heart but now you're telling me that I've always had one. You were right, this has shocked me... but I'm absolutely OK with it...' After a few moments wrestling in his mind with the stark facts, Jim went on, 'How come my father married a Jewess – that's what you call them,

184

isn't it – when he brought me up to hate all Jews? That just can't be right.'

'Dr Jäger is pretty sure that he didn't know she was Jewish when he married her – he thought she was Catholic, having been brought up by nuns in a Catholic children's home – but divorced her when he somehow discovered that she was, around the time that you were born,' Edwin explained.

'How does he think he got to know?'

'Well, he says it's now impossible to know for certain but he suggests that it's probably something to do with the fact that your mum, who learned to play the piano at the children's home, went on to become a very famous concert pianist and she may have been asked about her family background.

'One of the other possibilities is that she spoke to your father about you being circumcised – which is traditional among Jewish baby boys – and that he then realised that you were both Jewish. It seems he then brainwashed you with all those old Nazi ideologies just as he was brainwashed by his father, and you would have grown up never for a second thinking that you were anything but a patriotic German, part of Hitler's Master Race.'

'I'm going to need some time to process all this. Let's leave it at that for now, can we? Just let me take the report home and go through it with Sylvia and a couple of staff brandies... me, Jewish, I can't get over that.'

'If you don't mind me asking, Jim – were you circumcised?'

'No – no, I wasn't,' he replied.

'I didn't think you would have been. I checked it out on

the Internet and by all accounts, only a minority of babies in Germany are circumcised, even though it's not just a Jewish practice. Jesus, I learned, was circumcised when he was eight days old and for many Christians, the day of his circumcision is celebrated.'

'I don't expect my brother, Uwe, was circumcised either... you know, just to change the subject, I am wondering how I would have reacted to all this if I'd found out I was Jewish when I was over in Liverpool causing mayhem. I reckon I would have just denied it. I'd have just told people they were talking utter bloody crap and carried on regardless. I know I wouldn't have believed them and wouldn't have spent time trying to dig around to find out. I guess I would have just thought they were all bloody cranks trying to upset me.'

'D'you think you'll adjust to it – get used to the fact you're Jewish? I can see that it won't happen overnight but I reckon you'll get used to the idea more quickly than you think – especially when you bear in mind that it's your true birthright and you'd never have been the way you were had it not been for your father.'

'I hope you're right, Edwin. I'll do my best. I suppose having now got used to the fact I've got a Jewish heart means I'm already more than halfway there.'

'There's one thing that's just struck me, Jim – you were asking me some time ago about how you can make amends for things you were involved with in the past. Well, I'm pretty certain that this is going to make that a whole lot easier. I'm not sure exactly how, but I just really believe that it will. I mean, you'll be accepted instantly by Jewish people because you are Jewish.'

'Yes, OK, I can see that. We'll see.'

Edwin felt that it was time to lighten the conversation, especially as they were sitting close to patients and visitors at other nearby tables within earshot.

'There's a lot of take in, Jim, I know, but there's also a lot of really fascinating stories about your mum and even some copies of articles and reviews of her concerts that appeared in local papers in various parts of Europe. I know you'll enjoy reading those and generally getting to know your mother. She sounds as if she was a really lovely and very talented lady.'

'Can I get you another tea or coffee?' asked Jim.

'No thanks, I'm fine. I need to get on my way soon. I'll give you a ring in a day or so when you've had a chance to plough through the report and had time to digest it.'

'Are you planning to write anything in your paper about all this, Edwin?'

'I'm not sure yet. It's obviously a strong news line and I know that the editor was interested, but if you are worried that it could lead to some problems for you and Sylvia at home, then I am sure they would either ditch it or put it on hold until you have moved to a new address. I can see that there is a risk of those car vandals coming back – especially when they find out that you are Jewish. What's your view?'

'My view? Well, I can't tell your editor how to do his job and I see that it's an interesting story, but I would certainly not want it in the paper right now while Sylvia and I are at Rossendale.'

'I don't think that will present a problem, but I'll keep you posted. Good to see you looking so well,' said Edwin, handing him a copy of Dr Jäger's report in a sealed envelope.

They stood up, shook hands and walked towards the hospital exit before heading in separate directions to pick up their cars.

*

As he headed back into the city centre, Edwin rehearsed in his head how he was going to persuade his editor to hold the story at least until Jim and his wife had found a new home at an address that would not be known to his aggrieved former neo-Nazi followers. The fact that the newspaper had paid a four-figure sum for Dr Jäger's report and that news editor Ross Hetherington had already earmarked the revelation that Jim was Jewish as a "great story", would considerably weaken his case, he feared.

But he need not have worried.

'Tell him we'll wait until he's moved house and we'll then reconsider it. We don't want to be accused of inciting neo-Nazi thugs,' said Ross in his usual succinct way. Then he added, '... but make it clear that we reserve the right to carry a piece at a later date.'

'He'll be happy with that, Ross, I'm sure,' said Edwin. 'He's also asking me how he can now atone for his old sins, so there's still a lot of mileage to come apart from the Jäger report.

Talking of the report, Jäger is asking if we are interested in taking it any further, in particular conducting further research to try and find the whereabouts of Jim's elder brother.'

'No. Thank him for what he's done to date but tell him we don't want to take it any further for the time being. I reckon we can find his elder brother ourselves. I'm sure you can crack that one, Edwin – you'd enjoy that.'

'Fine by me. You're right. I would enjoy having a shot at that.'

Tracking people down with even the sketchiest of information was one of Edwin's journalistic fortes and one he was frequently called upon to put into practice by the news desk.

*

Apart from writing up a short piece appealing to the elderly to seek regular eye tests in order to identify any signs of macular degeneration at an early and treatable stage, Edwin was able to begin his genealogical detective work that same afternoon.

He knew it was most likely that Jim's brother had probably not changed the spelling of his family name, so he would be looking for an Uwe Wilhelm Fischer somewhere in the USA. A search via the *Ancestry* family history website proved inconclusive, but when he punched the name into the Facebook search engine, he instantly struck gold. There were several Uwe Fischers but only one with the middle initial W, and he lived in a beach resort just north of San Diego in California. In the "about" section, it didn't give his date or place of birth but there was a photograph alongside his profile that Edwin concluded was of a man who looked five or six years older than Jim and certainly looked Jewish.

Edwin was fairly certain he had found his man – and with considerably less difficulty than he had anticipated. Other than the name of the beach resort, there was no email address or contact telephone number, but there was the Facebook Messenger facility which enabled him to send a short message.

My name is Edwin Benn, Medical Correspondent of The Informer *newspaper in the UK. During the past year, we have published numerous articles about James Karl Fisher, who just over a year ago, had a heart transplant operation at Roundthorn Hospital in Manchester. He told us that he had an elder brother, Uwe Wilhelm Fischer (James anglicised the spelling of his family name from Fischer to Fisher), but that he had lost touch with him and, for reasons that would not be appropriate to discuss here, he had not attempted to discover his whereabouts. Suffice to say that James has found a new, positive purpose in life following his transplant and is now keen to reconnect with his brother. My newspaper recently commissioned the services of a professional genealogist who confirmed that James had a brother named Uwe Wilhelm Fischer and suggested he had emigrated to the USA. If you are the brother in question, James would love to make contact with you.*

We look forward to hearing from you.
Kind regards, Edwin Benn.

Edwin sent off the email when it would have been around mid-morning in California and was pleasantly surprised to receive a fulsome response just before he ended his shift.

It contained a number of inconsequential changes in semantics, revealing that the author's native language was not English but, more importantly, it confirmed that Uwe Wilhelm Fischer was indeed Jim's elder brother.

You have found the right person, Mr Benn. I am the brother of Karl Fischer. We lived together in Karlsruhe in Germany. I think Karl emigrated to the UK around the time that our father died and from the tone of your correspondence, I suspect you know that he became involved in pro-Nazi activities as a result of the evil that was instilled in his young head by our father. I am most pleased to hear that he has now found a new and, what you say, positive direction in life following his operation – I am interested to know more about his transplant, especially as I work in the medical world.

I was luckier than my brother because I was not influenced by my father. I am sure you will understand when I tell you that I had many Jewish friends – including for a time a Jewish girlfriend called Rosa – and also other Jewish friends when I attended the Univesitatsmedizen in Hamburg. My father tried to discourage me from having those friendships and when I refused, we fell out and I decided to move here to the United States. But my mother never had any objection and I have since learned that she was Jewish, with Jewish parents. Your researcher may have told you that she became a celebrated concert pianist.

I had contact with her for several years before she died – I went to Hungary to meet her on two occasions – and have many photographs here that I can share with my brother and you. I can perhaps make plans to come to England to meet him but I am not yet retired and would need to make arrangements at the hospital where I work. I am married to an American lady, Nicole, who was a nurse at the hospital where we met. We have two sons and one daughter born here in California. We are all in the family photographs I have attached.

This is all very exciting.

Kindest regards, Uwe Fischer.

Underneath his signature, he inserted what appeared to be the logo from his letterhead that included his medical qualifications and details of his specialism in gastroenterology.

Edwin sent him an immediate reply, thanking him for responding so promptly and positively. "I will forward your email to Karl, who goes by the name of Jim, and suggest that he makes direct contact with you. I am sure he will have lots of questions to ask you and, no doubt, there are many questions that you will want to ask him," Edwin wrote.

*

Before heading off for home, Edwin recounted this latest significant development to his news editor.

'You'll be interested to hear that I've found Jim's brother and I have already had a full reply from him in California – I couldn't believe how easy it was.'

'Tell me why we're paying all this money to some professional when you have done just as well!'

'I'm OK with certain things, Ross, but I couldn't have found out all the things Dr Jäger discovered about Jim's mother and the fact he wasn't related to the Nazi professor. We would still have needed a pro for that, Ross. It's a whole different ballgame tracing ancestry in Europe.'

'Have we learned anything new?'

'We have, yes. His brother seems to know all about Jim's criminal days on Merseyside and confirms that he was brainwashed by his father. He also tells me that he's got a lot of archive material, including pics, relating to their mother.'

'Does he say what he does?' asked Ross.

'He's a senior gastroenterologist in California, with a wife and three children – two sons and a daughter. He's hoping now that he can correspond with Jim directly and possibly arrange to fly over. I'll print off his email and let you have a read.'

'We'll need to run a follow-up story soon, Edwin. We can't just keep spending time and money on this Fisher saga and not write anything.'

'You're right. I reckon that as soon as Jim moves house and can become anonymous, we'll have no problem in running another exclusive encapsulating all the new info.'

'OK, keep me posted.'

Ross took a call that came through the news desk, signalling that his conversation with Edwin was at an end. Edwin closed down his PC, picked up his briefcase and went home satisfied that it had been a productive day.

*

It was almost a month later, with real warmth in the midday sunshine and the first early daffodils opening their petals in Edwin's garden, that he next heard from Jim Fisher. He assumed he must be calling to discuss the response from his elder brother, Uwe, and the report from the genealogist, but not so. He wanted to update Edwin about his house-moving plans.

'Sylvia and I think we may have found a new place in Bowdon, a modern apartment in one of those secure gated developments, and we've already had quite a bit of interest in our place at Rossendale... Bowdon is near to where you are, Edwin, isn't it?'

'Just a few minutes down the road. Yes, we often go into Bowdon. It's a nice area and as I'm sure you already know, it's very convenient for the hospital.'

'So, you think it could be a good move then? If we happen to sell our Rossendale place first, it wouldn't be a problem. We could stay at the pub.'

'I do know it well, yes. If you and Sylvia like the place and if as you say, it's in a safe gated development, I'm pretty sure you'd like the area. It's not like Rossendale but it's on the doorstep of some lovely places in Cheshire. I wish you luck with that.' Edwin did not feel that it was prudent to tell him that Bowdon and the surrounding areas had a high Jewish population.

'We've certainly made our minds up that we're going to move and just hope it'll be soon.'

'Just to change the subject, Jim – have you had time to digest Dr Jäger's report and have you made contact with Uwe in California yet?'

'Yes, I've done both. I've written back to my brother, told him the whole story and how genuinely thrilled I was to make contact with him again after all these years. I never thought for a minute that I'd have a brother who was a top medical man like Uwe. He puts me to shame. Anyway, he's written back and all being well, he's planning to come over and meet up again, hopefully, this summer. If we've moved by then, he would be able to stay with us.'

'And what about Dr Jäger's report? Did you manage to look through it?'

'I've been through it several times. I think I understand now why I ended up being the way I used to be... it wasn't really my fault... I didn't stand a chance... but I ended up being the bloody ringleader over on Merseyside and I can never deny that. So, I still want to find some way of putting things right, to make amends, and I know you're happy to help me with that.'

'Of course, but I'm still not precisely sure how and where. We'll have to work out a plan together, Jim.'

'One thing that I would now really like to do, is go over to Europe and follow in the footsteps of my mother in Poland, Hungary and Austria. I'd be especially keen to visit her grave in Vienna. You could perhaps persuade your newspaper to let you come with me and write up a piece for your paper. That, I reckon, would go some way to making amends for the past.'

'That's not a bad idea at all. I like the sound of that. After you've moved house, we can sit down and see if we can come up with a workable plan. If you're OK with it by then, it would also be the right time to reveal that Dr Jäger's research discovered that you are in, in fact, Jewish. Does that make sense?'

'I'd have no problem with that. If I've moved and you keep my new address out of the paper, I'd be happy to go along with that. It would sort of be one big news story of me following in the footsteps of my famous Jewish mother.'

Edwin felt that he had to ask one rather searching question. 'Jim, how does it feel to know that you had a Jewish mother and that you are Jewish? I'm just wondering if that has really sunk in yet. I'm just asking out of personal interest.'

'That's a difficult one. I'm really not sure I can answer that just yet. To be honest, I don't feel much different at all. I might have done when I was the old Jim Fisher in Liverpool – I'd have just said it was all bloody nonsense and dismissed it – but now I guess it's a bit too soon to know how it might change my life. Sylvia said that I should have a Star of David tattooed over my new heart. That would make a good photo for your paper, wouldn't it?'

'It would, yes. Just let me know if you ever have it done.'

'For one thing, it would show the world that I'm serious about paying my debts for all the nasty stuff I got involved with in the old days. I'm lucky enough to have a few bob in the bank, so I'd happily give some of that away if you can help me find the right people and places. I don't know what else I could do but I'm sure that you'll be able to suggest a few things, Edwin.'

'We'll definitely work something out after you have moved house, Jim.'

*

When they had finished their conversation, Edwin realised that when he last spoke with Rabbi Goldbladt about how Jim might atone for his past sins and crimes, it was not known that he was Jewish. Would that make any difference? Would it make his reparation any easier or more difficult?

He called him from the office but was advised that he was conducting a funeral service and he was not able to speak until early evening when they would both be at home.

'There's been a surprising and fascinating development with our heart transplant recipient that I feel I must bring to your attention, Rabbi,' said Edwin after dispensing with the pleasantries.

'Is he well?' the rabbi asked.

'He is absolutely fine. Nothing to do with his health. The fact is we've now heard back from the genealogist who we asked to look into his family history and, remarkably, he's discovered that Jim is, in fact, Jewish – that his mother was Jewish.'

'I did not expect you to say that, of all things. He is Jewish! How come he did not know he was Jewish?'

'It's a long story but, basically, his grandmother died in childbirth and his mother was brought up by nuns in a Catholic children's home in the countryside about an hour's drive from Lodz which, we believe, has since been converted into a residential home for the elderly. His father never knew she was Jewish when they met and later married, but it seems he did discover she was Jewish sometime after Jim was born and he then divorced her. As it happens, Jim's mother went on to become a well-known concert pianist and composer and that helped the researcher to find out more about her early years.'

'Where was he born?'

'In Ulm in Germany. His mother was Polish, born in Lodz and died in Vienna after giving a recital there.'

'And I presume he has seen the report from the genealogist and now knows he's Jewish?'

'Yes, he's read the report and I was talking to him about it earlier today. He says it hasn't made him feel much different, although I'm not sure if it has really sunk in yet. Interestingly, though, he's keen to trace his mother's footsteps around Europe and visit her grave... and wonders if I might be able to accompany him.'

'So, there certainly doesn't seem to be any suggestion that this rapport with Jewish people following his transplant is only temporary?'

'No, not at all. It all seems very permanent, hopefully, like his new heart... I was just wondering if his resolve to repay his debt to society and repent would need to be any different now that we know he's Jewish?'

Rabbi Goldbladt remained silent for several seconds before responding.

'This is a very interesting question and I would simply say this: if he were a religious man – and I suspect that he is not and never has been – I would have suggested that on Yom Kippur, our Day of Atonement, he comes to the synagogue to confess his sins, makes his peace with God and, perhaps, even goes to the ritual baths, the mikvah, the day before Yom Kippur.

'These days, I know that even secular Jews who do not attend the synagogue during the year, do make a special point of attending on Yom Kippur, which is the holiest day in the Jewish calendar, but in Mr Fisher's case, I do not believe that this would be appropriate. By all means, ask him, but I feel that as we alluded to earlier, it would be preferable for him to atone in his way by giving to appropriate charities.

'There are many dozens of Jewish charities and one of the most appropriate in this case might be the World Jewish Relief appeal, which among many other groups and organisations, supports the Abayudaya Jewish community in Uganda. Of course, there are also several specific anti-racism charities and others that are dedicated to helping disadvantaged communities that he might also want to consider. It would have to be his decision finally.'

'That's all really useful, Rabbi. I will spend a bit of time having a trawl through all the different charities to see which would seem to be the most suitable and reduce them to a shortlist that I can discuss with him. I think I can safely say that he would go along with whatever we suggest.'

'Always glad to be of help. I'm sure it will all work out satisfactorily.'

*

As soon as they finished speaking, Edwin could not resist opening up his Internet browser and taking a look at the World Jewish Relief charity website. He was personally interested in learning more about their work in Uganda as well as the charity's appropriateness for Jim.

The Abayudaya Jewish community in eastern Uganda, he learned, had been practising Judaism for more than a hundred years and their name had its roots in the Luganda word for the "people of Judah".

Edwin printed off and highlighted a number of key facts, knowing that he would be able to weave them into his article at the appropriate time. He learned that:

The community was established in 1919 when a local chieftain began to study the fundamental tenets of Judaism and the fledgling community became deeply connected to Jewish tradition and Jewish people around the globe.

The Abayudaya set up their first rabbinical studies educational institution in 1920 and three years later their first synagogue, but when Idi Amin came to power in Uganda in 1971, he banned the Jewish faith and the synagogue was destroyed.

A core of some three hundred Jews remained, practising their religion in secret and by the turn of the millennium, the community had risen to around three thousand and was now approximately two thousand.

Two other historical facts about the charity interested Edwin convincing him that it would be the one that he would recommend to Jim: the first was that under its former name, the Central British Fund for German Jewry (the CBF), it was instrumental in effecting the Transportation in which some ten thousand German and Austrian Jewish children were rescued from the Nazis and brought to Britain.

And secondly, after the liberation of the Nazi concentration camps, the charity rescued and rehabilitated more than seven hundred child Holocaust survivors, initially bringing them to the safety of a camp in Windermere in the Lake District and later to other hostels around Britain. The children were known as The Boys, even though almost two hundred of them were girls.

Having satisfied himself that he had identified the ideal Jewish charity for Jim to support, Edwin turned his attention to those who supported the disadvantaged communities and devoted their resources and energies to fighting racism and hate crimes. Eventually, he settled on three: Show Racism the Red Card, the UK's leading anti-racism educational charity; Blueprint for All, the former Stephen Lawrence Charitable Trust set up after the British black teenager was murdered in a racially-motivated attack in April 1993 and The Stand Against Racism and Inequality (SARI), supporting victims of hate and run by people who, in most cases, have themselves been victims of race-hate behaviour.

He typed out the names of the charities with the relevant contact details and emailed the list as an attachment to Jim, along with a short note, which read:

Hi Jim,

Here is the list of charities with contact details which we feel would be the most appropriate in the circumstances. When I spoke to the rabbi, he said that under Jewish religious law whenever people are making donations to repay wrongs from the past, they should really do so anonymously but I will leave that entirely up to you.

He also said you would be welcome to go to the synagogue on the Day of Atonement (Yom Kippur) in September, which is the holiest day of the year in the Jewish calendar and the day on which people confess their sins and make their peace with God. But I suspect that this is something that you would not want to do – at least for the foreseeable future. Just thinking ahead; if and when you go over to Europe and follow in your mother's footsteps, there is every possibility that you may then visit a synagogue and, thereafter, feel differently about attending on the Day of Atonement.

Within the hour, Edwin received a response:

Thanks for the list – seems good to me. You're right about going to a synagogue. As you know, all the old hate has gone since my transplant but it's not made me a religious guy, you understand. I'd be a bloody hypocrite if I went confessing sins in a synagogue – I don't think that's for me.

But I approve of the charity that helps Jews in Africa. To be honest with you, even in the old days when I was having a go at the Blacks over on Merseyside, I always had a bit of a soft spot for the lads who looked after the orphan elephants. Perhaps it was just that I had a soft spot for the animals – I don't really know now. Anyway, if my donation helps those people in Uganda, I would have no problem with that.

You can be sure that I'll send off my donation ASAP, but right now, I'm a bit bogged down with selling our place and finding somewhere new to live – but, fingers crossed, we'll sort that out soon.

Edwin made a mental note of the fact that Jim did not refer to the rabbi's suggestion that any donations he made should be anonymous and that he did not give any indication of how much he was proposing to donate. There was every possibility that it would emerge in conversation in due course but for the time being, Edwin decided that they were two private areas of Jim's proposed reparation that he should not pursue.

Instead, he would take another look at Dr Jäger's genealogical report and see if he could work out an outline itinerary that he could develop further should Jim begin talking seriously about following in his mother's footsteps in Europe.

It was a prospect that Edwin found both personally and professionally exciting.

CHAPTER 8

Some two months had elapsed since Edwin had last spoken with Jim and he was the last thing on his mind as he and his wife, Marion, packed their suitcases for a two-week holiday in rural Tuscany. They were due to fly from Manchester Airport to Pisa the following morning.

By a little before 10 p.m., they decided to take a break – leaving their toiletry essentials like toothbrushes, toothpaste and shampoos until after their ablutions the following morning – and make themselves a pot of tea while listening to the late BBC News before turning in for the night. Just as the news was finishing, Edwin was alarmed by a call on his mobile. He walked over to his bedside table and saw from the display that it was from Jim Fisher.

Rarely did anyone ever call him at home at that time of night and his first thought was that there must be a problem. In the same instant, he just hoped that it was nothing that was going to jeopardize their holiday.

'Jim, it's Edwin. Is everything all right?' he asked in a tone of voice straddling concern and surprise.

'Yes, everything is going well. Am I calling at a bad time? Sorry, I've just realised the time. It's just that I've had some news – good news – and wanted to update you on a couple of things. We've not spoken for a while.'

Edwin sat down on the edge of the bed and could feel himself beginning to relax into the conversation.

'No, it's no problem, Jim. It's just that people don't usually call us at this time of night and I thought there must be a problem of some sort... as it happens, we were just finishing off packing and planning to make ourselves a cup of tea before turning in. We're flying off to Italy tomorrow for a couple of weeks in Tuscany.'

'Very nice. Have you been there before?'

'Several times, yes. It's our favourite place in the world for holidays.'

'I've never been. I must take Sylvia there sometime... anyway, I'd better let you guys get some shut-eye. I just felt that I had to tell you that I had an email from my brother earlier tonight saying that he's going to come over with his wife this summer... he has some photos of our mother that he wants me to see... all very exciting and all thanks to you.'

'I'm really pleased for you, Jim. Will they be staying with you?'

'Well, that's the other thing I have to tell you – we've signed the contract for the apartment we saw in Cheshire and we're pretty sure we've also found a buyer for the place here. With a bit of luck, we should be moving in the next fortnight. So, yes, we should be settled in the new place by the time Uwe comes over and they will hopefully stay with us.'

'Do you know how long they will be staying? If it's possible, I'd like to meet him and see those photographs of your mother. Perhaps you could arrange to have some copies made. I am not sure right now, but we might be able to use them in the paper. Anyway, good luck with the move.'

'Fingers crossed but, so far, everything has gone like clockwork and it looks like when I've done all the sums, I'll be able to put a few extra quid in the bank.'

'Great. That can't be bad.'

'Oh, yes, and talking of money, you'll be pleased to hear that I've made those donations to the charities you gave me. It took a bit of setting up but I managed to make them anonymously through Western Union, so they won't know where the money came from but I can check that it was received. Of course, Western Union knows who sent it but they don't pass that information on to the recipient. All good, I reckon!'

'You've done a good job, Jim. And it's really great news about your brother and his wife coming over and your move to Cheshire. By the time we get back from Italy, it's possible that you may already have moved. I'll give you a call when I'm back and you can give me an update.'

'Are you staying in a hotel?'

'We are, yes – a little gem of a place where we have stayed once before in a small village called Pancole which is about halfway between Florence and Siena. We'll be picking up a hire car at Pisa Airport.'

'I'd better let you go then. I'll talk to you when you get back. I hope you both have a great time.'

'Thanks, Jim. I'm sure we will. I hope all goes well with the move. Give my regards to Sylvia. Bye for now.'

*

As he finished his conversation, Marion came into the bedroom carrying two china cups of tea, each with a plain digestive biscuit on the saucer.

'Your new friend, Mr Fisher, I gather. What did he want that was so urgent at this time of night?' she asked.

'Nothing urgent, nothing that wouldn't have waited. He just wanted to tell me that his brother and his wife in California are coming over in the summer and that it looks like he'll be moving to his new house within the next couple of weeks. And, perhaps most importantly, he has donated to the charities I suggested to him.'

'Did he tell you how much he donated?'

'No, and I didn't feel that I should ask him.'

Marion, whose focus was still on their imminent holiday, changed the subject.

'I have just closed the suitcases for tonight. All we have to do in the morning is put our toiletry bags and a few other bits and pieces in in the morning, take them down into the hall and then sit back and wait for the taxi. Then we'll be on our way to our beloved Tuscany.'

Edwin drank some of his tea and ate his biscuit. He then opened up his desktop PC to print off his nightly cryptic crossword puzzle and, just in case it slipped his mind, he opened up his diary and made a note to call Jim when he returned home.

When he eventually put his head on the pillow with his mind switching between the Fisher case and the delights of Tuscany, Edwin realised that he had not told him that he had provisionally mapped out an itinerary for his pilgrimage to follow in the footsteps of his mother. But it was still largely a work in progress and, in any event, it was highly unlikely that Jim would be able to make the trip until after his brother and his wife had visited from the United States.

'You know, Edwin, the way that Jim Fisher rings you up and chats, you'd think he was a long-time old buddy. I still find it hard to believe he's the same guy who, not that long ago, would happily have had all minority groups wiped off the face of the earth,' said Marion.

'It is amazing, yes. You could call it a medical miracle... but he's just not the same person now,' he replied sleepily without opening his eyes.

'I hope you're right. I sometimes worry that the old Jim will come back like the proverbial bad penny. Anyway, don't let's worry about that... we're on holiday.'

Within a few minutes, they were both asleep.

*

When they awoke the following morning, Edwin switched on his mobile and found a short text message from Jim. It read: "Apologies for the late call last night – just didn't realise the time. Have a great break, mate." It was the first time that he had called Edwin "mate" and it made him feel slightly uncomfortable – although he wasn't quite sure why. With his focus fixed firmly on their imminent flight to Pisa, he did not dwell on it.

Their taxi arrived at 3:30 p.m. and after the airport check-in formalities and a brief excursion to Duty Free for a "medicinal" bottle of brandy – which Edwin always contended was the best prophylactic against gippy tummy – they boarded their flight a little before 6 p.m. Some two and a half hours later, they landed safely at Pisa where they picked up a small Fiat hire car for the fifty-mile drive to their hotel.

With a brief stop for refreshments en route, they arrived after the restaurant's dinner service had ended but a young woman on the reception desk said the chef would happily make them a light snack.

'*Grazie*,' said Edwin, then adding in English, 'That would be perfect.'

'You like bruschetta – it is very good?' said the receptionist.

'*Eccellente* – and *due caffè, per favore, se possibile*?' asked Edwin.

Although it was well after 10 p.m., the night air was still comfortingly warm and redolent with the perfume of the bougainvillea vines that were just beginning to come into bloom around the hotel's terrace. Edwin and Marion sat down in two wicker chairs with a view over the garden and the hotel pool and chatted about their plans.

'How come they always taste so much better here than they do back at home?' asked Edwin rhetorically.

'It's everything really – the bread, the tomatoes, the oil, the fresh basil plus the atmosphere, the ambience. But, you're right, they don't taste anything like this if you have them in England,' said Marion.

They were already beginning to relax – to succumb to the tastes, aromas and the distinctive beauty of Tuscany. Although they were a little travel-weary, they remained chatting over their coffee for another half an hour before going to bed, eagerly looking forward to their first full day being wooed by the magic of Tuscany.

Over the next two weeks, they explored some of the off-the-tourist-trail areas that they had not visited on previous visits. In the Via Luigi Carlo Farini in Florence, they chanced upon the 19th century Tempio Maggiore, the Great Synagogue, with its 155-feet high green dome that competes in the city's skyline with Brunelleschi's terracotta-lined dome towering above the Duomo di Firenze and the 312-feet tower of the Uffizi Gallery.

'It's hard to believe that this is just the sort of place that the Jim Fisher I first met would have delighted in desecrating in his bad old days. I wonder what he would make of such a beautiful building now – now that he's both a reformed character and is also Jewish himself!' Edwin remarked.

'I've no idea. I expect that he would not give it much thought at all. I know he's Jewish by birth but he's not a religious man. Anyway, Mr Benn, you're on your holidays and you shouldn't be thinking or worrying about Jim Fisher,' said Marion, mildly reprimanding him.

'Sorry, you're right. I promise you I won't mention him again – at least not until after we get back home,' Edwin replied.

In Siena, after ambling haphazardly through the fiercely independent Palio Contrade, they decided it was time to stop for lunch and tried to find a small bakery-cum-deli, where on a previous visit they had relished a home-roasted herb and pork sandwich that always stimulated their taste buds every time they thought or spoke of Siena. They remembered that it was on a side road just off the Piazza del Campo, but they failed to find it again and had to opt for a pasta lunch in a small restaurant that seemed to be a favourite with locals.

On other days, they returned to absorb the culture and elegance of Lucca; the film-set town of San Gimignano, with its bristling towers built by wealthy warring families to outdo each other; Montepulciano, where they sampled the much-revered ruby-coloured Vino Nobile from a restaurant terrace with a panoramic vista over the Tuscan countryside with its distinctive conical cypress trees; and, for pure nostalgia, they returned to the beach resort of Pietrasanta, where a decade or more earlier they had enjoyed many of their most memorable meals and had made a wealth of happy memories.

Edwin also kept his promise to take Marion to the epicurean utopia of Fattoria La Vialla (The Plough), an extensive patchwork amalgam of organic farms at Castiglion Fibocchi near Arezzo, which produced a cornucopia of gourmet foods

211

and fine wines. Some years earlier, on a news assignment, he had sampled its culinary delights at an alfresco buffet and ever since he and Marion had salivated as they thumbed through their brochures sent to their home through the mail.

'What do you think then – was I right to keep my promise?' Edwin asked as they drove out along the tree-lined drive after an escorted tour around the farm and a superb but simple pasta lunch served on a chequered red and white tablecloth alongside the farm's delicatessen.

'Even better than I ever imagined – just magical and memorable. I wouldn't have missed it for the world,' she replied, smacking her lips in appreciation.

'I knew you'd enjoy it. I always wanted to bring you here. It is undoubtedly a very special place.'

*

After two enriching and magical weeks in the warm, spring Tuscan sunshine, their holiday was at an end and they returned home to find that winter was still clinging on by its fingertips with cold, wet days. Edwin was also brought back to reality with another text on his mobile from Jim, which read: "Give me a call when you get back. Will be moving on Monday. My brother is now coming over in July. Hope you had a great holiday."

It was early on a Saturday evening when Edwin and Marion stepped back through their own front door, less than forty hours before Jim and Sylvia Fisher would be moving to their new apartment in Bowdon and, by comparison with Rossendale, they would almost be neighbours.

After a cup of tea and unpacking a few essentials, he phoned.

'Just got back about an hour ago. Had a great time – good weather and good food. You asked me to call. How are things with you?'

'All good, too. The hospital tells me my new ticker is ticking over normally and I feel a million dollars. You'll have seen we are moving house on Monday... more importantly, I can now tell you that Uwe and his wife, Nicole, will be coming over in July and staying with us for at least a week,' said Jim excitedly.

'It's all happening for you. New heart, new wife, new house and now a new brother, well, a brother that you haven't seen since you were a child in Germany. Pity you won't be able to meet his children, your nephews and nieces.'

'They'll be staying with Nicole's sister, I gather. All being well, Sylvia and I will go over there before too long so we'll get to know them then. All exciting stuff.'

'Do you think that I'll get a chance to meet your brother and his wife when they're here? I think he said that he had some photos of your mother and, as I might have mentioned, we would love to use them in the paper along with a piece about your reunion with Uwe. It would make a really nice, happy human-interest story, Jim.'

'Yes, I'd have no problem with that. I'll make sure that we have some photocopies for you. What's most exciting is that he also has a short black-and-white film of my mother taken

when she played at some concert hall – I can't wait to see that...
it's on a DVD so I should be able to make a copy of it for you.'

'That will be fascinating to see. Perhaps when you go over
to Europe you might be able to visit the concert hall, if we can
find out which one it was.'

'As I said, they will be staying with us for a week or so, so we
can fix a date for you to come and meet them nearer the time.
It'll probably be best a day or so before they go back, when
we've had a chance to get to know each other again.'

'Sounds good to me. Anyway, I must make a move now.
We haven't unpacked properly yet, there's a whole mountain
of mail to open and, although it's Sunday, I'm back in the
newsroom tomorrow. Good luck with the house move!'

'I'll let you go then. We can talk about your trip to Europe
and hopefully arrange something for August or September
after my brother and Nicole have gone back to California.'

'That should fall into place nicely. Cheers for now.'

*

Before he went on holiday, Edwin left his news editor with
an outline plan of his proposal to accompany Jim on his trip,
stressing that he was confident it would produce an impactful
feature article with wide reader appeal. Crucially, he made the
point that it would be highly unlikely that Jim would attempt
to undertake the trip on his own.

It proved to be a convincing argument.

'Edwin, whilst you were away, I had words with the editor
about your proposal to accompany Fisher on his trip, and as

long as it's no longer than one week, he said he's happy to go with it,' said Ross.

'It'll make a good piece; quite possibly, more than one. I've been roughing out an itinerary and it's all fascinating stuff... but what about pictures? Will we be sending a photographer as well?'

'We'll work something out nearer the time. You say that Fisher hopes to visit his mother's grave and we may just need to send someone over for that, as it seems to be the picture we are most likely to use. When is it you'd be going anyway?'

'Probably in August or September. His brother, the consultant from California, and his wife are coming over to stay with him for a week in July, so it's going to be just after that. Jim says he's happy for me to meet them towards the end of his week, just before his brother goes back to the States.'

'Keep me posted on that, Edwin – and keep the picture desk up to speed. We'll certainly need to have a pic of the two brothers and their wives. Should make a nice piece.'

'It will, I'm sure. Judging by the email exchange I've had with the brother, he seems like a really nice guy.'

Ross switched his focus to the matters of the day. 'What have you got on today, Edwin?'

'Nothing of any great importance. I was just thinking of firming up the itinerary – emailing some of the archive departments in Lodz and Vienna, contacting the press attaché at the Hungarian Consulate here and checking out the address in Budapest which we believe was the last place Jim's mother lived.'

Ross paused and glanced at the news desk diary and schedule. 'OK, you get on with that, but if anything crops up I will have to take you off it for now.'

'Fine. I'll plough on,' Edwin replied, returning to his desk.

As it transpired, there was no breaking news of any great significance, so, apart from breaking off to take a number of calls and arrange interviews during the coming week, Edwin was able to flesh out the itinerary in fairly fine detail. Broadly, he reckoned he and Jim would need to spend two days in Poland visiting Lodz and the Catholic children's home where Jim was brought up, perhaps two days in Budapest visiting Jim's mother's home and any venues with which she had a close association, and perhaps a further two days in Vienna where they would visit her grave in the city's Jewish cemetery.

In discussions he had over the months with Jim, Edwin had asked him if he wanted to return to his birthplace in Germany and to visit places that would have been familiar to both his mother and father – and to a lesser extent, his brother, Uwe – but he had made it clear that he did not want to return to his homeland.

'I don't have very happy memories of my childhood or growing up in Germany, and I now know that's where I was brainwashed with all that Nazi propaganda by my father. I can remember he used to give me comics with grotesque drawings of Jews with big, hooked noses who were counting bags of money – no, I'd not be happy going back there,' he told Edwin.

Edwin did not pursue it any further.

*

When he drove home that evening after his first day back at work, Edwin felt content that he had devised an itinerary that would enable Jim to feel close to his mother and learn something of her life and lifestyle, while bearing in mind the passage of time and the many changes that would have occurred over the years. Journalistically, he was confident that it would also produce a fascinating and poignant human-interest article that would touch the heartstrings.

'Hi, honey. How's your day been?' Edwin asked his wife as he opened his front door and greeted her with an affectionate kiss on the cheek.

'Back to domesticity with a vengeance. Washing, ironing all the holiday clothes and a quick sortie to the supermarket... but, mentally, I'm still in Tuscany. What about your day?' she asked.

'Remarkably uneventful. I fixed up a few interviews for next week, but for most of the day, I was able to work on the itinerary of Jim's trip. Ross spoke to the editor whilst we were away and he's rubber-stamped it as long as it takes no longer than a week – and that should be about right.'

'Do you reckon this saga is ever going to end?'

'Not for a good while yet – but it will in time, I guess. Jim's long-lost brother and his American wife are supposed to be coming over for a week shortly and then, in August or September, all being well, he'll be going off with me on this pilgrimage to Europe. After that, I don't know but there will undoubtedly be something.'

'I just worry that the bubble will burst and he'll revert back to being the nasty racist.'

'It could happen, I suppose, but I honestly believe that he would have done so by now. I sometimes find it difficult to believe what a normal, nice guy he now is, but he genuinely is. I suppose you could say that his mental change of heart is just as big a miracle as his physical change of heart – probably even more miraculous or whatever you want to call it. Anyway, enough of that, do you fancy going out to the Italian for a bite to eat to stay in holiday mode for a few hours longer?'

'If that's what you'd like to do, OK. Give me ten minutes to change and we can go.'

Three-quarters of an hour later, Marion was enjoying a linguine gamberoni and Edwin a king prawn risotto as they reminisced about their two weeks under the Tuscan sun.

*

For the next few weeks, Edwin had a welcome respite from the James Karl Fisher saga, but it was short-lived. In mid-July, the story was back at the top of the news desk schedule when Jim's brother, Uwe, and his wife, Nicole, arrived from their home in California for their week-long visit.

As arranged, Edwin and photographer Mike Wolff drove over to Jim's new Cheshire apartment on the day before Uwe and Nicole were due to return to America. They arrived at the gated apartment block around midday on what was the fifth day in succession that the temperature was in the upper seventies.

There were headlines in the newspapers and bulletins on TV about Britain "sizzling" in a heatwave, as well as warnings about grassland and forest fires and gloomy, worrying predictions about the effects of climate change.

Edwin pressed the intercom bell and a moment later he heard Jim's voice.

'Push the door and I'll meet you inside,' he said.

They stepped into the communal vestibule and Jim, who was wearing a hospital transplant charity tee shirt and below-the-knee shorts, greeted them with a handshake, ushered them into the apartment and made the introductions.

'This is Edwin Benn and Mike Wolff from *The Informer* who have been following my story. We've got to know each other pretty well over the months, haven't we, guys?'

Edwin nodded in agreement as they sat themselves down on a beige fabric three-seater sofa that was almost identical to the uniform colours of the carpet, curtains and other soft furnishings. The only contrasting colour was provided by two large Andy Warhol prints in silver frames, some wooden ethnic sculptures and a rectangular glass vase of pink and mauve hydrangeas in the middle of a square glass and chrome coffee table.

Sylvia, whose facial tan suggested that she had been taking advantage of five days of wall-to-wall sunshine in Palma, asked her guests if they wanted tea or coffee and took herself off to the kitchen.

'Great weather you guys are having here. I'm told it's hotter here today than back home in California,' said Uwe in an American accent that contained occasional vestiges of his native German. He was taller and slimmer than his brother, had thinning grey hair, a youthful complexion and surgeon's hands.

'Jim has probably told you but it could be cold and wet in a couple of days. We can pretty well get all four seasons in one day in England. All you can predict is that it's never boring,' said Edwin.

'The weather's not a big topic of conversation back home. We pretty well know from day to day what it's going to be like and so there's not a lot to say about it. Here in Britain, everyone talks about the weather, we're told,' said Nicole.

'Yes, I would say that's right – wouldn't you, Mike? It's a sort of national preoccupation.'

Edwin felt that it was time to dispense with the formalities and niceties and start gathering the information that he would need for his article and then hand it over to Mike to take the accompanying photographs. But, as always, Edwin opted to draw out the facts through natural conversation rather than by way of persistent but polite interrogation.

He began with a general question, which he hoped would set the tone for the rest of the interview.

'What sort of week have you guys been having so far? You certainly picked the right week weather-wise,' he enquired, opening his shorthand notebook.

Jim looked at his brother and the two wives and replied, 'I'll answer that. I think we agree it has been bloody amazing, just fantastic. We all admitted that we were a bit nervous and not sure how we'd get on and all that. But it's like we've all known each other forever and Uwe and I had never been apart.'

'That's great to hear. I am so pleased for you all,' said Edwin.

'And perhaps the best bit of all is that, thanks to Uwe, I have now got to know my mother who disappeared from my life when she and my father divorced when I was a baby. I really never knew her and thought she had died, but Uwe brought over an album of photos of her and a short black-and-white film of her playing the piano at a concert she gave in Budapest. That's a still taken from it. Uwe and Nicole had it framed for me.'

Jim pointed to an A4-sized photograph on the sideboard which showed the slim, elegant figure of his mother wearing a black sequined dress seated at a Bechstein piano during a recital at the Liszt Ferenc Academy in the Hungarian capital.

'I can't help noticing that she had such beautiful hands. She looked really lovely,' said Jim.

'I think you said that you would be able to make some copies of the photos for me. That one of her seated at the piano would be just brilliant,' said Edwin.

'I will. I'll email them over in a photo file later.'

Whilst they were talking, Sylvia placed a tray of cups of tea and a selection of biscuits on the coffee table. Uwe picked up the plate of biscuits and offered them round – referring to them as cookies.

'How much did you know about what happened to Jim over the years, Uwe?' Edwin was cautious about saying too much, in particular about Jim's criminal past, in case his brother and Nicole had no, or only sketchy, knowledge of that unsavoury period of his life. But he need not have worried.

'I pretty well knew everything except where he was living until I received your email,' said Uwe. 'Let me start at the beginning. It's one hell of a story. Just stop me if there's anything that you want me to clarify. I know you're taking notes and will be writing an article for your newspaper.'

'I will, thanks, Uwe.'

'I think the first thing to say is that Jim never really knew our mother. When our parents divorced, he was only about a year old and we just carried on living with our father and, for a time, some woman who was a housekeeper-cum-nanny. Whether he actually said it in so many words or not, I cannot remember, but he led us to believe that our mother had died. I was only about six so I never questioned it.

'There were no real problems when we were young, but when I was around twelve or thirteen and Jim had started school, our father started telling us all about Prof. Fischer, who he said was a great patriot and visionary – and also one of our family. I guess that I was lucky because I had a lot of Jewish friends – mostly from families that my mother knew – and even though I was young, I used to tell my father that all the Jewish people I knew were very nice and just like everybody else. He tried to stop me from seeing them but I didn't take any notice and he got pretty angry with me sometimes.

'But, of course, young Jim didn't really stand a chance. He was too young and our father just brainwashed him with all this racial hygiene nonsense and there wasn't much I could do about it.'

Edwin felt the need to ask a question. 'The genealogist we hired suggested that your parents divorced when your father discovered that your mother was Jewish. Do you think that was the reason?'

'I'm sure it was. My father was probably always anti-Semitic but after he latched on to Prof. Fischer and was told by his father that he was some sort of messiah – he became fanatical and it must have been one hell of a shock to him to find out that our mother was Jewish. We'll never know exactly how he found out, but are certain that is why he divorced her.'

Jim and Nicole nodded in agreement.

'And, of course, after the divorce, we didn't really know what happened to our mother and we still don't know exactly where she lived, whether she found somewhere else to live in Germany or whether she went back to Poland. We know that she lived in Budapest for some years and I visited her there, but I still don't know when she first went to Hungary or much about her life there. Hopefully, we will now find out.'

'If your mother was brought up in an orphanage or children's home by nuns, how do you think she found out herself that she was Jewish – presumably as a young child, she would have thought she was a Catholic?' Edwin asked.

'Jim and I have thought about that, and we cannot be absolutely sure,' said Uwe. 'It's possible, of course, that when she was old enough, the nuns may have told her but we think that was unlikely. It's more likely that as she started to become well known and people – perhaps even journalists like yourself – started asking questions about her background and family and then she applied for her birth certificate.

'She may even have visited her parents' graves and realised that they were buried in Jewish cemeteries, and there's also a possibility that she discovered she had close relatives perhaps, even siblings, who told her that she was Jewish. There are all manner of possibilities, some that we probably haven't even thought of.'

'They are all very plausible theories,' said Edwin, adding, 'Of course, it's worth noting that the genealogist we hired said that it was only a preliminary report and that given more time – and, of course, an additional payment – he is confident that he will find out a good deal more. I might be able to persuade my editor that it would be worth doing, but there's every possibility that Jim and I will find out a good deal when we go over there and follow in her footsteps.'

Several more questions were queuing up in Edwin's mind.

'Uwe, sorry for all the questions, but after you eventually discovered where your mother was living, how did you first make contact with her?'

'It wasn't easy in those days. But, yes, we first of all just exchanged letters during the time that she was living in Budapest, and when I started earning a reasonable salary in California, I flew over to meet her on two occasions, staying with her for around a week each time. On one of them, I went to a recital she gave at the Liszt Academy and that was where I managed to take that short movie film on a camera I borrowed.

'I also went to her funeral service in Vienna, but when the stone-setting took place about ten months later, I was, unfortunately, unable to be there and have always regretted that. I was just amazed by the turnout in Vienna for her funeral at the Wiener Zentralfriedhof – apart from a number of local civic dignitaries, several fellow performers, directors from the concert halls and several leading figures from the Jewish community, dozens of her fans lined the cemetery drive to see the hearse pass by.

'I never really realised until then how revered she was in the world of classical music. But, more importantly, she was a lovely and very beautiful lady.' Then, directly addressing his brother, he went on, 'If you and Edwin are going over there this summer, you must find her headstone and place a pebble on it for me. It's a common practice in the Jewish faith: within a year of a burial one must place stones or pebbles on the grave, as opposed to flowers, as a tangible and permanent token of a visit to pay respects. The headstone was erected with money raised by the Jewish Community in both Budapest and Vienna and I was asked to make a contribution. I gather it is a very impressive headstone, although I have sadly not been able to get back to see it – but I am sure I will one of these days.'

'I'll let you have photos in the meantime,' said Jim.

'Did she ever come to you in California?' asked Edwin, each of Uwe's answers prompting yet another question.

'No, she never did – although, when I last saw her, she said that she would try one day to come. I used to send her photos of the grandchildren but sadly she never met them.'

'We would love to have had her over in California. Uwe told me all about her, but, of course, I never met her either. Apparently, she was frightened of flying and that made it even more difficult,' said Nicole, who, until then, had sat quietly in a voluminous easy chair, which seemed to swallow up her diminutive frame.

Jim chipped in, 'I must take after her. I'm not happy about flying either. I know that I'll need something to knock me out when I go on the trip with Edwin in the summer. But I'm still looking forward to it all the same.'

Edwin accepted a top-up cup of tea from Sylvia and consumed a digestive biscuit, before taking a drink and continuing with the interview – or conversation, as he preferred to think of it.

'This is all really most interesting... but tell me, Uwe, did your mother ever ask about Jim?' he asked.

Uwe looked over at his brother and touched him affectionately on his arm. 'That was one of the first things that Jim asked me – which isn't at all surprising. I'll tell you what I told him, even though I know it now upsets Jim.'

'There's no need to go into any detail, Uwe.'

'No, it's OK really. Our mother never really got to know what happened to Jim when he came to England and, after trying for some years to find him, eventually gave up. Apart from me, there was really no one else she could ask, but when I got to know about all his old criminal activities – sorry, Jim, but it's important that Edwin knows – I decided that there was no way I was going to tell her.

'She was upset not knowing what had happened to him and what he was doing, but I'm sure she would have been more upset if she had known how he felt about Jews and all that. In fact, she once or twice asked me if I thought that he had died and I just said that it was always possible. I just kept searching and said I would let her know if I found anything.

'I think that she had an idea that our father had been feeding him with that anti-Semitic, racist garbage but she had no idea that Jim had taken it to the lengths that he did. She never became a religious Jewish woman and I've never been religious either, but she lived in the Jewish area in Budapest, had a lot of Jewish friends and had a great respect for Jewish culture. If she'd known about the old Jim and all his old neo-Nazi activities, it could have killed her and, quite apart from anything else, I did not want to have any contact with him either.'

'Are you OK, Jim?' asked Edwin.

'Don't worry about me. I'm just fine. I've had this conversation with Uwe and he's just telling you the truth. It's my loss though. I would love to have been close to my mother in later years but it just wasn't to be. I will just have to try and make amends in my own way when we follow in her footsteps in the summer. If there's a God, he'll know that I'm sorry for everything and she'll get the message in heaven.'

Edwin smiled softly. 'That's a nice thought.'

'There's just another thing you ought to know,' said Uwe. 'When you have a chance to look through all the photographs, you'll see two or three pictures of our mother taken with a

Jewish-looking guy at a holiday resort on Lake Balaton and at a Jewish restaurant in the centre of Budapest.

'On the back of one of the photos, she has written, "me and Gyorgy", but I never found out who he was. He may have been another classical musician or composer or may have owned the restaurant where they were pictured together. I've discussed it with Jim and we've agreed that it looks as though they were very close, probably romantically involved. It's nice to think that she may well have found a soulmate in her later years.'

'Do we know the name of the restaurant?' Edwin asked Uwe.

'Well, you can see part of the name on the photograph but we've never followed it up. Someone will recognise it, I'm sure, if it's still there. It's perhaps something that you and Jim may want to look into when you go over there. It would certainly be interesting to find out more about Gyorgy and his connection to our mother. I suppose there's even a chance that he could still be around.'

'We will most certainly follow that up,' said Jim. 'It sounds like it will be a priority.'

'Most definitely,' said Edwin with real enthusiasm. Resolving mysteries of that kind was one of Edwin's journalistic fortes.

*

Apart from the odd brief comment, Uwe's wife, Nicole, had sat quietly in her easy chair through most of the exchange.

But just as the conversation seemed to be reaching its natural conclusion, she felt the need to make a contribution.

'There are one or two things that I feel I ought to say,' she began. 'When Uwe first told me that he wanted to come over here to meet Jim and Sylvia, I thought that it might be a big mistake. Uwe had told me all about Jim's background and I suppose I just found it hard to believe that anyone could have changed that much. It almost certainly had a lot to do with the fact that I had family members who perished in the Holocaust, but I couldn't help thinking that Jim would remind me of all that every time I looked into his eyes. I even said to Uwe that he should perhaps go over on his own.'

She leaned forward and looked directly at Jim.

'But I am really pleased to say, Jim, that I was entirely wrong. I've got to know you pretty well over the past week and I'm proud to call you my brother-in-law. I know that there's not one bit of hate in that new heart of yours – except perhaps for the old Jim!'

'Thanks for that, Nicole. I'm proud to call you my sister-in-law, too. You're a lovely lady and my big brother is lucky to have you.'

Nicole continued, 'You know, when Uwe told me that everything changed for you after your transplant, I was very sceptical at first. As a nurse, I have never actually met any heart transplant recipients back home, but shortly after Uwe told me about your transplant, Jim, I made a point of speaking to one of the cardiologists and he told me that the phenomenon of cell memory was now pretty well universally accepted.

'He told me about one heart transplant patient he had seen – a woman in her late thirties – who had been something of a rock chick with bright red spiky hair, all manner of facial piercings and who had heart failure as a result of years of drug abuse, but who completely changed her look and lifestyle after her transplant.

'When she came back for her outpatient assessments, he said she had a normal, natural hairstyle and colour, she had had all her piercings removed and she was dressed smartly and wore classy make-up and perfume. She had never met her donor but it turned out she was a former fashion model about the same age as herself who had been on life support in hospital after being involved in an automobile accident. And I've heard of other similar stories since.'

'It's most certainly an interesting area for further academic research,' said Uwe.

*

There was a natural lull in the conversation in which Sylvia asked if anyone would like another drink. Edwin closed his notebook. Mike spoke for the first time and asked if he could take some photographs to accompany Edwin's article. Everyone agreed.

'First of all, I'd just like a shot of Jim and Uwe holding the framed photograph of their mother – with the photo facing the camera,' he said, removing his Nikon from a large black camera bag that he carried on a strap around his shoulder.

He took perhaps half a dozen different shots in different parts of the room, some standing and some sitting, and then he repeated the exercise with their wives included.

'That's brilliant, thank you, folks.'

'We'd better head back to the office. It's been lovely to meet you, Uwe, and you, Nicole. It's tomorrow you fly back home, I gather. I hope that you have a pleasant journey. I'm not sure when the article will appear but I will let Jim know and he should be able to send you copies of the paper or email it over to you.'

'Good to meet you too, Edwin. I'm sure that you and Jim are going to have a fascinating and fruitful expedition over in Europe. I can't wait to hear all about it. It's going to be quite an adventure and lots of fun, too, I hope,' said Uwe, shaking Edwin and Mike by the hand as he spoke.

Jim and Sylvia accompanied them to the front door and thanked them for coming.

'I hope that you got all the material you wanted,' said Jim. 'I look forward to reading the next instalment.'

'It will be soon, I hope. I'll just have to spend some time writing it up and having a proper look through the file of photos you have given me – especially the ones of the mystery gentleman with your mother in Budapest. Then, of course, I'll be back in touch to fix a date for our trip and go through some of the details.'

It was around three o'clock in the afternoon when they started their drive back to Manchester and the temperature had risen another two degrees.

'I don't know about you, Mike, but I'd welcome a half-hour break and a glass of shandy.'

'Great idea, we deserve one,' Mike replied.

Ten minutes later, they found themselves sitting in the garden of a south Manchester hostelry. They put the world to rights and discussed the merits of the next instalment of the saga, before heading into the office.

*

The article appeared in *The Informer* three days later accompanied by three photographs: one of the brothers and their wives, a close-up shot of Jim's mother seated at the piano at a concert hall and a third of her by Lake Balaton with her companion, Gyorgy. Edwin emailed it as promised to Uwe in California with a brief note saying how much he had enjoyed meeting him and his wife, Nicole.

Jim telephoned Edwin to tell him that he was delighted with the way it had been written and presented and how much he was looking forward to their imminent trip to Europe to "discover" his mother.

The next time that Edwin would sit down at his PC to wrestle with the next instalment of the James Karl Fisher ongoing saga would be after they returned to the UK.

CHAPTER 9

Summer had said its last hurrahs when on a rainy day in mid-September, Edwin and Jim flew from Manchester to Warsaw on the first leg of their journey to Lodz, the birthplace of Jim's mother and the city ironically dubbed the "Manchester of Poland" because of its textile heritage.

When they landed around midday at Warsaw Modlin, a former military airfield on the outskirts of the city with a terminal building resembling a giant aircraft hangar, they were greeted by clear blue skies and warm sunshine that bode well for the rest of their week-long visit.

Edwin was especially excited at the prospect of visiting Lodz for reasons he had not mentioned to Jim. He had Jewish ancestry himself and had been told by his late father that his great-grandfather, Markus Ezekiel Benovitz, and other members of his extended family originated from Lodz. At some point when the family fled from the pogroms in the late 19th century and were among the first Jews to settle in the mining valleys of South Wales, the name had been changed from Benovitz to Benn. Edwin was called Edwin Mark in deference to his Polish great-grandfather.

For many years, Edwin had attempted to trace his ancestral roots in Lodz, but despite taking a DNA test, comparing notes with other members of the family and seeking professional help, they had remained frustratingly elusive. As he left for what was his first-ever visit to Poland, Edwin hoped that in helping Jim to follow in his mother's footsteps, he would also serendipitously stumble across people and places that would help with his own family research.

Even though Edwin felt sure that Jim was no longer the anti-Semite he first met in his hospital bed following his transplant, he did not feel it would have been prudent to apprise him of his own Jewish ancestry. But as they made their way to Lodz, the thought implanted itself in Edwin's mind that at some point during the trip, he might feel that the time was right to make him aware of his Jewish heritage.

Jim, like his mother, confessed that he was frightened of flying and, apart from very brief monosyllabic exchanges, he did not speak to Edwin during the two-and-a-half-hour flight. But as they walked out of the terminal building into the sunshine and took a taxi to the railway station for the journey to Lodz Fabryczna, he began to relax and became considerably more talkative.

'Thank God that's over! I was just the same when Syl and I went on our honeymoon to Spain. I've never liked flying... anyway, remind me where it is we are going now, Edwin?' he enquired as they took their seats aboard the train.

'Lodz, the city where your mother was born and your grandparents lived. We should be there in just over a couple

234

of hours, I think. We're told she was born in a house near the old Jewish cemetery in an area that became the Lodz ghetto in 1940 when the Germans moved in. But, luckily, your mother was born a year earlier and had been moved out before the ghetto was formed.'

'Are we going there today?' Jim asked.

'It will be a bit late by the time we get there to go today. We'll head there straight after breakfast in the morning. Today, we just need to check into our hotel, perhaps have a stroll around, relax and something to eat.'

'Sounds good to me.' Jim scanned the Polish countryside for the first time through the train window.

'Are you now beginning to look forward to it all?' Edwin enquired. 'I'm sure we are going to have some pleasant surprises.'

Jim pursed his lips and nodded from side to side before answering. 'Yes and no, I suppose. I mean, yes, I am looking forward to it but I'm just not sure how I'm going to be when I meet certain people and go to certain places.'

'Why's that?'

'Well, I suppose whenever I meet anyone Jewish, I'll be thinking that they will look me in the eyes, see the old Jim Fisher and want to bloody lynch me. I think it's going to take time before I start accepting the fact that my mother was Jewish and that I'm Jewish, and that people I meet are going to accept me for what I am now.'

'I promise you, no one will want to lynch you. If anything, my only worry is that we could encounter the reverse – that we might just come across Polish, Hungarian and Austrian people who are anti-Semitic. But I honestly don't believe we are going to run into any problems at all, anywhere. You'll find that most people will be bending over backwards, wanting to help.'

It was in the middle of the evening rush hour when Edwin and Jim checked into The Loom Hotel in Lodz alongside the city's Manufaktura Shopping Centre, the area that for some two hundred years, was the largest textile centre in Poland and the second largest in the Russian Empire, after Moscow.

Various features of the hotel's contemporary decor and furnishings recognised its long textile heritage and the irony did not escape Edwin that he travelled several hundred miles from the city dubbed the UK's Cottonopolis to a hotel with a Club Cotton bar. Edwin was also very conscious of the fact that he was there to follow in the footsteps of Jim's mother, but as he scanned the skyline from his bedroom window, he could not help thinking that many of his own ancestors had lived and worked in the area before moving to Wales in the late 19th century, where they sold drapery and boots to local coal miners.

After freshening up, they agreed to meet in reception before stretching their legs to familiarise themselves with the immediate area around the hotel and find somewhere, first for a coffee and then for an early evening meal. Almost right away, they came across yet another reminder of the city's textile heritage, the Muzeum Sztuki, an avant-garde modern art museum housed in a gigantic, five-storey red-brick mill indistinguishable from those back home, which were once the powerhouses of the cotton industry in Manchester and neighbouring Salford.

Just a short distance away, they found themselves in old Baluty Square, now developed as a modern piazza with open-air bars, restaurants and cafés, serving everything from burgers to Italian pizza to Japanese sushi. The evening was still pleasantly warm, so they stopped for a coffee at the bizarrely named The Beach Bar, a Hawaiian-style café bar with potted palm trees, surfboard props and straw huts situated at least two hundred miles from the nearest ocean.

'Funny old place, isn't it?' said Edwin rhetorically. 'What I've seen so far is like old Manchester, Bondi Beach and parts of the US all rolled into one. It's not what I expected.'

'Much more, what's the word – cosmopolitan – than I imagined. Seems like quite a fun place to me.'

'I think we'll see a totally different side of it tomorrow. From what I've seen of much of the old ghetto area on Google Maps street view, it all seems a bit drab and dreary but I could be wrong.'

'Well, we'll find out for ourselves tomorrow. I suggest that we now pay the bill here, go and find somewhere to eat and then get an early night. It's getting a bit chilly to sit out here any longer.'

'Fine by me,' said Jim as they paid for the coffee and prepared to leave.

They followed their noses down a side street that looked inviting and quickly came across a modest Polish restaurant simply called Lodzkie Menu – the Lodz Menu.

'This looks all right to me, Jim. What do think?'

'Yes, let's give it a whirl. I have never tried Polish food before but there's always a first time.'

Inside, there were no more than a dozen tables and only two or three of them were occupied by diners who were all speaking Polish and who they took to be locals.

A young woman in a white blouse and a short black skirt showed them to a corner table and handed them two menus with everything written in Polish. As she walked away towards the kitchen, Edwin beckoned her back.

'Excuse me, do you speak English? Do you have a menu in English?' he asked.

'Sorry, no speak English... moment,' she replied indicating that she would find someone who could.

A few moments later, a man who they took to be manager approached their table.

'Can I help you, gentlemen?' he asked in a strong Polish accent.

'Thank you, yes,' said Edwin. 'Do you have a menu in English?'

'Polish only, sorry, but I can translate for you,' he replied.

'That'll be just fine,' said Edwin.

The man pointed to an item on the menu listed as *Kotlet Schabowy*. 'This is our speciality. Very good. Breaded pork cutlet with green cabbage, potatoes and dill. I am, sure you like.'

'Sounds like the *scaloppine milanese*, the breaded veal they have in Italy – which I like a lot,' said Edwin.

'We also, if you like, have very good pork spare ribs in honey,' said the manager, who they later found out had learned to speak English when he had worked for a number of years in the Earl's Court area of London.

Edwin looked at Jim. 'I think I'm going to have their speciality.'

'That'll do for me. Quite honestly, I'm bloody starving now and could eat anything.'

Edwin pointed to the *Kotlet Schabowy* on the menu and indicated they would like to order two.

'You like something to drink, gentlemen?' the manager asked.

'Just two beers, thank you,' Edwin replied.

'Two *kotlet*, two beers. *Dziekuje ci*,' said the manager, thanking them for the order in his native tongue.

'Does the hospital say that you can drink alcohol, Jim?'

'In moderation, yes. But I don't drink spirits any longer. I used to be a whisky man but now I just stick to a glass of beer or red wine – reckon it does me more good than harm,' he said.

'You're probably right.'

'It's just dawned on me, this *kotlet* we've just ordered. Am I OK eating it?'

'I'm sure you are, why? What makes you think you shouldn't be eating it?'

'Well, it's pork and Jews don't eat pork, do they? I know I've eaten it all my life but should I now be giving it up? I'm not quite sure what it's all about.'

Edwin put his hand on Jim's shoulder in a sort of brotherly gesture. 'It's not a problem. You're right. Jews are not supposed to eat anything from the pig because, in biblical times, it was regarded as an unclean animal. They are not supposed to eat any shellfish either because they feed on the detritus on the sea bed. They are only supposed to eat fish with fins that swim freely.

'But, honestly, Jim, you needn't worry. If they are very religious, they certainly wouldn't eat pork or shellfish – and there are a lot of other religious rules as well that they would observe, like not eating milk products with meat. But, by the same rule, there are a lot of Jewish people who do eat pork and shellfish and others who won't eat them, even though they are not at all religious but because they have been brought up that way.

'Your mother was Jewish, so that makes you Jewish, Jim, but you're not religious and you obviously were not brought up to feel Jewish, so you can eat what you like. I wouldn't even give it a second thought.'

Jim paused and looked slightly perplexed. 'How do you know all this stuff, Edwin?'

'I didn't think I should mention it when we first met – we would not have been here now if I had. My mother was a Roman Catholic but my late father was Jewish. Strictly, that does not make me Jewish, but a lot of my close relatives are and I have always felt Jewish. And, as a matter of interest, my father ate pork and shellfish and so do I. In fact, I used to have an uncle, a famous Jewish barrister, who used to come up to our house every now and again and ask my mother to make him a bacon sandwich because he did not feel that he should eat it at his own home,' Edwin explained.

'Bloody hell. It's really no problem. You're a nice guy and I'm not bothered what you are. But I guess if I'd known this when we first met, the old Jim Fisher wouldn't have wanted to have had anything to do with you – at best. I think I'm going to order another beer.'

Edwin did not believe that it was an appropriate time to tell him that his father's ancestors came from Eastern Europe and most probably from Lodz and the neighbouring areas. He felt that it would have been an unnecessary distraction from their mission to "find" Jim's mother.

Having eaten very little since leaving Manchester, they were both hungry and by the time their meals arrived, all religious and ethical considerations about eating pork had evaporated and they tucked into their breaded cutlets with gusto. The portions were generous, to say the least, and they declined a dessert, opting instead for coffee which was accompanied by two Polish-made truffles.

'I feel a lot better for that,' said Jim patting his stomach as he spoke. 'I shall be asking Sylvia to have a go at making this when I get back.'

After a free top-up of their coffee, they paid the bill and walked briskly back to their hotel where they chatted in reception for a few minutes before taking the lift to their separate rooms.

'See you down in the lobby for breakfast about 8 a.m., if that's OK with you, Jim,' said Edwin.

'Fine by me. I reckon I'm going to crash out.'

'Me, too. I'll probably just whizz through the TV channels to relax; see if I can find any UK news, and then get my head down. See you in the morning.'

As his head sank into his pillow, Edwin made a promise to himself that he would return to Lodz with his wife to research his own family history and, in particular, try and unravel the mystery surrounding the roots of his paternal grandfather.

*

After breakfast at the hotel the following morning, they set off for their first port of call: the apartment block in Franciszkańska Street where, according to Dr Jäger's research, Jim's grandparents, Hans Zederbaum and his wife, Ida Rachela (nee Bermann), had lived and where his mother was born.

The day was noticeably cooler, although still dry and windless, so, with the aid of a rudimentary street map Edwin had printed off from the Internet, they decided to walk. They passed the modern art museum they had seen the previous evening, quickly entering the green oasis of Park Staromiejski and what would have been the original southern boundary of the Lodz ghetto.

In the knowledge that approaching ninety percent of Poles are Roman Catholic, Edwin was surprised to see two tangible and evocative reminders of the time, prior to the start of World War II, when the city was home to almost a quarter of a million Jews. The first was a statue of Moses holding the Ten Commandments, the Tablets of the Law, and the second was a memorial marking the site of the old fifteen-hundred-seater Alte Szil Synagogue in Wolborska Street that was burned to the ground by the Nazis in November 1939 just before the formation of the ghetto.

'I don't think that there was a public park here in your grandparents' day, but they would certainly have known of the synagogue and very likely worshipped in it and attended weddings, funerals and the like,' said Edwin.

'It's near where they lived, is it?'

'Just about ten or twelve minutes' walk, I reckon.'

The thought flashed through Jim's mind that in the not-too-distant past he and his racist henchmen would have rejoiced to hear that a synagogue had been reduced to ashes but he kept the thought to himself and said nothing.

*

As they emerged from the park, the suburban landscape became a dreary, unimaginative amalgam of grey, boxy apartment blocks, older tenements, many daubed with graffiti, sundry office buildings and the occasional shop. The old stone-built tenements, which would have been there when the area was within the confines of the ghetto, now looked flaky and tired.

Not far along Franciszkańska Street, close to the junction with Wojska Polskiego, they calculated that they had reached the street number of the dwelling where Dr Jäger's research revealed that Jim's mother was born and her parents had lived.

But over seven decades, most of the old ghetto buildings had been demolished, and the Zederbaum home was among them.

The site where it would once have stood was now the entrance to a small car park, overlooked by a copse of trees on the far side of a high concrete wall. A tram line ran past what would probably have been the frontage of their property, and some fifty yards to the left, they were surprised to see a whitewashed old building that was a Tesco supermarket.

'Well, that's a bit disappointing but probably only to be expected,' said Edwin.

'What do we do now then?' Jim asked.

'I'll just take a photo of the site where the house would once have stood and then we need to move on to the old Jewish Cemetery where your grandparents are buried. We can either take a taxi or try and fathom out the tram system.'

'What do you suggest? Do you think if we're going to the cemetery, I should go and buy some flowers to put on the grave?'

'No, Jim, not flowers. Jewish people don't put flowers on graves. They always leave a pebble or a stone on the headstone to indicate that they have visited – and to let other people know that someone has visited,' Edwin reminded him.

'Of course, you know those kinds of things – I forgot.'

'I wouldn't mind going in for a bottle of water though. That Polish bacon we had for breakfast plus the walk has given me quite a thirst.'

'Good idea. I could manage a drink myself and there don't seem to be any cafés around these parts.'

Inside the store, it was not like any other Tesco they had ever seen before. The building was obviously old, its front entrance facing the road had been bricked up and it had clearly been used for other purposes in its past. But it was not until they returned to the hotel, after completing their visit to the ghetto and the Jewish cemetery, and Edwin Googled it on his laptop, that he discovered it had formerly been the Bajka movie cinema and theatre – popularly known as the Fairy Tale Cinema Theatre – and had been subjected to several other reincarnations before becoming a supermarket.

In its heyday, they learned that international stars such as the American-born singer, actress and dancer Josephine Baker had performed there and that old and young alike from across the city had flocked there to see the latest comedy legend, Buster Keaton, in his blockbuster film of the day. By all accounts, the cinema had employed the use of a megaphone to announce to passers-by in the neighbouring streets that a performance was due to start and tickets were available at the box office.

When the ghetto was formed, all performances and film showings came to an abrupt halt and the local Jewish population used the building for prayer meetings. But its use for worship was short-lived. When the occupying Nazis commandeered the building, initially using it to house German Jews, it was eventually earmarked for demolition. But before it could be dynamited or bulldozed, the Soviet military marched into Lodz and the building was saved. It later became the Pioneer Theatre and, in more recent years, a Tesco supermarket.

Edwin had researched the cemetery records in advance and, furnished with details of the plot numbers and their location, it did not take them long to find the resting place of Jim's grandparents. By comparison with many of the ornately extravagant tombstones bearing fruit and flower motifs from the Tree of Life, the Lion of Judah, as well as candlesticks, sheep's heads symbolising maternal loss, birds, water jugs and bowls, their shared grave was a modest affair, comprising a plain rectangular slab and a small, equally-plain upright headstone bearing their names.

The inscriptions were in Hebrew but Edwin could deduce that Hans Zederbaum, Jim's grandfather, was born in 1912 and had died in 1938, aged only 26. In his report, Dr Jäger said the records he had researched suggested that he had died as a result of an accident during the early part of his wife, Ida Rachela's pregnancy – although there was no mention of this on the headstone. Ida, they knew, had died in childbirth, aged 24, in 1939 shortly before the Lodz ghetto was formed.

'I would have thought that the simplicity of their grave is a reflection of the time, Jim,' said Edwin.

'How do you mean?'

'Well, the ghetto was formed in the spring of 1940, very soon after your grandmother died, and it lasted for four years. After that, there would really have been no one left to erect a proper headstone. In that sense, it's probably quite historic – your grandmother's burial being one of the last before the cemetery was under Nazi control when it became known as the Cemetery at Marysin.'

'You know, Edwin, it's a very strange feeling for me being here, not just because it's my grandparents' resting place, but simply because it's a Jewish cemetery. I keep thinking of my bad old days when I'd happily have gone around here with a sledgehammer smashing the headstones. I just can't now believe I ever did that sort of thing – and why.'

'That's all in the past, Jim. We now know that it wasn't really your fault anyway. But I can understand that it must be an odd feeling for you to be here. Shall we put some pebbles on their grave?'

They scoured the ground around them and a few moments later, Jim placed two pebbles on the side of the headstone.

'That's one for me and one for my brother,' he said.

Edwin placed a third next to them. 'Would you like a photograph, Jim?'

'I think we should, don't you?' he replied.

Jim knelt down by the side of the grave and Edwin took two of three shots on his mobile phone camera before they slowly moved away reverentially and in silence.

Before leaving the cemetery, they looked at some of the 65,000 headstones and mausoleums, many of them partially obscured under a green blanket of ivy and in the shadow of old trees. At the southern end of the forty-four-hectare site, they also visited the area known as the Ghetto Field, the mass grave area for some 43,000 Jews killed during the Nazi occupation, and the eerie area where the remaining eight-hundred Jews were forced to dig their own graves – but were mercifully saved by the sudden advance of the Russians. The empty graves have been left unchanged as a chilling reminder of the Holocaust.

Both Edwin – who could not suppress the thought that some of his own ancestors could be buried in the cemetery – and Jim were in a sober and contemplative frame of mind when they eventually walked back into the outside world through one of the gates in the high red-brick perimeter wall.

'I don't know about you but I'm bloody starving and could do with a glass of something alcoholic,' said Jim.

'I could certainly eat and drink something. Let's get a taxi back to that elegant avenue near our hotel which is lined with bistros and restaurants, and find somewhere where we can have a relaxing lunch. I think we deserve it.'

'That'll do for me. Let's go.'

A local passer-by pointed out the nearest taxi rank and within fifteen minutes, they were in Piotrkowska Street, where they selected a chic street corner bistro and were shown to two seats on the outside terrace.

The menu was a melange of European cuisines.

'I'm just going to have a burger with fries and gherkins and a bottle of beer,' said Edwin.

'Sounds good to me. Make it two.'

They gave their order to a young waiter who indicated it would be about ten minutes. As they waited, they surveyed their surroundings.

'If I'm not mistaken, there's a sculpture of a man seated at a grand piano just over the road,' Edwin noted. 'I'm just going to walk over a have a closer look.'

Jim took a drink from the beer that arrived during the time that he was away from their table.

'You won't believe this,' Edwin exclaimed upon his return. 'I think fate must have led us to this place.'

'Why's that then?'

'It's a life-size sculpture of the great Polish pianist, Artur Rubinstein, whose childhood home was just over there at number 78. He lived to the grand old age of ninety-five. Obviously, this city produced great classical pianists.'

'I've never heard of the guy,' Jim replied, taking another drink of his beer.

'He was born here in Lodz on January 28th, 1887, and was generally regarded as one of the greatest exponents of the works of Chopin and one of the world's greatest pianists of his time. And, like your mum, he was Jewish.'

'Perhaps one day they might put up a statue of my mum, too. From what you've told me, she was in the same sort of league as this Rubinstein chap.'

'Why not, Jim? It's something that we can look into when we get back home. I am sure there are people here who would be interested – if only a plaque near the site of the house where she was born. It's obviously a city of culture with an appreciation for classical music and so I would think there's every possibility something could be done.'

'What's our plan for the rest of the day, then?'

'Well, from here, we need to walk back to the hotel, relax for an hour or two and find our way to the old folks' retirement home about an hour out of the city, where your mother was raised by nuns when it was a children's home. We've got to move on to Budapest tomorrow, so there's really no option but to go tonight.'

'How are we going to get there?'

'One of the ladies on the reception desk at the hotel speaks good English and I asked her before breakfast. She said there's a regular bus service and that the journey takes a little over an hour.'

'Do they know we're coming?' Jim asked.

'They do, yes. I spoke to someone at the Lodz Tourist Information Office, who rang the management on our behalf and she called me back to say that they would be delighted to see us – at whatever time we can make it. But we don't want to get there too late otherwise we might not be able to get a bus back.'

'What do you think we will see there?'

'I'm hoping we will see the room where your mum lived. But, whatever, I'm sure it will be interesting. It'll be the first place we have been where your mum lived. I am sure it will have changed a bit, but it's the same place all the same.'

'All exciting stuff. You never know, this new heart of mine could get a bit emotional.'

*

When they arrived at the Dom Mieszkalny Sanktuarium – the Sanctuary Residential Home – it was early evening and the light was beginning to fade. A long gravel driveway led from the gate to the home, and it wasn't until they walked past a screen of tall trees that the impressive 19th-century neoclassical building came into view.

With its portico supported by four pillars and tapered wooden steps leading to the main entrance, it reminded Edwin of the clapperboard ranch-type manor houses that were featured in American TV dramas such as *Dynasty* and *Dallas*. But it was the national flag of Poland which fluttered from the centre of the portico and not the Stars and Stripes of the US.

Some rudimentary research that Edwin carried out on the Internet in advance revealed that the two-storey building had been built by a local nobleman as his family home, but in the early 1930s it was converted into an orphanage that was run for more than half a century by a Catholic order of nuns. Since then, it had been a private residential home for the elderly.

Edwin and Jim mounted the front steps and looked for a doorbell to alert staff of their arrival. But they assumed that they must have been seen approaching the entrance by a CCTV camera because the door was almost instantly opened by a well-built blonde lady in a white blouse and a navy trouser suit, who shook their hands and introduced herself as Magdalena, the home's manageress. There was a name badge on her lapel.

'Very pleased to meet you. Good evening... I'm Edwin Benn and this is Mr James Fisher. I gather you are expecting us,' said Edwin as they walked across the expansive carpeted hallway, now the home's reception area.

'Yes, we are pleased to welcome you. Please, come with me.' She gestured for them to follow, leading them to a front room overlooking the driveway that she used as her office.

It had been around a quarter of a century since the sisters and orphaned children had occupied the building, but tangible signs of its many years as The Sanctuary were still evident. An arched alcove alongside the reception desk contained a colourful statue of the Madonna and Child, and inside Magdalena's office, several black-and-white photographs of the children and the nuns decorated the walls. On the window-ledge, there was also a large plain wooden cross draped with rosary beads.

'Would you gentlemen like a drink – tea or coffee, perhaps?'

They both opted for coffee and Magdalena rang through to the kitchen to order them.

Edwin and Jim sat down in two rattan bucket chairs and Magdalena sat behind her large antique mahogany desk.

'I understand, Mr Fisher, that your mother was here as a child but that she and your late father divorced and you did not know until recently that she was ever here. Is that right?'

'That's right, yes. It's a long story.'

'You know, of course, that she became one of our country's great pianists and composers – a national treasure?' Magdalena continued.

'I did not know until Edwin arranged for an expert to research my family history. It produced a whole lot of things that I did not know about my family and myself. It was quite a shock in many ways.'

Edwin explained that as his newspaper's health and medical correspondent, he had been in the operating theatre as an observer when Jim had his heart transplant and since then had written several articles about milestone developments in his life. He felt it necessary to put their visit into the context of the whole story.

'James and I are now spending a week in Europe following, as it were, in the footsteps of his mother. Tomorrow we will be going to Budapest and then we will be moving on to Vienna, where, as you probably already know, she died and is buried in the large Central Cemetery,' Edwin explained.

'It must be a very emotional journey for you, Mr Fisher... but very exciting, too, I am sure,' said Magdalena.

Edwin continued before Jim could respond, 'If it is at all possible, we would love to see the room where James's mother lived.'

'I am so sorry but that is now not possible. When it was a children's home, the boys and girls were accommodated on wards but the interior of the building has now been converted into separate living quarters for our residents with their own bathroom and toilet facilities. But I do have something to show you that I am sure will be of great interest.'

'That sounds intriguing.'

A young woman wearing a white apron over a plain cotton dress entered the room with their coffee.

'I will let you drink your refreshments and I will show you. We will need to go through to the residents' lounge,' Magdalena informed them.

Fascinated to discover what she had to show them, Edwin and Jim finished their coffees in a matter of a few minutes.

'Please, gentlemen, follow me,' she said, standing up from behind her desk.

They followed her down a wide corridor that led to the residents' lounge and dining room at the end of the right-hand wing of the home. Inside, a dozen or more elderly men and women were seated in easy chairs watching what appeared to be a game show on a large television. A number of them were eating their evening meal on dedicated trays that could be wheeled on trolleys to the side of their chairs.

'Hello, everyone,' said Edwin as a number of residents looked up, clearly not expecting to see strangers in their dining room at that time of the day. Others ignored them and carried on, oblivious of their presence.

Magdalena walked over to an expanse of wall between two window seats that had a panoramic view of lawns, flower beds and distant woodland.

'Well, what you think of that!' she said enthusiastically.

She was standing by an ornate oak upright piano with two brass candle holders at each end. There were two framed photographs resting on the top: one of Jim's mother as a child seated with her fingers on the keyboard and another of her as an adult seated at a grand piano at the Liszt Academy in Budapest with a printed legend within the same picture frame.

It was on this modest piano that the celebrated concert pianist and composer, Perla Bermann (Zuzanna Perla Zederbaum), learned to play when she lived in The Sanctuary children's home from her birth in 1939 until she was aged 17 years.

'Would you like me to unlock the lid so that you can touch the ebony and ivory keys that your mother would have touched, Mr Fisher? Normally, we keep it locked because it is so precious to us,' said Magdalena.

Jim was speechless for several seconds, obviously overcome at seeing an inanimate object that had played such a pivotal role in his mother's life.

'Yes... please. That would be wonderful... thank you,' he stuttered, stepping slightly back so that Magdalena could open the lid with a key she had in her pocket.

'Sit down on the piano stool, Mr Fisher. That, too, is the one that your mother would have used,' she said.

Jim sat down and placed his hands gingerly on the keyboard.

'You can press the keys, Mr Fisher. It is some years since it was tuned but you will hear the notes that your mother heard. Do you play yourself?'

'No, I have never learned any instrument,' he replied, randomly pressing a few keys and hearing the strings respond. 'Well, I didn't expect that, I have to say. My mother's first piano – who'd have thought I'd ever be seeing and playing on that.'

'Would it be possible to take a photograph of James sitting at the keyboard?' asked Edwin.

'Of course, you must. Go ahead, please.'

Edwin opened the camera on his mobile and took several different shots: some with Jim holding the framed photographs and others with Magdalena standing beside him.

'If you have not heard them, you must listen to some of her many compositions. You will, I am sure, be able to buy many of her recordings – they are often played on Polskie Radio 2 and our other classical stations.

'She was greatly inspired by her countryman, Frederic Chopin, and composed many etudes, polonaises and mazurkas. One of her nocturnes has been compared to *Chopin's Nocturne in C-sharp minor*, which was the theme music for Roman Polanski's film *The Pianist*.'

'We will most certainly make a point of starting a collection of her work. Hopefully, we will be able to find a shop in Budapest or Vienna. It will be too late when we get back to Lodz tonight,' said Edwin.

'It was really in Budapest where she achieved international acclaim, so I am sure that there will be many places there where you will be able to buy recordings of her own compositions, as well as recordings of her many live concert recitals.' Magdalena closed the piano and locked it again.

Jim, who was still emotionally overcome, remained silent but caressed the patina of the aged oak before the threesome slowly walked back to Magdalena's office.

'Would it be possible to have a copy of the photograph of Perla sitting at the keyboard? We have seen other photographs of her that James's brother showed us when he came over from the US, but that is something special and we don't have that one.'

'Of course, that will not be a problem. I will arrange to have it sent to you.'

Edwin handed her one of his business cards that included his email address. 'Could you send it to that email, please?'

'Yes, of course.' After a brief pause, she added, 'I think you may find that there is now no bus from here to take you back to Lodz. My husband, Marek, would be happy to drive you to your hotel. It would take only thirty or thirty-five minutes by car.'

'That is really most kind of you. Thank you,' said Edwin.

Some fifteen minutes later, Marek, a stockily-built man in his mid-fifties who they learned was one of the directors of the home, showed them into a Volkswagen people carrier and they set off back to central Lodz.

On arrival at their hotel, they headed straight for the restaurant where, without perusing the menu, they simply ordered two ham and cheese omelettes with French fries and two bottles of Polish beer.

'That was quite a day, I'd say. I have to admit seeing that Old Joanna really got to me. I could see my mother sitting there. God knows what on earth we'll next do or see.'

'I know it's not my mother but it's all pretty exciting for me, too, Jim. I reckon that archaeologists must feel the same way when they unearth some hidden treasure on a dig. This is certainly the journalistic equivalent and I'm sure there is more to come.'

'We'll see what tomorrow brings. Budapest here we come, Mum!'

'When we've had our meal, I suggest we get a reasonably early night. We need to be down here for breakfast at 7 a.m.

257

and be at the main Lodz airport at around nine. All being well, we should be in Budapest by midday.'

After a long day, they were both hungry and when their omelettes arrived they devoured them with relish in a matter of five or ten minutes.

Edwin signed the bill and with mutual pats on the back, they headed for their rooms.

'Till the morning then, Edwin.'

'See you around seven. Have a good night's sleep.'

CHAPTER 10

Their flight from Lodz the following morning left precisely on time and ninety minutes later, they landed at Budapest Ferenc Liszt International Airport, where they stepped out into warm sunshine and a cloudless blue sky.

'How are you feeling now, Jim?' asked Edwin, aware that because of his flying phobia, his companion had hardly spoken a word during the journey.

'I'm just fine now. I don't think I feel as anxious as I did flying from Manchester – I'm getting used to it, I suppose,' he replied as they waited for their suitcases on the carousel in the arrivals hall.

'That's good to hear. If this sunny weather is anything to go by, I think it bodes well for a successful day. Who knows, perhaps your mother fixed it for us!'

'Could be, you're right. Perhaps she's up there keeping her eye on us.'

As they spoke, their luggage appeared on the carousel and within five minutes, they were in a taxi en route to the Párisi Udvar Hotel alongside the Danube, a ten or twelve minute walk from the heart of District 7, the historic and bustling Jewish area of the city where Jim's mother had lived.

The hotel with its Arabic, Moorish and Gothic architectural features had been recommended to Edwin by a press attaché at the Hungarian Embassy in London because of its unique characterful ambience and because it would almost certainly have been frequented by Jim's mother and fellow musicians.

Jim and Edwin had only eaten a light breakfast before leaving Lodz, so, after checking into the hotel shortly after midday, they made straight for the sumptuous Párisi Passage Café and Brasserie with its cathedral-like vaulted ceiling. The international menu and the all-enveloping atmosphere enticed them to linger, but anxious to make the most of their afternoon, they opted for two croque monsieur and a pot of coffee.

Refreshed and replete, they set off on foot to an address in Kazinczy Street, close to the 19th century Dohány Street Synagogue in the heart of the Jewish quarter, which genealogist Dr Jäger's research suggested was almost certainly the last place where Jim's mother had lived before her tragic death in Vienna.

As they neared their destination, they became increasingly aware that the area was still very much the beating heart of Budapest's Jewish community. Within an area no bigger than perhaps a couple of football pitches, there were at least two other synagogues, several kosher restaurants and cafés, and many of the orthodox men and boys were going about their business in white shirts, black trousers and sporting pe'ot sidelocks and yarmulke skullcaps.

'We're obviously in the right place, Jim. It's interesting that your mother was brought up by nuns in a Catholic children's home, but there was obviously a time in her life when she realised that she was Jewish and decided to live in a Jewish community.

'Of course, that doesn't mean that she was Orthodox or even very religious – it could just be like a lot of Jewish people the world over, she felt comfortable and safer living in an area where there were people like her and where they was no prejudice or hostility.'

'It's not something the old Jim Fisher would have known anything about – or cared even less – but I'm keen to learn. And I'm pleased to say, Edwin, that you were right.'

'About what?' he asked, clearly puzzled.

'Right about people looking at me and seeing the old criminal and nasty racist bugger that I used to be. I thought that they would look at me as though I had a swastika tattooed on my forehead, but I can see now that I need not have worried. You were dead right, I'm pleased to say.'

'Well, I don't know about you, but I could do with a quick drink before we start knocking on doors.'

'I was thinking the same thing. I'm not used to all this walking when it's hot,' Jim replied.

There was an appealing looking café bar with an unpronounceable name just across the road, and a few minutes later, Edwin was drinking from a tumbler of freshly squeezed orange juice and Jim had a milky coffee served in a tall glass in a metal container with a handle.

Edwin showed the address he had been given by Dr Jäger to the café proprietor, who took him to the café door and directed him with right and left-hand gestures to what they discovered was a fine-looking apartment block which backed onto a small suburban park. It had an impressive central entrance, with two steps to an internal glass door that could only be opened electronically by the residents. There was a panel of doorbells to the right with the apartment numbers and, in some cases, the name of the occupiers alongside, in dedicated metal strips covered in plastic.

'Well, here goes, Jim. Fingers crossed,' said Edwin, as he pressed the bell for number eleven with the names Hanna and Boris Polgar typed alongside.

'*Igen, hello,*' said a woman's voice speaking in her native Hungarian.

'Hello, do you speak a little English?' Edwin asked hesitantly.

'Little, only little,' she replied. 'Wait, please.'

Barely a minute later, a tall, slim lady with thick, grey swept-back hair appeared on the other side of the plate glass doors. Edwin smiled and raised his hand in a friendly gesture. She looked him straight in the eye and opened the door a matter of a few inches.

'How I help you, please? I speak no good English,' she said.

Edwin explained who they were and why they were there as simply and succinctly as he could, but was not sure how much she understood. But when he mentioned the name of Perla

Bermann and indicated that Jim was her son, she appeared less concerned and willing to help in any way that she could.

'Moment, please,' she said, ushering them into the communal hallway and making it clear that they should remain there whilst she went for someone she knew who could help.

She returned in a few minutes with a younger woman, perhaps in her forties, who gave her name as Kamilla.

'I am an English teacher here in Budapest. How can we help you, gentlemen? My friend, Hanna, says it's something concerning Perla Bermann who lived in her apartment – is that right?'

Jim and Edwin could not believe their good fortune. Not only was she able to speak English fluently, but she had already confirmed that it was the apartment where Jim's mother had lived.

Edwin repeated the explanation for their visit.

Kamilla smiled and nodded her head as he spoke, then passed on the explanation to Hanna in her native tongue, who instantly looked less anxious and smiled.

'She understands and asks if you would like to see inside the apartment. She says that she and her husband – who is a pharmacist at the local hospital – never met your mother in person but attended one of her recitals here in Budapest. She says they bought the apartment through the solicitors who handled her estate after she died,' Kamilla explained.

'If it's no trouble, we would love to see inside and, if she does not mind, perhaps take a few photographs,' said Jim.

'No problem, OK,' said Hanna, gesturing that they should take the lift to her apartment which was on the second floor. Kamilla accompanied them.

Hanna ushered them through a wide hallway into a spacious and elegantly furnished sitting room with tall windows looking out over the neighbouring park. She invited them to sit on a striped sofa in front of which was a square glass-topped Chinese lacquer table with inlaid peony motifs. Alongside one of the walls stood a Dutch marquetry cabinet with barley sugar twist legs, and in the corner an ornate cabinet with a glass bow frontage. Several oil paintings, mostly of landscapes, adorned the walls.

Edwin and Jim were also aware of a pervading, delicate floral aroma – either patchouli, jasmine or both – that emanated from a large lighted candle that stood on a small side table.

'Mrs Polgar asks if there is anything in particular you would like to know,' said Kamilla.

Jim looked across at Edwin before speaking. 'Could you ask her if there's anything in the apartment that belonged to my mother?'

Kamilla translated. 'She says that when she and her husband bought the apartment, they were simply told that certain items were for sale and that they bought the dining room table and chairs, the Dutch cabinet you see over there, some of the paintings and two marble busts – the small one of Liszt and the larger one of Chopin.'

'Please tell Mrs Polgar that we are really most grateful for allowing us into her home and that if we could just take a few photographs, perhaps with the busts of Chopin and Liszt, we will be on our way,' said Edwin.

'She says "would you like a hot drink?"' Kamilla informed them.

'That is very kind of her but we would not want to take any more of her time and we have other places that we have to go this afternoon,' said Edwin.

Kamilla translated as Edwin opened up the camera on his mobile and began taking photographs of Jim with the marble busts.

As he arranged the various poses and took a general shot of the skyline from the window, Mrs Polgar left the room, returning a few minutes later carrying a strong carrier bag with cord handles, a length of bubble wrap and some Sellotape. She spoke in Hungarian to Kamilla.

'Hanna says that she would like Mr Fisher to have the small bust of Liszt that belonged to his mother. She says she knows that if her husband were here, he would want him to have it. She says they have had the pleasure of it for many years and know that it will mean a lot to Mr Fisher and he will treasure it.'

As Kamilla faithfully translated her comments, Mrs Polgar protected the six or seven-inch high bust in the bubble wrap, secured it with the tape, placed it in the bag and handed it to Jim. Such acts of spontaneous kindness were largely unknown to him and he seemed lost for words.

'Is she sure? I don't know what to say. Thank you,' he spluttered.

'She is quite sure, Mr Fisher. It is yours now,' said Kamilla. Jim and Edwin stood up and prepared to leave.

'Before we go, ladies, I have a photograph here taken of Perla Bermann that we believe was taken here in Budapest outside one of your cafés or bistros. All we can see is part of the name – "ryktu 7" above the entrance and we are wondering if you recognise it. We would like to go there,' said Edwin.

Kamilla and Mrs Polar took the photograph into the light by the window, and a moment later, they both became animated.

'Yes, yes, we are sure we know this place,' Kamilla exclaimed. 'It is very well known here, a famous place. We are sure it is Perla Dystryktu 7, or as you would say in English, the Pearl of District 7. It is the café named after your mother, Mr Fisher.'

'I told you this morning, Jim, that we would have a successful day... thank you both so much. That is really brilliant. Is it far from here?' asked Edwin.

Kamilla took a small piece of paper, wrote down the name of the street and drew a rudimentary map for them to follow.

'Perhaps six or seven minutes from here. Everyone will know it if you get lost,' she added.

After an exchange of smiles, handshakes and pleasantries, Jim and Edwin took the lift back to the ground floor, walked out into the late afternoon sunshine and breathed deeply. They were both feeling elated.

*

With the aid of Kamilla's map, they found themselves standing outside the small, inviting-looking bistro in no time at all. An awning, to shield customers seated at the outside tables from the sun, obscured the name, but when they approached the entrance, they could see it clearly: *Perla Dystryktu 7* written in gold arts-and-crafts style lettering on the inside of the window.

'This is it then. It looks pretty much exactly the same as in the photo,' said Jim.

'Who'd have thought when we got up this morning that you'd be given a marble bust that belonged to your mother and find the café named after her all in just one afternoon? I take it we're going in,' said Edwin.

'Absolutely! I want to find out how it comes to be named after her.'

As they stepped over the threshold, their senses were overcome by the aroma of freshly ground coffee and herbs and, visually, by the distinctive, old-world ambience evident in every nook and cranny. Old prints of Budapest and photographs hung from the walls, but two, in particular, stopped them in their tracks – one, similar to the one they had seen at the residential home, of Perla seated at her piano and another larger one, that looked like a studio portrait of her wearing a black beaded dress and a pearl necklace.

'It's only just beginning to dawn on me just how well-known my mother was in these parts. It seems she was quite a star,' said Jim, unable to take his eyes off the two photographs.

'You can safely say that I've no doubt. In Poland, Hungary, Austria, in fact, most of Europe, classical music has a devoted following, and there's no doubt that your mother, as one of the great exponents of the works of Chopin and Liszt, would have been much celebrated in these parts.'

As Edwin spoke, a young waiter with a mane of thick black hair showed them to a table and presented them each with a menu.

'English,' he said, obviously having heard them speaking. 'I come back in a few minutes.'

Edwin scanned the menu – which was in English and Hungarian – and became instantly aware that it was a Jewish establishment, although not observing the strict culinary rules practised by the kosher eateries he had seen as they walked through the district.

Edwin spotted several dishes on the menu with which he was familiar: the clear chicken soup with matzo balls, the chicken liver with egg, the bagels with smoked salmon and cream cheese and the ubiquitous Hungarian goulash.

'Jim, they obviously serve traditional Jewish food here, which looks pretty good to me. I think I'm going to have the chicken livers.'

'What's Hungarian goulash like, do you know?'

'It's a beef and vegetable stew with paprika and other spices. It's the national dish. Should be good here, I reckon.'

'Sounds like my sort of thing. I'll have that.'

'Is there anything that the hospital told you that you shouldn't eat or drink,' Edwin enquired.

'Not too much fatty food, not too much sugar or salt, and alcohol in moderation. Anything in moderation, I suppose.

Sylvia makes sure I stick to it at home, and if we go out, I'm always pretty careful. This goulash will be just fine,' he said.

'And, of course, you're getting plenty of healthy outdoor exercise with all this walking about – so that will help to burn off any excess calories,' said Edwin.

As they spoke, a bearded middle-aged man wearing a suit and tie entered the bistro and immediately went behind the cash till, where he thumbed through a notepad and started to make a telephone call. Edwin assumed he was either the owner or the manager.

When he had finished his call and came from behind the cash desk, he acknowledged Edwin and Jim with a smile and a nod of his head.

'Excuse, me, may I ask if you speak English?' asked Edwin.

'I understand a little. Can I help you?' he said.

'I hope so,' Edwin replied, removing from the folder he was carrying the black-and-white photograph of Jim's mother sitting at a table outside the bistro with a man of Jewish appearance. On the back, she had simply written "Gyorgy and me". 'This is an old photograph of Perla Bermann outside this bistro, and we are wondering if you know the name of the gentlemen with her – his first name is Gyorgy?' He then gestured towards Jim and added, 'This is Perla's son. We are here to—'

Before he could complete the sentence, the man interrupted, 'I know him well. That is Gyorgy Herczel. I bought this place from him. He is now retired. He was planning to marry your mother, Mr Fisher. Very nice man... my name, by the way, is Rudi,' he said, pulling up a chair at their table.

'Do you know if he is still alive?' asked Edwin.

'Yes, he is. He was here only one month ago for lunch. He now lives at Siófok on Lake Balaton about an hour's drive away.'

'Is it possible for us to contact him?' Jim asked.

'Why do you want to see him?' asked Rudi, naturally a little concerned about giving any personal details to two people he had only just met.

Edwin explained as simply and succinctly as he could that Jim had lost contact with his mother when he was very young and they were spending a week in Poland, Hungary and Austria to learn what they could about her life in all the intervening years.

'We have just been to the apartment where she used to live. The new owner very kindly gave us one of her possessions, a marble bust of Liszt, that once belonged to Perla,' said Edwin. 'We are going to Vienna next to visit her grave in the Central Cemetery.'

'I understand. I can let you have Gyorgy's address and telephone number if you like. I think he would be pleased to see you,' said Rudi, clearly content that there was nothing untoward or sinister about their request.

Edwin handed him his notebook and ballpoint pen and Rudi wrote down the address and phone number after first checking it on his mobile phone.

'Does Gyorgy speak English? Thank you,' asked Edwin, taking back the pen and notebook.

'Like me, a little. Maybe better than me,' said Rudi.

When their meals arrived, Rudi stood up and shook their hands.

'I will leave you to enjoy your food – I think you will like. I wish you good luck with Gyorgy and your adventure. You come again sometime, perhaps,' he said as he walked away towards the kitchen.

Jim and Edwin attacked their meal with relish, energised by the fact that they had just discovered that Perla Bermann had planned to re-marry and that Gyorgy Herczel, the man who would have become her husband, was living only an hour or so away.

'I am guessing that he must be a man well into his eighties, but he sounds fit and well,' said Edwin.

'Do you think there's any chance we could meet up with him?'

'We should try, Jim. We might not get another chance.'

'It's too late today and tomorrow we're going to Vienna, aren't we – so how will we find the time?'

'I suggest we get back to the hotel and give him a call. If we have a language problem, we can find someone at the reception desk who can speak English and translate for us.'

'And if he's happy to meet up with us, what then?'

'We'll just have to postpone our trip to Vienna until the day after. All we are planning to do there is visit your mother's grave, so that shouldn't be a problem. We might even be able

271

to visit the cemetery and fly back home later the same day. I just don't think we should miss the opportunity to meet your mother's fiancé.

'We were planning to visit the site of the Kistarcsa concentration and internment camp on the outskirts of Budapest tomorrow, but I don't think that would be the right thing to do now anyway. I know that before your transplant, you denied that the Holocaust ever happened, but that's not what you believe now – so there wouldn't really be much point in taking you to one of the concentration camp sites. It'll be far more productive for you to meet up with Gyorgy.'

'I wonder what he will be able to tell us about her, how long he'd known her, whether he knew about my brother, whether they lived together... there's a lot we need to ask him.'

'You're right, there is.'

Anxious to make the call, they finished their meal, paid the bill and walked briskly back to the hotel.

*

Back at the Párisi, Edwin went straight to the reception desk where he explained that he had an important local call to make and would very likely need the help of someone who could translate.

'No problem, sir. Jozsua here will help you. He worked long time in New York and speaks very good English,' said the young woman pointing to her male colleague who was wearing a different uniform which Edwin presumed indicated he was in a more senior position.

Edwin decided that it would be prudent to ask Jozsua to make the call for him and explain briefly why they were calling.

'Of course, sir. What is the gentleman's name and what shall I tell him?'

'His name is Gyorgy Herczel. Tell him that I am a British journalist here in Budapest with James Karl Fisher, the youngest son of Perla Bermann and that we would very much like to meet him tomorrow before we return home to England. We are happy to come over to Lake Balaton any time,' said Edwin, handing over his mobile to Jozsua.

Everything went much more smoothly than they had anticipated. Gyorgy answered the phone immediately, Jozsua faithfully relayed the message in Hungarian, listened to his reply and, within a minute or so, handed the mobile back to Edwin.

'He sounds very excited and will be very glad to meet you. He says you should go to the Balaton Lakeside Residence in Siófok at midday and he will meet you in the reception area. He says he will have completed his daily swim and will be wearing a blue tracksuit. You can speak to him,' said Jozsua.

'Hello, Gyorgy, this is James Fisher. My friend, Edwin, and I will see you tomorrow,' said Jim not knowing if he would understand or not. But he obviously did.

'It will be good to meet you,' said Gyorgy in good English.

'Thank you. We are excited to meet you. Goodbye for now.'

'Well, that was all pretty straightforward. I thought we would have had all kinds of difficulties. I think it's now time that we got ourselves the drink we didn't have after our lunch,' said Edwin.

A few minutes later, as they relaxed in the café bar with their drinks, Jim said, 'He sounds like quite a character and certainly bloody fit. I could hardly believe it when he said he'd have been for his swim and would be wearing a tracksuit. He must be in his mid-eighties, I'm sure!'

'Probably done it all his life. Apparently, Lake Balaton has got beaches and a promenade, and Siófok is a very popular holiday resort,' said Edwin, checking it out on the Internet on his mobile as they spoke.

'How do we get there?'

'I'll ask our friend on the reception desk. I'm sure he'll know.'

He did. He told them that there was a train service from Budapest-Kelenföld station to Siófok that took anything from one-and-a-quarter hours to one-and-a-three-quarter hours depending on the number of stops and time of day.

'Thanks. You have been most helpful,' said Edwin.

'You're welcome, sir. You have a nice trip,' he replied.

*

Straight after an early breakfast, Jim and Edwin made their way to the station and a good half-hour before their midday meeting with Gyorgy, they were standing on the promenade outside the hotel on what was yet another gloriously sunny day.

Even though all the signs, notices and building names were in Hungarian, Edwin could not suppress the thought that Siófok had the appearance and trappings of an English seaside resort. People of all ages were strolling along the promenade in beach and swimwear. Others were sunbathing on the strip of sand lapped by waves whipped up by a wind blowing across the lake. There was a children's play park, a marina and a big wheel like the London Eye, too.

'Do you fancy an ice cream, Jim, before we head inside the hotel to meet Gyorgy?' Edwin asked.

'I'll have a plain vanilla cornet, thanks.'

They ate their ice creams whilst sitting on a bench overlooking what they learned was the largest lake in Hungary and then, suitably refreshed, headed inside the hotel to wait for Gyorgy in the reception area. On the dot of midday, a man in a sky blue tracksuit and carrying a sports bag walked purposefully into the foyer.

'Gyorgy!' said Edwin offering an outstretched hand. 'Edwin Benn and this is James, Perla's son. Thanks so much for coming.'

'My pleasure,' said Gyorgy clasping Jim's hand with both of his, followed by a welcoming hug.

Edwin thought that he looked no older than a man in his late sixties but realised that he was considerably older. There was something about his looks and stature that reminded him of Pablo Picasso.

The trio sat around a corner table in the hotel bar where they ordered drinks. Gyorgy, who was clearly well known to the staff, had a pineapple juice in a tall glass with a straw. Edwin and Jim had coffee.

Edwin broke the ice. 'Do you swim every day, Gyorgy?'

'Every day if possible. In winter not always possible. It is good way to keep fit,' he said in clear but broken English.

'You knew my mother very well, Gyorgy. Did you meet in Budapest?'

'She was my best friend. We met when I had a restaurant in Budapest, maybe now twelve years ago, which I renamed after your mother — it is now the *Perla Dystryktu 7*. Very good bistro with good food.'

'We were there for lunch yesterday. It was Rudi who told us about you. You are right; excellent food,' said Edwin.

'Your mother, she agreed to marry me but only a few weeks later, she had the bad fall in Wien and died in hospital three days later. My heart, it was broken and is still broken. She was the love of my life,' said Gyorgy, his voice breaking with emotion.

'We went to her apartment in Budapest yesterday and the lady who lives there now gave me a little statue of Liszt that belonged to my mother. Did you both live there?'

'We did, yes. I lived there for many years with your mother. I remember the statues. I have many things here in Siófok that belonged to your mother. You are welcome to come to my house and I show you. Do you think you come again to Hungary?'

'I would love to, Gyorgy. I will tell my wife, Sylvia, that we should come here for a holiday by the lake next spring. We could meet up again then.'

'It would be good to meet her, tell you more about your mother and show you many things,' said Gyorgy.

It was clear to Edwin that the two men had instantly struck up a mutual rapport, suggesting that Gyorgy knew nothing of Jim's unsavoury criminal past. Had he known anything about the old racist, anti-Semitic James Karl Fisher, Edwin felt certain that he would not have welcomed him so warmly and invited him to visit him at home – especially as Gyorgy himself was Jewish, albeit one who was proud of his heritage but who was not in any way religious.

In the hope it would shed further light into this grey area, Edwin asked, 'Did James's mother ever speak about him?'

'She did but it upset her. She would ask Uwe about him but she never told me much. She would just say sometimes to me that she had lost contact and that his father was to blame. But she did not explain why and I did not want to ask.' Then, turning to Jim, he said, 'But I know she loved you and Uwe the same and I knew she wanted very much to see you again. She used to tell me about you as a baby and showed me many pictures of you. I have brought some here today to show you.'

Emotionally disturbed by Gyorgy's words, Jim stood up from his chair and announced that he was going to get himself a drink from the bar.

'I need a brandy. Would anyone else like a drink?' he asked.

Gyorgy said he would have another pineapple juice. Edwin said that he, too, would have a brandy.

When Jim returned with the drinks, Gyorgy was placing his sports bag on the table which he unzipped and removed a plastic wallet containing a miscellany of photographs, including several of Jim as a baby.

'Your mother often looked at these pictures of you,' said Gyorgy, as he laid out the photographs on the table.

There were a number of photographs of baby Jim in a cot, another in a pram, one on a sofa stroking a dachshund and the most evocative of all, a colour photograph of him on his mother's lap.

Jim just stared blankly at the photographs and drank his brandy to suppress his tears. 'I can remember that dog. He was called Nivo, I think. I wonder whatever happened to him? These are the only photographs I've seen of myself when I was a baby. Amazing, just amazing,' he said with a noticeable tremor in his voice.

'And I have these, too,' said Gyorgy removing several small items from his sports bag, a little like a magician pulling rabbits out of a hat. He handed each in turn to Jim: first a pair of baby shoes that looked as good as the day they were bought, followed by a little outfit that looked like a baby's version of lederhosen and the pièce de résistance, a Steiff teddy bear with the company's hallmark button still in its ear.

'Were all these mine?' asked Jim, unable to say more.

'They were all yours, yes. They were your mother's treasures – her memories of you. They are now for you to keep,' said Gyorgy.

Edwin, who had always had an interest in antiques and collectables, noticed the Steiff button in the bear's ear.

'I know that you would not part with it, Jim, but that is a Steiff bear and probably now worth a lot of money. You'll need to treasure that.'

Jim confessed that he knew nothing about Steiff or their teddy bears.

'Are you sure I can keep all these things?' he asked.

'They are for you, yes,' Gyorgy replied.

'Thank you, thank you,' said Jim, still choked with emotion.

Edwin had never really seen this tender and sensitive side of Jim and could not help thinking to himself how differently he would probably have reacted before his life-changing transplant, even though they were photographs of himself and were his mother's possessions. Almost certainly, Edwin thought, he would not have believed that his mother was Jewish had he been told before his transplant and he would have rejected anything that she had kept and treasured because of their Jewish associations.

'This calls for a couple of photographs,' said Edwin, switching into his journalistic mode. 'If you could hold up the teddy bear, Jim, and the baby shoes, arrange some of the photos in front of you and Gyorgy could sit up close next to you; that would be perfect.'

Gyorgy removed his sports bag from the table top and Edwin moved their drinks onto an adjacent empty table and spent a minute or so arranging the pose. He then opened up the camera on his mobile and took half a dozen shots.

'Excellent, gentlemen, thanks. There should be at least one good one,' he said.

When all the excitement had calmed, Edwin suggested that they found somewhere for a light lunch before he and Jim had to catch their train back to Budapest. Gyorgy said that he, too, had to return home in an hour or so because he was meeting a friend for a game of chess.

'I recently learned to play chess, Gyorgy, but I haven't played for a while.'

'When you come back with your wife, we have a game,' said Gyorgy.

'I'll keep you to that. I look forward to it,' said Jim whose equilibrium had all but returned to normal.

At Gyorgy's recommendation, they lunched in the hotel's own restaurant, each selecting something different from the extensive buffet. As they finished their meal with coffee, Edwin looked at his watch.

'Jim, Gyorgy, I'm afraid we now have to go for our train. It has been wonderful to meet you,' he said.

Outside the front entrance, they all shook hands and Jim gave Gyorgy a hug.

'Great to meet you, Gyorgy. I promise I'll be back. It's been fantastic. Now you go and enjoy your game of chess.'

Gyorgy walked further along the promenade, turning around once to give them a wave. Edwin and Jim headed inland for the short walk back to the railway station.

'It was worth coming, Jim, that's for sure. What a nice guy.'

'He'd have been a match for some of the young guys who used to come down my old gym. I wouldn't have missed that for the world.'

Twenty minutes after they arrived at the station, their train arrived and they headed back to the city and their hotel. Jim slept for much of the journey, emotionally drained by what he had learned about his mother.

That night, as his head hit the pillow, he wondered how he would feel the following day when he visited his mother's grave in the Central Cemetery of Vienna.

CHAPTER 11

After a continental breakfast of croissants and coffee served in their rooms, Jim and Edwin left the hotel at first light the following day for an early flight to Vienna – their last destination on their European ancestral odyssey before returning home.

Edwin calculated that if they could visit the Zentralfriedhof Cemetery around the middle of the day, they would have enough time to travel into the city centre, buy a selection of Perla Bermann's classical CDs and return to the airport for an evening flight to Manchester Airport.

If all went according to plan, it would mean they could avoid the cost of another night's accommodation in a hotel in Vienna and, more importantly for Edwin, he would not have to explain to his editor why he would have to charge additional expenses for an extended stay.

The flight time to Vienna International was only fifty minutes and, as an added bonus, Jim said that, for the first time, he was not feeling at all tense and nervous. Edwin presumed it was because his mind was preoccupied, both with the prospect of standing by his mother's headstone and the events of the previous day. Or possibly he had just simply conquered his phobia.

Their flight took off on time and a few minutes before noon, after a short taxi ride from the airport, they were walking through the gate of one of the largest cemeteries in the world. A sign directed them to the newer of two Jewish burial grounds and, having established the location and plot number in advance, it did not take them long to find Perla Bermann's grave and memorial.

They stood in silence for some considerable time just looking at the impressive, dignified black marble structure with, at the base of the arched headstone, the representation in relief of an octave of ebony-and-ivory piano keys in black and white marble. A menorah was carved into the top of the arch and beneath it the Tree of Life.

The inscription in Hebrew was appropriately simple.

Here lies Perla Bermann, Pianist and Composer. Born Zuzanna Perla Zerderbaum, August 14, 1915 – November 1, 1939. In her music and our memory, she lives.

And beneath that, the Hebrew text from 1 Samuel 25:29.

May her soul be bound in the bond of eternal life.

Edwin broke the silence. 'There are many others who have visited her before us, Jim.'

'How do you know that?'

'Look at all the stones and pebbles that have been left on her headstone.' Edwin counted them as he spoke. 'There are eleven – but people may have placed more than just one and we don't know how recently.'

'Who do you think could have put them there?'

'It's a good question. Friends, admirers, fellow musicians and, I suppose, possibly even relatives we know nothing about. We can be pretty certain that she didn't have any other children after you were born but she could well have had cousins.'

'It would be interesting to know if she did have other relatives who are still alive.'

'We should have asked Gyorgy – he may well know. If you go over to visit him with Sylvia, you should ask him. Or we could ask Dr Jäger to dig a little deeper, but he'd charge a fairly hefty fee for that.'

Jim sighed audibly and shook his head from side to side. 'You know, I feel all churned up inside standing here and don't like myself very much. It's not a nice feeling.'

'Do you know why? Can you explain?' asked Edwin, somewhat taken aback by his comment.

'I just can't help thinking of my bad old days when I went into Jewish cemeteries with the lads and got a thrill out of daubing and smashing the headstones. What a horrible, nasty bastard I was. I just cannot believe now how anyone could do such a thing.'

'Just remember that it wasn't your fault. You were brainwashed – and it's certainly not you now. The old Jim Fisher doesn't exist any longer.'

'You're right, I know. It just freaks me out sometimes when I think about these things.'

'Anyway, you need to mark your respect and place a pebble on the headstone and I'll take a few photographs. It's one of the pictures that they are most likely to use with the article when I get back.'

Jim scanned the ground around him and picked up three pebbles, which he placed sedately on the edge of the grave.

'That's one for me, one for Uwe and also one for Gyorgy,' he said.

Edwin then placed one for himself before taking several photographs.

As they walked slowly away from the grave, Edwin could see that Jim was still understandably feeling a little unsettled and he decided to lighten the mood.

'You know what they say about this place, Jim. They say the cemetery is half the size of Zurich but twice as much fun. It's an old Viennese joke that presumably says something about their views of their Swiss neighbours or, at least, those in Zurich. I think that it's probably a bit of a dig at the so-called Gnomes of Zurich, the Swiss bankers, all the boring money-men.'

Jim gave a polite chuckle, but did not respond.

*

Outside the main cemetery gate, they managed to pick up a taxi which took them to The Graben, one of the main shopping and eating boulevards in the city centre, where they planned, firstly, to find somewhere for lunch and then visit one of the specialist classical record shops, where they hoped to purchase CDs of Perla's recordings and live concert recitals.

'This will be our last proper restaurant meal before we get back home, so I suggest we treat ourselves to a Wiener schnitzel. They will use veal here, unlike the one we had in Lodz which was pork,' said Edwin.

'Best idea you've had today, Mr Benn,' said Jim sarcastically.

There were numerous inviting-looking eateries on each side of the boulevard. They selected the first one they came across that listed schnitzel on its menu.

A waiter presented them with an extensive menu and wine list which Edwin indicated that they did not need.

'We have already decided, thank you. Two Wiener schnitzels and two beers,' he said.

The waiter seemed to understand what he said, took back the menus and disappeared into the kitchen to place the order.

'How are you feeling now, Jim?' asked Edwin as they relaxed with their drinks.

'Just fine now, honestly. The cemetery got to me a bit but that's because I kept getting flashes of the old me. Actually, seeing my mother's grave didn't upset me. I just wish that I had gotten to know her. But I sure know her better now after everything that I've heard and seen over the past few days. I certainly never knew what a talented and famous mother I had. I'll now just have to start listening to all this classical stuff she played and, hopefully, get to like it.'

'What type of music do you like? Have you ever played an instrument yourself?'

'Rock n roll, heavy metal, a lot of country and western stuff, Neil Diamond – until I found out that he is Jewish, I'm now ashamed to admit – but I've never really listened to any classical stuff. All that's about to change though. I did buy a guitar many years ago when some of the lads thought we should start a band, but I never learned to play and the plans to form a band just fizzled out.'

'Well, with a bit of luck, the music shop should have your mother's recordings and you'll be able to start your classical education as soon as you get back home. I wouldn't mind betting that you'll have heard a lot of pieces even though you might not know what they are. They use a lot of classics as background music in TV shows and films.'

'You're right, I'm sure.'

*

Replete and rested after their schnitzels – which they both agreed was the best meal they had during the whole trip – they made the short walk along the boulevard to the record shop.

Edwin went straight up to one of the shop assistants and asked, 'Do you have music by the pianist Perla Bermann?'

'*Jawohl*, you please follow me,' the young man replied, leading them to a section of the shop dedicated to piano music and recitals.

Everything was categorised in alphabetical order and they were pleased to find ten or a dozen Perla Bermann CDs. They selected four: one with a studio photograph of Perla on the cover that they had never seen before, a second featuring much-loved pieces by Chopin and Liszt, a third of her last recital at the Vienna Concert Hall where she had her fatal accident and a fourth that the assistant recommended which included many of her own compositions.

As they left the shop, Edwin asked for one of their business cards listing their contact details, just in case they wanted others and couldn't find any of her work back in the UK.

'It's going to be quite something, Jim, when you get back home and can sit back and hear your mother playing. It will almost be like having her in the room with you.'

'It'll be emotional, that's for sure.'

There was a taxi rank just a short distance from the shop and, within five minutes, they were heading back to the airport for an early evening flight to Manchester. On arrival, they picked up their luggage which they had left in secure lockers, sat down in one of the café areas for coffee and a cake and then made their way to the duty-free shop.

Edwin bought his usual bottle of brandy and a bottle of Twilly d'Hermès perfume for his wife. Jim bought some Coco Mademoiselle parfum by Chanel for his wife.

On the short flight back, Jim seemed to have overcome all his fears of flying and was much more talkative. At one point, he even told Edwin that he was "enjoying" the flight and was hopeful that he had conquered his flying phobia for good.

'It's been pretty successful and productive in every way, I'd say, Jim. I felt sure that we would learn something about your mother but, if I'm honest, not as much as we actually did. For me, finding Gyorgy, the man she had planned to marry, was the highlight and meeting up with him was a real bonus.'

'Seeing myself as a baby with my mother in those old photos – and, of course, being given the bust of Chopin, my baby things and that teddy bear – were the most thrilling things for me. I'm going to have to find somewhere special to show them off when I get back home – a special cabinet or something.'

'And I reckon all the walking would have been very good exercise for you, Jim. Presumably, the transplant centre encourages you to take regular light exercise. Have you got any routine check-ups soon?'

'Yes, next week, as it happens. Will you have written up your article by then, Edwin? Do you know what you are planning to write this time?'

'Not really. I haven't thought about that just yet. But it's going to make an interesting piece, that's for sure All being well, I'm hoping to make a start on it when I'm back in the office on Monday. I'll let you know when it's going to appear.'

'Thanks – I would appreciate that. And thanks for all the organising. You did a bloody good job – everything went like clockwork. All that research you did beforehand really paid off.'

'No problem, I enjoyed it. Digging and delving around is my sort of thing.'

The two-and-a-half-hour journey to Manchester seemed to fly by, and before they knew it, the engine noise changed and the pilot announced that he was beginning the descent into

Manchester Airport – adding that the temperature was sixteen degrees centigrade with light rain showers.

'Surprise, surprise – it's raining in Manchester. Who would have thought that...' said Edwin mournfully.

'We were lucky – didn't have a drop whilst we were away. Anyway, I'm not bothered. I'm just looking forward to putting my feet up for a bit and telling Sylvia about everything.'

After going through passport control and collecting their baggage, they shared a black cab for the short journey to their homes in Altrincham and neighbouring Bowdon.

Jim was dropped off first. 'See you, Edwin. Don't forget to let me know when your piece is going to appear. Bye for now,' he said as he stepped out of the cab and collected his case.

'I will. I enjoyed your company. Give my best to Sylvia. Cheers for now,' said Edwin as the cab drove off.

*

It was late on a Friday when Edwin arrived back home and he was looking forward to a relaxing weekend with his wife, Marion, before returning to the frenetic, deadline-centric world of the newsroom on Monday morning.

Although he was physically tired and it was getting late, he felt the need to wind down with a cup of tea, a light snack and a catch-up chat with his wife before going to bed. Edwin rambled on in no particular chronological order about the various highlights of the trip. Marion acquainted him with sundry domestic issues that had arisen whilst he was away. One of their two cats had to go to the vet to have a thorn removed from its foot – but was now perfectly fit and well again. British Gas had been to service their boiler and their outside security light no longer functioned and needed replacing – a job for Edwin on Saturday morning.

Edwin had phoned Marion every day during the trip and acquainted her with the highlights of their various encounters and discoveries. But she was interested to hear some of the finer details, especially about their visit to Lodz because of its association with the paternal side of Edwin's own family.

'One of these days, we really ought to go over there and see what we can find out. It's a fine city with a wealth of interesting places to visit – and I didn't realise that, like Manchester, it was the major hub of the cotton and textile industry in Poland. It's almost certainly why my grandparents were involved in the textile, clothing and drapery business when they settled in Wales. Just fascinating stuff.'

'Sounds like you had an interesting and very successful trip. Your new friend, Mr Fisher, must be delighted,' said Marion.

'You could certainly say that. I was a bit worried that when we went round the Jewish cemeteries, the old Jim Fisher would somehow bubble up to the surface, but he was really great to be with all the time. We got on famously and he now thinks of me as one of his pals, not just the reporter covering his story. He's honestly a really nice guy, really pleasant to be with – it's an amazing transformation, I must admit.'

The following day, Edwin replaced their security light, and in the evening, he and Marion went out to their favourite Indian restaurant for a curry. On the Sunday, the weather was

291

dry and so they headed out into the Cheshire countryside for a five-mile circular walk that took them through woodland, undulating fields and a section of canal. They enjoyed a picnic lunch of prawn sandwiches and hard-boiled eggs sitting on a grassy embankment alongside a dry-stone wall.

*

Monday morning came around all too quickly and with it the harsh realities and cut-and-thrust of a daily national newspaper. Edwin had been back at his desk for only enough time to switch on his PC, when he was summoned to the news desk by his news editor, Ross.

'Edwin, you're back, great. Good trip I gather. I need a word,' he said with his Glasgow accent undiluted after several years away from his native Scotland.

'It was excellent, Ross. It'll make for a cracking read,' Edwin assured him.

'I'm sure it will. It's the photographs I'm worried about. We have a problem.'

'What's that?'

'The photographers' chapel is not happy about using any of the pics that you have taken. They say that if we intended to use photographs, then you should have gone with a photographer. I told them that in the circumstances, it would not have been possible and I'm hoping they'll relent – that they will realise this is a special case.

'I want you to download all the photographs you took and email them to me in a folder – then you can start knocking something out. From what you told me, I think we'll use two pieces of around twelve hundred words each. I'll leave you to make a start.'

When Edwin walked into the office, he was still feeling exuberant and energised from his whirlwind European adventure but the brief conversation with Ross had left him feeling deflated and irritated. The thought had crossed his mind fleetingly whilst he was away that there could be a problem with the photographers' union chapel, but he had dismissed it from his mind, believing that they were exceptional circumstances and common sense would prevail.

Still hoping that would be the case, Edwin sent an internal email to the news desk attaching a folder of all the photographs he had taken with explanatory captions. He then settled down, feeling a little less anxious, to start writing the first of the proposed two articles. He wrestled with various options for his intro and having satisfied himself that he had found the right punchy and colourful approach, the rest began to flow freely.

'You'll be pleased to hear we've come to an agreement with the chapel,' said Ross, coming over to Edwin's desk and placing an avuncular hand on his shoulder.

'That's great news. I was worried, I must admit,' said Edwin.

'Mike is going to make arrangements to go round to Jim's house and take some shots of him and his wife with the teddy bear, the Chopin bust and all the other things he brought back, but they've agreed to use four token photos of yours: Jim at his mother's grave, the one with the guy in the tracksuit,

Gyorgy, Jim at his grandparents' grave and maybe one at the apartment where his mother lived. They're prepared to make an exception on this occasion but only this once, they say. The editor has had to agree it's a one-off.'

'Thanks, Ross. That's quite a relief. Jim knows Mike and he'll be happy to go along with that, I'm sure. I can tell him if you like. I promised to call him and let him know when we're using the article, so I could tell him about Mike wanting to go round at the same time.'

'Fine. You do that. I'll tell the picture desk.'

Edwin broke off from his article and immediately called Jim, who answered the phone after just a couple of rings.

'Jim, it's Edwin. I'm just ringing to tell you that the articles will be in the paper towards the end of next week and that the picture desk wants to send Mike Wolff round to take some shots of you and Sylvia with all the things you were given by Gyorgy and Mrs Polgar at your mother's apartment.'

'Not a problem. When do they want to come?'

'I'm not sure. I'll tell Mike to call you and you can fix up a time – sometime in the next couple of days ideally.' He paused, then asked briskly, 'How have you been, by the way? Have you had a good weekend?'

'I've been boring the pants off Sylvia; telling her all about everything – but she is genuinely interested and says she'd love to go over to Lake Balaton for a little holiday, to meet Gyorgy and take a trip to that bistro in Budapest where they have all those photos of my mother on the wall – the place named after her.

'And you'll be pleased to know that Mr Chopin is looking over at me as we speak. Sylvia shuffled a few bits and bobs around and found a place for him in the middle of the dresser. And how was your weekend, Edwin?'

'Very relaxing. I went for an Indian with Marion on Saturday and yesterday we went on a country walk and took a picnic lunch. I'm now back in front of the PC and ploughing into the articles and it's going well, I'm pleased to say. Anyway, I'd better make a move. I will be in touch soon, no doubt.'

'I'll leave you in peace then. It sounds busy there.'

'Talk soon then, Jim. Keep well.'

*

Despite several minor interruptions from sundry telephone callers and members of the public calling with a miscellany of potential news stories, Edwin managed to complete both articles by the middle of the week. Overall, he was pleased with the end result and just hoped that the news and features editors would feel the same.

'Obviously, it all worked out, Edwin – an interesting read,' said the features editor, Graham Ditchfield, when their paths crossed in the corridor as Edwin was making his way to the cuttings library. 'We're planning to use them on Thursday and Friday. We should get a good show.'

'Yes, it went like clockwork. We were pretty confident that we'd find out something about Jim's mother but we ended up with much more than we'd expected. Finding the guy who was planning to marry her was a real bonus. In fact, Jim and his wife are planning to go over next summer for a short holiday and they will have the opportunity to chat again.'

'Tell him to let you know when he goes. It could make another piece,' said Graham.

'Already arranged.'

'Should certainly make a news story, if not a feature.'

*

The two feature articles under Edwin's byline, accompanied by some professional photographs taken by Mike Wolff that Edwin had not previously seen, were given a prominent show on the inside pages Thursday and Friday as planned.

As Edwin was driving home early on Friday evening, he took a hands-free call in his car. He could see from the display who it was.

'Hi, Jim. How are things? I'm just in the car, driving home. Good, as always, to hear from you.'

'I could have called you yesterday but I decided to read both pieces first. Great job, mate, thanks. It brought the whole trip back again. In fact, Sylvia's already been out to buy a scrapbook to put them in, and all the other articles you did from day one.'

'Glad you liked them. I'm not sure now when we'll next meet, but don't forget to let me know if and when you go over to see Gyorgy with Sylvia.'

'Will do, I promise.'

*

And he did. The following August, Jim called him to let him know that he and his wife were about to fly out for a week at the Balaton Hotel and, in an exchange of emails with Gyorgy, had arranged to meet him, this time, at his home.

'Don't forget to ask him if he knows if your mother had any cousins or other relatives who could have left the pebbles on her headstone in Vienna,' said Edwin.

'I haven't forgotten. I'll let you know what he says when I get back home.'

Just over a week later, as promised, Jim phoned Edwin again to tell him that he and Sylvia had had a great time in and around Siófok. They had spent several hours with Gyorgy at his home. Gyorgy told him that he was fairly certain that his mother had a younger brother called Jerzy Zederbaum and that he had a son called Aleksander Anatol Zederbaum who would probably now be in his late fifties.

'He also told me that he thought my grandfather, Hans, had siblings, who may also have had children of their own but did not know any more than that. He said that my mother didn't really talk much about her father's side of the family, probably because he died before she was born – in some sort of accident, I think.'

'Well, it looks as if you could have at least one cousin who could be alive and well, Jim, and may be other relatives, too. Did he tell you where Jerzy and Aleksander were born or where Aleksander might be living now?'

'He was pretty sure that they were born in Poland and he thought that Aleksander could have been living in Lublin, but that's all he knew. If they are still around, they could be anywhere now.'

'Send me the details you have and I may get a chance to do a bit of research and see if I can come up with anything. You and Sylvia could do the same. Keep me posted.'

'Will do, Edwin. Anyway, thanks again for everything. I'm not sure when we'll meet again but, hopefully, it won't be before too long.'

'You keep well. See you around. Best wishes to Sylvia. Bye for now.'

*

When he was next in the office, Edwin relayed his conversation to the news and feature editors, who were both of the opinion that the discovery of a possible cousin, whilst interesting and exciting for Jim, did not warrant any further coverage in the paper – and Edwin agreed.

In one form or another, from the initial coverage of his heart transplant to his journey of discovery around Europe, the James Karl Fisher story had occupied several thousand words of newsprint. But, for the time being, at least, it was agreed it had reached its natural conclusion.

CHAPTER 12

It was, in fact, another four years before Edwin next saw Jim, ironically in an intensive care bed in the same ward at the hospital where he had interviewed him after his transplant.

Edwin was no longer employed as *The Informer's* health and medical correspondent, and for all of two years had been running his own specialist medical public relations company from offices near his home in Altrincham. The hospital's heart transplant charity was one of his clients, and at least once a week, he would meet the transplant coordinator and invariably the surgical team, too, to identify newsworthy topics that could help promote the work of the centre and raise funds.

More often than not, there was a feel-good human-interest story that Edwin would write up and distribute in the form of a news release to all of the relevant media, including his old newspaper. Usually, they focused on individual patients whose transplant had given them a new lease of life and who had gone on to achieve all manner of dreams and goals that would previously have been unthinkable.

There were men and women who, prior to their transplants, could hardly put one leg in front of the other, but who only months after their surgery, could return to their jobs, walk down the aisle at their wedding, enjoy active days out with their children or take part in the hospital's own "Olympics", the Transplant Games.

It was on one such routine weekly meeting in February with Transplant Coordinator Anna Dickson in her office at the hospital, that Edwin learned that Jim was back in hospital and his condition was giving cause for concern.

As usual, he had sat down in her office with a cup of coffee and opened his spiral-bound notebook.

'Anything especially interesting or exciting since last week, Anna?'

He was not prepared for her response.

'Yes, but not good news, Edwin. Our friend, James Fisher, has been with us for the past three days and is receiving treatment back on the ward. He's not at all well and the consultants are worried about him.'

'Oh that is bad news. I'm so sorry to hear that,' said Edwin, genuinely shocked. 'The last time I saw him he was literally full of the joys of spring when we flew back into Manchester from Vienna after we'd been visiting places around Europe that had special association with his mother. He looked so fit and well – the picture of health. That's quite taken the wind out of my sails.'

'His wife has been coming down to sit with him every day. In fact, I am pretty sure that she will be on the ward with him now. I could probably ring the ward and see if you could go over and see them, if you would like.'

'Yes, please, I'd like to see them, Anna. We got to know each other when we were travelling around in Europe and I think he regarded me as one of his pals by the time we got home.' After a brief pause, he asked, 'What actually went wrong, Anna, do you know? What's the prognosis?'

'You'd need to talk with one of the consultants for an authoritative answer, but I gather he started feeling poorly a few weeks ago after going down with a chest infection. As you know, he's been taking immunosuppressants like all transplant recipients, which would have weakened his immune system and made his body much more vulnerable to infection.

'I gather he was given antiviral medication and he appeared to be much improved, but shortly afterwards, he developed a fever, swelling of the ankles, shortness of breath, debilitating fatigue and nausea, and it was feared that he was rejecting his new heart and should be admitted to hospital. And, as I said, he's been with us now for the past three days.'

Edwin quite forgot that the purpose of his meeting was to identify uplifting stories that illustrated the success of heart transplantation.

'That really doesn't sound good at all. Can you say what the likely prognosis is?' he asked.

'I suggest you have a word with his consultant. All I know is that they increased the dosage of his immunosuppressant drugs but that did not seem to have any beneficial effect. I gather he is now on prednisolone, steroids, and is being monitored around the clock.

'Anyway, if you would like to see him, I'd better ring the ward and check if all is OK. He may be dozing or asleep but you can always speak to his wife. I'll let her know it's you. I know you know each other.'

Anna picked up her phone and spoke to the sister on the ward, who said she had no objection to Edwin going along to sit with him for a short time.

'Thanks, Anna, I know we've not discussed any PR initiatives but perhaps we could do that later or tomorrow, if that's OK with you.'

'I wouldn't worry this week, Edwin. There's not much news to report but tomorrow would be just fine if that suits you."

When he arrived on the ward, he was directed by a nurse to an adjacent side room where Jim was being nursed away from other patients. Sylvia was sitting on an upright chair alongside the bed, holding her husband's hand. Jim himself had his eyes closed and did not appear to be aware of Edwin's presence. His face looked puffy and his complexion flushed.

'Sylvia, hello. I've just been told about Jim. I'm so sorry... how are you?' Edwin asked hesitantly.

'I'm OK, I suppose, given the circumstances. Just trying to be strong for Jim. He was fine a couple of weeks or so back, then he picked up some chest infection and he's gone rapidly downhill. We are all very worried about him.'

'I'm sure everything is going to be all right, Sylvia. He couldn't be in better hands,' said Edwin reassuringly.

'It's only last month we went out for a meal to celebrate the fourth anniversary of his transplant and we'd been planning to go away for a short holiday in April. We'd been looking through all the brochures just before he fell ill.'

'Does he know you're here, Sylvia? Has he just fallen asleep?'

'He was awake when I arrived about an hour ago but he keeps dozing off. It might be all the drugs he's taking, I don't know. But I'm pretty sure he knows I'm here.'

'I'm sure he does... please let him know I've been, Sylvia, and I'll come and see him when he's up and about again.'

'I will.'

'I don't suppose you will know, but I'm not with *The Informer* now. I'm now running my own medical public relations business and, among other things, I look after the PR for the heart transplant charity here. I usually come to see the coordinator once a week and I didn't know about Jim until she mentioned it just now,' Edwin explained.

'He'd appreciate you calling, Edwin. He often talked about his trip to Europe with you and said how much he had enjoyed it... and, of course, you know he took me back to Hungary to see Gyorgy at his home by the lake,' said Sylvia.

'I'll never forget it. It was a great trip and we discovered more about his mother than we ever expected. Does he ever listen to any of the music we brought back?'

'He does, yes, quite often. He'd never been into classical music but there are several pieces he really likes – the famous one by Chopin that was in the film and several of his mother's own compositions.'

As she spoke, Sylvia gently stroked the back of her husband's hand, hoping that he might open his eyes and wake up. But his eyes remained shut.

A nurse entered the room saying that she needed to carry out some routine checks and take various readings from the monitors. Edwin felt that it was time that he made his exit.

'I think that I'd better make a move, Sylvia. I'll keep in touch. Please let me know if there's anything I can do. My mobile number is still the same,' he said, handing her one of his business cards before walking back to the main entrance and the hospital car park.

*

In his office the following day, Edwin called the hospital and managed to speak with Jim's surgeon, Mr Barr-White. Over the years, they had got to know each other well and saw each other regularly to discuss the work of the transplant centre and its charity activities.

'Edwin, what can I do for you? I've just got a few minutes before I need to scrub up. Is it something I can deal with quickly?' he asked.

'I think so, Jonathan. I went to see Jim Fisher yesterday and I am just wondering what the prognosis is. I sat with his wife at his bedside for a short time but he didn't seem at all well and didn't wake up during the time I was with him.'

'His condition is giving us cause for concern, Edwin, and to be brutally frank, the prognosis is not good. We have been taking regular heart biopsies and they indicate clear signs of organ rejection, which is always worrying. We have increased immunosuppression with three different drugs, but this has proved ineffective and he is now on steroids. There is not much else that we can do.'

'It does not sound good,' said Edwin soberly.

'It is not. I suggest that you keep in touch either with me or Anna. Certainly, the next few days will be critical,' said the consultant, stressing that he could not talk any longer because he was shortly expected in theatre.

'Thanks, Jonathan. I will.'

*

As arranged, Edwin returned to the hospital the following day for his postponed weekly meeting with Anna Dickson.

'I managed to speak with Jonathan yesterday and he told me that the prognosis for Jim Fisher is not good. Have you heard anything further today, Anna?' he asked.

'I checked when I came in this morning because I thought that's the first thing you would ask me and the ward sister told me that, in fact, his condition has deteriorated and that he is now receiving palliative care – in addition to his ongoing treatment.'

'Is that, in effect, end-of-life care?'

'I wouldn't like to say for certain, but I know that has been the case for other patients in the past. I gather that he's had to have oxygen for severe breathlessness. But, of course, every case is different.'

'As I said to Jonathan, I'll just have to keep in touch. I suppose every twenty-four hours could be crucial.'

'I would say so,' said Anna.

Satisfied that there was nothing more to be said or done about the future prospects for Jim Fisher, Edwin and Anna spent the next hour discussing a miscellany of promotional initiatives. Top of the agenda was a story about a teenage girl who had spent much of her time confined to a wheelchair with a serious heart condition but who, less than a year after her transplant, was taking part in the swimming events at the hospital's transplant games in the summer.

*

Edwin left Anna's office towards the end of the working day on a Friday afternoon and drove straight home from the hospital. She did not work at weekends so he did not telephone her for a condition update until early on Monday morning.

'Anna, apologies for the early call but I am just anxious to know if you have heard anything about Jim Fisher,' he said.

'I have and it is very bad news, Edwin. I'm sorry to have to tell you that he passed away in the early hours of Sunday morning. His wife has obviously been informed. I'm told she was with him until quite late on Saturday night and was told then that there was nothing more that could be done and she should prepare for the worst. I don't know where she is now but I am sure that she would be happy for you to call her.'

'God, that's terrible, though it's not come as a great surprise, I suppose. I was half hoping that he might just miraculously start responding to treatment but I guess it was just not to be. I will call Sylvia later.'

'I know that the consultant had told her last week to expect the worst, and in that sense, she would have been prepared, but I know that she is really very upset and would welcome being with someone who knew him, like yourself. She could be on her own.'

*

Edwin waited until around midday to call.

'Hello, can I help you? Who's speaking?' said a woman, whose voice he did not recognise.

'It's Edwin Benn here, a friend of Jim and Sylvia's. Do I have the right number?' he asked, somewhat confused.

'You do. It's Sylvia's sister here, Evelyn. I've come over to stay with her,' she said.

'It's just that I have heard the very sad news about Jim and wanted to offer my condolences and see if there's anything I can do.'

He went on to explain briefly how he knew Jim and how he was now looking after the public relations for the hospital's heart transplant charity.

'Hold on please – I'll see if she is able to have a word with you,' said Evelyn.

Just a few moments later, he heard Sylvia's voice.

'Edwin, it's me,' she said almost inaudibly.

'Sylvia, I felt I just had to give you a call to say how very sorry I am to hear about Jim. I'm pleased to hear that your sister is there to give you some support. If you can, just tell me if there's anything you want me to do.'

'I've been in touch with Uwe and his friends at the pub to tell them, but no one else yet. You can tell anyone else you feel ought to know, like our friend in Hungary and his donor's widow – I'll leave it up to you, Edwin.'

'Yes, of course, I will, Sylvia.'

'Edwin, I have to tell you that I'm sure that Jim knew that he was going,' said Sylvia, her voice suddenly strengthening. 'When he came round for a few hours, he told me that if anything happened to him, he didn't want a Jewish funeral with a big headstone because he said that the yobbos who daubed his car on our wedding day would end smashing it up and probably other people's graves as well.'

'I can understand that… Jim was Jewish, I know, but there's absolutely no reason why he would have to have a Jewish funeral,' said Edwin reassuringly.

'He even told me that he would just like to have a farewell ceremony conducted by the same lady who celebrated our wedding, so that's what we're doing. Would you be able to put a short piece in the paper letting people know about Jim?'

'Of course I can. I would suggest that we keep it short and formal but stressing that it will be a small humanist funeral for close family and friends at whatever venue you choose. I'll let you have all the names and addresses.'

'Thank you, Edwin. I'll leave it to you It will be in the chapel building at the Altrincham Crematorium but it won't be a religious service, of course.'

Edwin could tell from her voice that she did not want to speak for much longer, so, after wishing her well and promising to keep in touch, he said his goodbyes and rang off.

Immediately after ending the call, Edwin made a list of the people he needed to tell that Jim Fisher had died and that they would receive an official invitation in due course. His list included: Leah Lieberman, the widow of his donor; Bernard Haworth, his chess tutor at Rossendale and Gyorgy Herczel in Hungary.

He then opened up a blank page on Word on his PC and started to draft a short news release which he would email to Sylvia and Anna Dickson at the hospital for their approval. It was very different from the news stories and feature articles he had written about Jim Fisher in his days in the newsroom at *The Informer*.

At the hospital and family's request, he kept the news release as brief and as formal as possible, alluding only to the fact that as a child he had been indoctrinated with racist ideology by his late Nazi father in Germany, but after receiving the heart of an Orthodox Jew, he had experienced both a physical and mental change of heart. He briefly mentioned, too, that he had later discovered that his late Polish-born mother, who became an acclaimed concert pianist, was Jewish and that he had made a pilgrimage to Europe to follow in her footsteps.

The text was subsequently approved by his widow, Sylvia, and the hospital and Edwin distributed it to all the relevant media outlets, including his former newspaper, *The Informer*, which had followed the story at every stage since the day of his transplant.

Over the next twenty-four hours, the story appeared in most of the national media and the local evening paper in the Greater Manchester area. *The Informer*, as Edwin had anticipated, gave the story more prominence, drawing on references to stories and articles that they had previously published. They also alluded to the fact that their former health and medical correspondent, Edwin Benn, had travelled with Fisher on his trip around Europe.

Edwin was worried that some of the so-called "red top" newspapers might carry the story under inflammatory, provocative headlines, with phrases such as "Ex-Jew hater" or "Ex-Neo-Nazi" but, without exception, it was handled sympathetically and sensitively.

He breathed a sigh of relief.

*

Leaden grey skies with low menacing black clouds hung shroud-like over the chapel crematorium as the mourners began to arrive for Jim's funeral. But, thankfully, there was no chilling March wind.

Edwin, who was accompanied by his wife, Marion, joined the small group of mourners assembled outside the chapel some twenty minutes before the funeral cortège was due to arrive. Among them was Leah Lieberman and her son, Daniel, and although it was some years since they had met, they recognised each other right away.

'Leah, Daniel, hello. How are you?' asked Edwin shaking their hands as he spoke. 'I don't think you've met my wife, Marion. It's lovely to see you again – I just wish it were under happier circumstances.'

'Yes, so very sad. After the way he was treated as a child, he deserved to have enjoyed life for many more years as the new nice man he had become,' said Mrs Lieberman.

'He did, most certainly. I got to know him very well when I took him over to Europe to learn about his mother, and he was a genuinely lovely guy who did everything he could to make amends for his bad old days – even though he knew it wasn't his fault,' said Edwin.

'I think I must have read most of your articles, Edwin, and I gather that you established more than just a working relationship with him. It must have been really so fascinating finding out all those things about his mother. What an interesting woman she must have been.'

'I'm so glad you could come today, Leah. I didn't know whether you would.'

'Daniel and I both felt that it was important for us to come for Marcus's sake as much as anything else. It was Marcus's heart that gave him those extra years – extra happy years – and now that has gone, too,' said Mrs Lieberman.

As they continued to talk, transplant coordinator Anna Dickson and consultant Mr Barr-White arrived together, followed by Bernard Haworth and two other pals from The Kettledrum Tavern at Rossendale. They all acknowledged each other with polite nods of the head and handshakes.

By the time the funeral cortège arrived on the dot of 11:30 a.m., some twenty or thirty people were waiting and chatting quietly in small groups, with some sheltering under umbrellas from the light rain that began to fall as the hearse stopped under the chapel's portico.

The undertakers opened the rear door of the hearse, then stood back as the main party of mourners: Sylvia Fisher, her sister, Evelyn, and Jim's brother and his wife, Uwe and Nicole Fisher, stepped out from the following car and walked towards the main entrance. Sylvia held onto her sister's arm and seemed oblivious to the rain.

Sylvia spoke briefly to the undertaker, and a moment later the wicker coffin, with a wreath made from branches bearing red and white berries lying on the top, was borne aloft into the chapel and placed on the catafalque in front of the tiered rows of chairs. Before taking her seat, Sylvia Fisher placed the Steiff teddy bear that her husband had as a child among the branches on the coffin lid.

To the accompaniment of piped soothing music, the mourners moved into their seats and, when everyone was settled, the celebrant, Evangelista de la Rosa, who had conducted Jim and Sylvia's wedding, took up her position behind the lectern.

'Good afternoon, ladies and gentlemen. I would like to welcome you all here today to celebrate James's life, to remember the many ways in which he enriched our lives and to say our goodbyes...

'It seems only such a very short time ago that I stood before many of the same faces I recognise here today on the occasion of James's wedding to Sylvia. What a wonderful and joyous day that was, and I know from Sylvia that the love they expressed for each other continued to grow and mature like good wine over the years .

'Their years together were happy, fulfilled and precious, all the more so because, had it not been for the generosity of his heart donor – whose widow we are honoured to have with us today – and the transplant surgery that saved his life, James and Sylvia would not have been able to share their lives at all.'

For the next five or six minutes she recalled how, with his new lease of life, James had not only found the love of his life but had been reunited with his brother, Uwe, and had travelled to Poland, Hungary and Austria to "rediscover" his mother with whom he had lost contact when he was only a baby.

'Many of you, I am sure, will know that James's mother was a composer and a virtuoso concert pianist, and before we leave here today we will be playing two pieces that were among James's favourites – one of her own compositions a stand-alone prelude appropriately called *The Heart's Awakening* (Przebudzenie Selca) and *Chopin's Nocturne No. 20 in C-sharp minor* which was featured in the film *The Pianist*. Chopin, of course, was one of James's mother's fellow countrymen, and throughout the classical world she was recognised as one of the great exponents of his work.

'But, first, I know that James's brother, Uwe, would like to give the eulogy... Uwe,' she said.

Evangelista stepped down from the rostrum and Uwe, who was sitting on the front row of seats next to Sylvia, stood up and took her place.

In an American accent that over his many years in California had obliterated almost all vestiges of his native German, he spoke of the happy early childhood years they had together but also of his sadness at their separation when, after their parents divorced, their father had attempted to indoctrinate them with his misguided Nazi ideology.

'I was lucky and rebelled against it. I had several young Jewish friends whose homes I often visited. I knew that they were not bad people who were going to destroy or corrupt our nation, but my brother was much younger than me and was not able to fight against all the evil that was being instilled in him. When I was able, I just left and emigrated to the USA, but Jim had no means of resisting the intolerance and hatred that our father taught him to believe.

'When I last saw Jim at his new home with his new and lovely wife, it was one of the greatest joys of my life to know that, following his heart transplant, quite miraculously all the hatred had disappeared for good, along with his old, diseased heart. It was such a pleasure to see him again and to know that the monster that our father had tried to create had gone, never to return.

'I really did not plan on saying so much about this unfortunate and distressing part of Jim's life but it is because

I was just getting to know the real Jim and, of course, Sylvia, and was looking forward to seeing so much more of them in the future, that I feel so sad and cheated that he has gone. Of course, I will make sure that we keep closely in touch with Sylvia, and I hope that in the very near future she will be able to come over to visit us in California.'

Sylvia, who frequently had to wipe tears from her eyes as he spoke, lifted her head and said under her breath, 'Of course I will.'

When he had given his eulogy and returned to his seat, Evangelista invited everyone simply to sit in quiet contemplation whilst they listened initially to the uplifting prelude, which the CD sleeve noted that she composed in 1959 when she was only twenty years old, and then to the Chopin nocturne before the ceremony ended and they left the chapel.

Edwin knew that he could never prove it, but always surmised that Perla had composed the piece around the time that Uwe was born and that it could also have been around that time in her life when she discovered she was Jewish, with a Jewish mother and father, and not, as she assumed as a child, a Catholic. Certainly, the title suggested that it was written to mark something pivotal and revelatory in her life, but it would always have to remain an interesting theory.

The speculation was occupying his thoughts as he, Marion and the other mourners moved in an orderly and sedate manner towards the exit to the appropriate accompaniment of Chopin's nocturne being played by Perla Bermann. But as they neared the door, Edwin was brought sharply back to the here-and-now by a recognisable male voice.

'Hi, Edwin. Thought I might see you here.' It was his old newspaper colleague, Mike, who had been sitting at the back of the chapel with an *Informer* reporter and two other journalists: one from the *Manchester Evening News* and another from a local weekly.

'Mike, how are you? Good to see you. You've met my wife, Marion, haven't you – at Jim Fisher's wedding, I think?'

'I did, yes – good to see you both again. This is Robin Richardson, our reporter who joined us after you left,' said Mike.

'Hi, Robin. Mike and I were in theatre when Jim Fisher had his transplant and I wrote several pieces about him over the years. I now, among other things, look after the PR for the hospital's heart transplant appeal.'

'Yes, Mike told me. I received your press release – and I've seen all the cuttings,' he said. Then, switching into reporter mode, he asked, 'Do you happen to know if we can follow the family down to the burial ground?'

'I think that could be a problem, Robin. The invitation says "followed by a private burial". You could ask Mrs Fisher's sister, but I know they were keen that the internment should be kept private just for close friends and family.' Edwin pointed out Sylvia's sister to Robin.

'Thanks, I'll ask her.'

*

316

As Edwin and Marion left the chapel, they were pleased to see that the rain had stopped and there were patches of blue sky permitting intermittent bursts of sunshine. Mike Wolff and the reporters were talking to Sylvia's sister and Jim's brother Uwe, but Edwin felt that it wasn't his place to get involved.

Instead, he and Marion made their way to the car park and pulled out onto the country lane in readiness to follow the cortège to the privately-owned burial ground in the heart of the Cheshire countryside where Jim Fisher would be laid to rest.

They did not have long to wait. In perhaps no more than ten minutes, the hearse and the black limousines drove slowly through the main gate and Edwin slipped in behind them for the half-hour journey to the oasis of meadow and woodland that he had seen once before on a Sunday walk.

'It doesn't look as though any of the journalists will be at the burial. They are certainly not following us,' said Edwin.

'Sylvia will have told them it was just for family and close friends,' said Marion.

'I am sure she did... and, anyway, news-wise I don't think it would add much to any story they might be carrying.'

On arrival at the burial ground, Edwin parked up in a dedicated area. The hearse and cortège came to a halt at the edge of a grassed area only perhaps twenty or thirty yards from the site of the grave.

The black clouds that loomed ominously earlier in the day had almost entirely disappeared and the whole area was bathed in weak sunlight as Sylvia, her sister, Uwe and his wife, Bernard

Haworth and the celebrant walked the short distance to the graveside.

Sylvia, who was battling to keep her emotions under control, was again holding on to her sister's arm. Edwin and his wife moved slowly into the group as the undertakers, assisted by two soberly-dressed men who were associated with the burial ground, lifted the coffin from the hearse, carried it to the grave and lowered it into the ground.

The undertaker then invited Sylvia to place a handful of earth onto the wicker surface of the coffin and everyone else followed suit. There was a water tap and a clean towel nearby for people to wash their hands.

Edwin and his wife were the last to wash their hands and as they returned to the group standing silently by the grave, Evangelista broke the silence.

'I had not planned to say anything further but I feel that I just could not leave without saying what a wonderfully peaceful and special place this is – I feel sure that you will all agree.

'We are now in the first flush of spring and as I look around, I can see daffodils, primroses and other flowers bursting into life accompanied by the sound of birdsong from the surrounding woodland. I am sure it must give you all comfort to know that James has been laid to rest in such a beautiful and tranquil place – and one that in time will in many ways become a joyous place for you to visit on bright, sunny days.'

Sylvia managed to say a few words. 'It does give me comfort, yes. Thank you, Evangelista.'

For a few minutes longer, everyone stood in the weak March sunshine, exchanging polite and subdued conversation. Edwin told Uwe how nice it was to see him again and wished him a safe journey back to California. Bernard Haworth told Sylvia how much he missed his games of chess with Jim. Evelyn told Evangelista what a "wonderful send-off" Jim had been given and how blessed they had been by the weather.

Edwin, who did not have an opportunity to speak with Sylvia at the chapel, offered her his hand and his condolences.

Her response was unexpected, 'We did invite Gyorgy but he said that he was now too old to make the journey on his own.'

Slowly and reverently, they began to move away from the graveside and head towards their cars for the short journey back to Jim and Sylvia's apartment, where she had arranged a modest sandwich buffet with tea, coffee and drinks.

'Will you be able to join us?' Sylvia asked Edwin and Marion.

'That's most kind of you but sadly, we have to get back home shortly,' said Edwin who did not feel the need for any further explanation.

As he and Marion drove back through the country lanes, he wondered if he would ever have any contact with the Fisher family ever again.

CHAPTER 13

Twice over the years, Edwin had convinced himself that his professional, and later personal, association with Jim Fisher and his family had reached its natural conclusion. First, when they went their separate ways after returning from their trip around Europe, and again when he drove away from the burial ground after Jim's funeral.

But this proved not to be so.

Five months after the funeral, Edwin and his wife received an invitation through the post from Sylvia Fisher to attend the unveiling of a memorial plaque and a tree planting at the burial ground. It was accompanied by a short hand-written note.

Dear Edwin and Marion,

I hope that you are both keeping well. I have been told by the groundsmen that now the earth has settled on Jim's grave, it would be possible to erect a small stone plaque in his memory and, at the same time, for me to plant a tree alongside the grave. It will just be a small ceremony for the family and close friends and we hope that you and Marion can be there.

Best Wishes,
Sylvia

'Who's the letter from, Edwin?' asked Marion as they prepared to go out for a pub lunch with one of his former newspaper colleagues and his wife.

'It's from Sylvia Fisher. She's inviting us to go the unveiling of a memorial plaque on Jim's grave and a tree-planting ceremony.'

'To a stone setting. I know he was Jewish but I did not think he'd have a stone setting or even whether it would be permitted there.'

'No, I don't think that Sylvia would know anything about the Jewish tradition of a headstone setting within a year of someone's death and, even if she did, I'm pretty sure the burial ground would not have permitted it. It's just a coincidence, I'm sure – but you could say a very appropriate one bearing in mind that Jim was not a religious man, although Jewish.'

'Do you think we should go then?' asked Marion.

'I think we should. She's inviting us as friends. She knows I don't work any longer for *The Informer*,' said Edwin, adding a moment or two later, 'It's ironic she should mention tree planting. When we were coming back from Vienna, Jim just said out of the blue that he would like to plant a tree in Israel one day and visit the Holocaust remembrance centre at Yad Vashem, which I'd told him about before we went on our trip around Europe. But sadly it wasn't to be...'

*

Three weeks later on a warm, sunny Saturday in August, Edwin and his wife drove down to the burial ground for the noon ceremony. They were some fifteen minutes early but four members of the family were already there: Sylvia, her sister, Evelyn, and Jim's brother, Uwe, with his wife, Nicole, who had come over from their home in California. They were all dressed smartly but not as soberly as they had for the funeral and burial.

They greeted one another with firm handshakes. Edwin was pleased to see that Sylvia was looking well and seemed very composed, even cheerful.

'Lovely to see you again, Sylvia, How are you keeping?' Edwin asked her.

'Most of the time I'm just fine. I occasionally go back to see my old friends at The Kettledrum – Bernard is still one of the regulars – and a couple of nights a week, I help out behind the bar at a lovely Italian restaurant near home. It keeps me occupied and I enjoy the company.'

'Who else are you expecting?'

'Leah Lieberman and her son said they are coming, but we're really very excited because Jim's mother's cousin, Aleksander Zederbaum, said he plans to come. We managed to trace him with Gyorgy's help and discovered that for many years he's been playing the cello in a string quartet in London. There's obviously a musical gene in the family.'

'How's he getting up here, do you know?'

'He's getting the train and then said he'd jump in a taxi. I've offered to put him up at the apartment tonight so I should have a chance to get to know him. Evelyn will also be staying over.'

'I look forward to meeting him. Who'd have thought there was another classical musician in the family and living in London.'

'It is amazing, I agree.'

As they spoke, a black cab pulled into the burial ground and a tall, slim man with angular features and slicked-back black hair stepped out, paid the driver and began walking over to where they were standing.

'This is Aleksander. I recognise him from a photo he sent us. He is obviously a man of his word,' said Sylvia, walking forward to greet him. 'Aleksander, how wonderful to meet you. It is so good of you to come. Did you have a good journey?' she asked, vigorously shaking his hand.

'No problems, I am pleased to say. I am really looking forward to meeting everyone and getting to know you. We have waited far too long,' he said.

'Much too long. But you are here now,' she said, introducing him to Edwin and his wife and then to everyone else before excusing herself and moving away to talk to one of the groundsmen who had arrived to help with the tree planting.

Edwin was curious to know more about Aleksander. So when all the introductions had been made and whilst Sylvia was preoccupied with the groundsman, he drew him into conversation.

'Am I right in thinking that you lived in Lublin, Aleksander? When Jim and Sylvia went over to meet with Gyorgy, I gather he told them that he thought you might have lived in Lublin, but they said he was not sure.'

'Gyorgy was right. My late parents lived in Lublin and I was born in Lublin,' he replied.

'So did you know Jim's mother?' Edwin asked.

'I did but I did not know her well. My parents told me that I had a cousin who was a concert pianist in Lodz, but that was more than three hundred miles from Lublin and I would have been too young to have travelled there on my own. But when I was older, I did go and see her at two of her recitals in Poland and we met afterwards at the hotel where she was staying. She was a really lovely, very humble lady, and I am sure that if she had not moved to Budapest, we would have seen much more of each other. And, of course, for the past twelve years, I have lived and worked in London.'

'Would you say that she had any influence on your career as a cellist?' asked Edwin, seamlessly slipping back into his former journalist mode.

'Yes, absolutely. Of that, I can be certain. My parents were musical but it was listening to my aunt's music and buying her records that was a real inspiration. I would not have become a cellist had it not been for her.'

Edwin would have continued his conversation with him but was interrupted by Sylvia who asked everyone if they would gather around the graveside for the unveiling of the memorial plaque and the tree planting.

Sylvia was standing to the side of the grave holding the corner of a green satin cloth that was draped over the memorial and much of the grass that, since the burial, had taken root in the bare earth.

'There is not much that I want to say other than thank you all so much for coming here today – especially to Uwe and Nicole, who have come all the way from their home in California, and to Aleksander, who has come up from London.

'As I am sure you will know, James learned after his heart transplant that his mother was Jewish, and that as such he too, was Jewish. With Edwin Benn's help, who I am delighted to say is here with his wife today, James made a pilgrimage to Europe to visit the places where she had lived and worked.

'James was not a religious man and told me that he did not want a religious service or any big stone memorials but he would certainly have been happy with this little memorial unveiling today, which I have learned could be the equivalent of the traditional Jewish stone-setting that takes place within a year after a person has passed away.

'I also know that in line with Jewish tradition, some of you would like to place pebbles on the grave as a tangible sign of your visit. That's all I want to say. Thank you again for being here.'

With that, Sylvia gently removed the satin cloth, revealing a small stone plaque engraved simply with his name, the date of death, his age and an appropriate quotation from Shakespeare.

I feel my heart new open'd.

Edwin did not know who had chosen the quotation but instantly thought of how, through the phenomenon of cell memory, James Karl Fisher had become a "new" man following his heart transplant.

As the plaque emerged into the sunlight, there was a spontaneous burst of subdued applause.

Sylvia and the groundsman then moved to the rear of the grave where the hole had already been dug for a rowan tree sapling. She placed the root ball into the hole, took a small pristine spade and placed two shovelfuls of earth into the hole. The groundsman drove a sturdy wooden support into the ground and tied the sapling to it with horticultural strapping.

'Would you like to place your pebbles now, Mrs Lieberman?' asked Sylvia.

'Thank you, yes,' she replied.

With help from her son, Daniel, she knelt down at the graveside and removed two smooth grey pebbles from her pocket that earlier in the day she had found in a flower bed in her garden.

Gently, she placed the first one on the side of the grave alongside the plaque, followed by the second one which she placed on the opposite side.

As her son helped her back on her feet, she spoke directly to Sylvia, 'I have left one for your dear husband and one also for my husband's heart.'

'Jim would have liked that,' said Sylvia.

With small pebbles and stones they found lying on the edge of the adjacent woodland, everyone else followed suit. Uwe and Aleksander also placed two pebbles on the grave, one for themselves and the second on behalf of their mother and aunt respectively.

'That was all very dignified,' said Marion as she and Edwin drove home.

'It was most certainly. Not sanctimonious, not religious but all very spiritual. One of these weekends, we must go on the walk that passes through that meadow and woodland. We can watch Jim's rowan tree grow.'

ACKNOWLEDGEMENTS

Ruth Sutcliffe, Transplant Coordinator, Wythenshawe Hospital Transplant Centre, Manchester; Dorota Wojciechowska, Director of the Polish National Tourist Office; Maciej Janik, State Archives of Lodz, Poland; Embassy of Hungary, London; Jewish Cemetery Simmering/ Zeltralfriedhof, Vienna, Austria; Friends of Nature Burial Ground, Mobberley, Knutsford, Cheshire; Geoffrey Green for his invaluable help with proofreading.

ABOUT THE AUTHOR

When I was fifteen, I wrote a poem entitled *Imitation Flowers*, which was published in the children's section of the *Manchester Evening News*. From these small beginnings, my passion for writing became irrevocably entrenched, and in my early 20s I was offered a reporting job in the editorial department of that same newspaper. I expressed my interest in health and medicine, and within a year I was appointed Health and Medical Correspondent, a post that for the next 25 years took me on assignments around the world and the rest of the UK.

After leaving the newspaper, I launched my own specialist Press and PR company and wrote my first book *God's Sabbatical Years*, a Holocaust memoir. My second book, *Salford at Work* (published by Amberley Books in 2018), was followed a year or so later by *A Doctor in Lowryland*, an account of life in post-war Salford. It won the 2020 Frank Mullineux Local History Award, presented annually by the Salford Local History Forum.

In 2022 I wrote my first novel, *The Filipino Doll*, a story which straddles three continents, America, Europe and Asia.

It was inspired by my personal interest in genealogy and, as with *The Blighted Son*, by my continuing interest in health and medicine.

Outside the literary world my interests include watercolour and oil painting, country walking, patio gardening and tracing my family history. My wife, Wendy, and I have lived for the past eight years in the Saxon market town of Sandbach in Cheshire.